# SUTTON'S SCANDAL
## THE SINFUL SUTTONS
### BOOK SIX

SCARLETT SCOTT

**Sutton's Scandal**

The Sinful Suttons Book 6

All rights reserved.

Copyright © 2022 by Scarlett Scott

Published by Happily Ever After Books, LLC

Edited by Grace Bradley

Cover Design by Wicked Smart Designs

This book or any portion thereof may not be reproduced or used in any manner whatsoever without the express written permission of the publisher except for the use of brief quotations in a book review.

The unauthorized reproduction or distribution of this copyrighted work is illegal. No part of this book may be scanned, uploaded, or distributed via the Internet or any other means, electronic or print, without the publisher's permission. Criminal copyright infringement, including infringement without monetary gain, is punishable by law.

This book is a work of fiction and any resemblance to persons, living or dead, or places, events, or locales, is purely coincidental. The characters are productions of the author's imagination and used fictitiously.

For more information, contact author Scarlett Scott.

https://scarlettscottauthor.com

*For my friend, Marietta S.*

AUTHOR'S NOTE:

The events within *Sutton's Scandal* are happening concurrently with events happening in previous books in the series. If you haven't read the rest of the series, have no fear. This is still standalone. But if you have read the rest of the series, you may find a few of these events familiar. Now you're seeing the story from Lily's and Tarquin's eyes…

Clementia's face was arranged in a perfectly pleasant manner. Alluring, even. She possessed all the requirements of a future spouse. She did not lack for suitors. She was considered a beauty. She was the daughter of an earl. She favored him. Tarquin's father had chosen her to be his bride.

And yet, he felt nothing for her save mild irritation whenever he was in her presence.

He ought to be thankful that Lady Clementia was so amenable to his suit, for he had spent his life fighting for the respectability he could achieve by such an alliance. It was through marriage to her that he would finally earn his father's approval. More importantly, he would secure the forgiveness of the tremendous loan the duke had provided him when Tarquin had bought his former partners out of Bellingham and Co. But Tarquin's gratitude was lacking this evening. It had been ever since he had discovered The Problem.

But never mind The Problem. He would not think on it now, for doing so would surely render false smiles and the pretense of amiability impossible.

"The lemonade here at Rivendale's is wonderful," Lady Clementia said suddenly, interrupting his thoughts. "Do you think we might fetch some for Mother?"

The lemonade was tart, and he had never witnessed the august Countess of Brownley perform such a plebian act as deigning to partake of food or drink, despite having been a guest at dinner.

Nonetheless, Tarquin changed his stride, moving them in the direction of the supper rooms where refreshments were on perpetual offering. If one considered dry cakes and buttered bread a refreshment. Tarquin himself did not. However, he had not scrabbled and clawed and bartered all but his soul to gain a voucher for Rivendale's for the lemonade and cakes. He had fought his way into these hallowed walls because his father had demanded it of him. And thanks to the financial threat looming over Tarquin's head—lose his shop or give the duke what he wanted—Tarquin was duty-bound to adhere to the latter.

It was not an entirely losing proposition, however. The shadow of his unfortunate birth would only be removed by the perpetual sun of a lady of good breeding and moral fortitude. Marriage with Lady Clementia was in his best interest, even if it was unpalatable.

"Mr. Bellingham?" Lady Clementia prodded. "You are quiet. I hope I have not shocked you in wishing for another moment of your company."

"Of course not," he reassured her hastily, whilst wondering when he might leave. This affair was as enlivening as a funeral, and he had a great deal of work awaiting him. "I am pleased to offer you my escort, my lady."

"Do you enjoy the lemonade, sir?" Lady Clementia asked.

"Yes," he lied.

In truth, he despised lemons.

"There is something so refreshing about lemonade," chattered Lady Clementia. "Do you not think so?"

"Refreshing," he repeated, his mind returning, as it inevitably had ever since he had discovered it, to The Problem. "Indeed."

Those blasted ledgers. He never should have stopped reviewing them. He ought never to have allowed Mr. Kenyon to take on the burden entirely himself. But Kenyon had lulled Tarquin into a false sense of security. For a time, Tarquin had believed he had found someone he could trust. Another mind and set of hands to oversee the vast needs of Bellingham and Co.

He had been wrong, and Mr. Kenyon was no longer in his employ.

"…jam?" Lady Clementia asked, the last word of her question cutting through Tarquin's ruminations.

Jam?

Lemonade?

The weather?

Had she nothing of substance to converse about?

A search of her countenance suggested not. Lady Clementia was gazing at him with an expression of childish adoration. Tarquin had done nothing worthy of such a reaction. He had merely partnered her in a Scotch reel, which was his least-preferred mode of dance. Far too lively, by his standards. However, apparently Lady Clementia liked leaping and galloping about.

It had only served to encourage a thumping ache in his temples.

"Jam," he repeated, for he had learned, over the course of his attempts at wooing Lady Clementia, that the mere act of repeating her words back to her pleased her.

Much like sour lemonade and dreadful dances.

"It is indeed," Lady Clementia agreed sagely as they approached the lemonade.

Tarquin wondered what he had agreed to, but then reckoned it could hardly have been sufficiently significant if it involved jam.

"Quite," he said again, dutifully fetching a lemonade for Lady Clementia, and then another for her mother.

"Will you not take one?" she asked. "Surely after our reel you have developed a thirst."

Yes, he had.

But not for lemonade.

Tarquin forced another smile. "I am well, my lady. Thank you for your kindhearted concern."

"Oh," she breathed, as if he had slayed a dragon instead of taking up a glass of bitter drink in each hand.

"The weather," he said, wondering if she would recall they had already discussed it.

Some devil in his soul had prompted him, he was sure.

"The weather is lovely," she said, smiling brilliantly, as if it were the first time they had broached the subject that evening. "Do you not think so?"

*Christ.*

He suppressed a wince.

"Indeed," he lied for the second time. "Lovely."

"So very lovely." Lady Clementia beamed.

This woman was going to be his wife.

The prospect ought not to make him so miserable. And yet, it seemed woefully undeserved that he should have to bind himself to a lady of such flimsy merit. But the duke was old friends with her father, the Earl of Brownley. Brownley was willing to overlook Tarquin's dubious lineage in favor of securing a familial bond with the hideously wealthy Duke of Hampton.

It seemed an unfair tradeoff for both himself and Lady Clementia. But then, his very existence was skin-and-bone proof of just how very imbalanced the world was. Tarquin Bellingham, the son of a duke who could never claim the title. He would not inherit. No one would ever address him as *Your Grace*. His mother had been an actress with a gin problem and a terrible temperament. His father had been her keeper. And a distant cousin was going to be the next Duke of Hampton instead of Tarquin.

He could never be the duke.

Would never truly be a part of the aristocracy.

He was fortunate he had managed to buy his way into Rivendale's. He was also damned fortunate that the Earl of Brownley had amassed such abundant debts that he required the Duke of Hampton's coin.

"...but I do think lemonade is such a delightful refreshment. So very civilized."

Lady Clementia's endless dialogue reached him.

Could he bear a lifetime of such meaningless prattle?

"Delightful," he repeated.

He would have to endure. There was no other choice. The Duke of Hampton had decreed the ultimate price for his money. And Tarquin had not raised himself to this position in life to surrender. Giving up everything he had worked for in Bellingham and Co. was not an option.

Grimly, he escorted his future bride back to her mother's side. Seeing both Lady Clementia and Lady Brownley settled with their lemonades, he made his excuses. With a bow, he took his leave. No more dancing for him this evening. Merriment was for fools and people who had never been forced to sell their souls to earn their daily bread.

Tarquin had a business to run.

# CHAPTER 1

*T*arquin Bellingham was an irritatingly comely man.

'Twas a deuced pity he was also an insufferable arsehole.

It was the latter, rather than the former, which made stealing from him that much more satisfying, Lily Sutton thought to herself as she carefully slid a handsome fan down her bodice. The ivory handle glided smoothly beneath her chemise, resting cool and forbidden between her breasts. Yet another secret to add to the ever-mounting pile.

One day, she would repent her sins.

But first, there was that damned enticing pair of gloves dangling fortuitously near her left hand from its place upon the shelf...

"Miss Sutton?"

Lily started at the unexpected voice at her back and spun about to find Mr. Smythe hovering in surprising proximity. The shop attendant was an obsequious cove if she'd ever met one. Always eager to please the patrons of the grand establishment that was Bellingham and Co. Easy to fool, just the way she preferred. But unless she was mistaken, there was a new hardness to his eyes and jaw this afternoon.

To his voice, as well.

She bestowed her best smile upon him. "Good afternoon, Mr. Smythe."

"Good afternoon, miss," he returned, looking distinctly uncomfortable. He shifted weight from one foot to the other, and then cleared his throat.

For several weeks, Lily had been making a regular jaunt to London's most prestigious shop. Bellingham and Co. boasted four different departments. Lily's favorite was furs and fans, because stuffing the costly goods to be had within its partitions was far easier than attempting certain others. Clocks, for instance. Bonnets, for another.

It was because of her frequent journeys from her family's gaming hell to Pall Mall that Lily had become quite familiar with Mr. Smythe by now. Their paths had crossed on numerous occasions. His demeanor on past excursions, however, had never seemed ominous as it did on this particular afternoon.

Something was amiss.

"What is troubling you, Mr. Smythe?" she asked kindly, keenly aware of the presence of her secreted fan. "Is it the weather? Dreadfully cold, with the portent of rain. Terribly grim, is it not?"

Lily was skilled at distraction. And deception, when the situation merited it.

Robbing Tarquin Bellingham's shop of its trifles was one of those situations.

"I have been asked to bring you with me, Miss Sutton," Mr. Smythe said, his countenance forbidding as ever. Nary a hint of a welcoming smile as he extended his arm, as if to offer her escort.

Lily stared at Mr. Smythe's brown, woolen sleeve, the

elbow crooked, and felt her guts twist and tighten into a knot. "And where do you intend to take me, sir?"

"I am to take you to Mr. Bellingham himself, miss." Mr. Smythe swallowed, the action making his Adam's apple bob above his simply tied neck cloth.

*Mr. Bellingham himself.*

Well, how do you do? The lofty Mr. Tarquin Bellingham, the owner of Bellingham and Co., the merciless scoundrel, wished an audience with Lily Sutton.

Without thought, her fingers lightly traced over her bodice above the fan she had so recently placed there, beneath the safe haven of her stays.

"Unfortunately, I don't wish to see Mr. Bellingham," she told Mr. Smythe, blunting the sting of her denial with a smile as she skirted around him to continue on her shopping excursion.

But Mr. Smythe was quicker-footed than he looked, moving to impede her further movement. "I am afraid the meeting is compulsory, Miss Sutton."

Her heart resumed a frantic pace once more.

"Compulsory," she repeated slowly, turning the word over on her tongue.

A large word for a man who believed himself far more important than all London. Of course he would issue such a decree. And as if she were Mr. Bellingham's grateful vassal, she was expected to follow Mr. Smythe to a place of his choosing.

"Yes, Miss Sutton," Mr. Smythe said, shifting again from foot to foot as a dull, red flush stole over his cheekbones. "That was Mr. Bellingham's word."

She took pity on the poor cove, but not so much that she was going to leap into the air when Tarquin Bellingham told her to jump. "If you please, Mr. Smythe, inform Mr.

Bellingham that I'm not his to order about. If you'll excuse me, I've a carriage awaiting me."

*And a stolen fan tickling my rib cage. I really must go before it unintentionally falls to the floor.*

Lily wisely kept that last to herself.

"But Miss Sutton…"

"That will be all, Mr. Smythe," said a cold, smooth-as-butter masculine voice.

And Mr. Smythe promptly scuttled away, for the devil himself had arrived.

Lily felt his stare on her back before she turned to face him slowly, gracefully.

Elegantly.

Secretly praying the fan would not slide free and land at her feet.

And he was every bit as handsome as she recalled. Tall and imposing, with thick, dark hair and eyes that were astoundingly blue. With a strong blade of a jaw and a proud chin. And a mouth that looked as if it had been sculpted by God for the sheer purpose of temptation. What a dreadful shame those lips were always held in such a tight, rigid line of disapproval. And what a waste for the rest of him to be every bit as bang up to the mark as his voice promised.

Because what was on the inside was rotten.

"Come with me, if you please, madam," Mr. Bellingham said curtly.

Lily held his stare, allowing all the defiant fire burning within to show. "No."

He raised a brow, his expression incredulous for a moment so brief Lily thought she may have imagined it. "No?"

Perhaps it was a word—a concept, even—with which he was unfamiliar. Refusal. Denial. Being told no.

*Too bloody bad, Bellingham.*

"You heard me," she said agreeably. "No."

And with that calm pronouncement, Lily sidestepped Mr. Bellingham.

"Perhaps I ought to have been clearer." His hand shot out, staying her. "I was not asking, Miss Sutton. I was *demanding*."

His arrogance was infuriating. But also alarming. Mr. Bellingham *knew who she was*. That did not bode well for either Lily or for the fan currently secreted in her stays.

Never mind that. This was not the first occasion Lily had confronted a self-important oaf, and nor would it prove the last. London was rife with men of Tarquin Bellingham's ilk. She could bring him low without blinking an eye.

To that end, it occurred to her that they were rather on display, much like Mr. Bellingham's wares. Curious customers surreptitiously gawked at them, heads cocked in the hope they might catch a brewing scandal.

"You would dare to accost me in plain sight of all your customers?" she hissed at him, hating the way his touch sent awareness careening through her.

His hand was large.

And warm.

Burning through her pelisse.

He released her at once, his lips thinning. "I am hardly accosting you, Miss Sutton."

His voice was low. Smooth. *Cunning.* It wrapped around her senses, settling in the same way his touch did. The man was a villain. She didn't even like him.

Her eyes narrowed. "Is that so?"

"Yes. That is so. Now, if you please, kindly come with me to my office where we can further discuss matters."

*Matters.* How deliberately vague of him.

Lily wasn't a fish. And she wasn't biting.

"I *don't* please," she said evenly, proud of herself for maintaining her composure and keeping her voice from carrying.

As the youngest in a large family—eight siblings in all—she often had to yell in order to be heard. But then, being the youngest also afforded her other luxuries. All her older brothers and sisters were too busy with their own lives to have a care for what Lily was about, and that was plummy in her opinion. She could do as she wished.

Nothing better.

Until it wasn't.

Now, for instance.

"Perhaps I should have parsed it differently," Mr. Bellingham bit out coldly. "You will accompany me without argument, or I will be forced to take measures."

His threat, like the one which had preceded it, was once again lacking in specificity.

The pronouncement startled a laugh from her, which was a problem. Her stolen fan slid deeper into her stays. She hadn't tightened herself properly before her shopping expedition, it was true. But that had been on account of needing space for the bounty she might relieve from Bellingham and Co. If the fan slid completely free and landed at her feet, the explanation for how such a feat had occurred would be painfully obvious.

*Blast.*

She swallowed hard and struggled to force a smile to her lips. "And why should you be demanding an excellent customer such as myself accompany you, sir?"

A muscle twitched in his rigid jaw. "A simple one. Thievery."

*Oh dear.*

He suspected.

But she would brazen it out nonetheless.

She pressed a gloved hand over her heart and affected a gasp. "Do you mean to say a thief has been beneath this very roof?"

Another tic of that telling muscle.

His nostrils flared. And curse the man, but even his nose was a thing of beauty, perfectly proportioned, the bridge strong and straight. No one had ever given Tarquin Bellingham an old click in the muns, that was for certain. But there was a first for every occasion, and if there ever lived a man more deserving of a fist to the face, Lily couldn't think of one at the moment.

"That is precisely what I mean to say, Miss Sutton," he said in clipped, measured tones. "Someone has been pilfering my fans."

His sharp gaze made it more than apparent he suspected she was the someone. And he was not wrong about that.

Lily didn't blink. "How dreadful. I'm terribly sorry to hear that, Mr. Burningham."

His lips compressed. "It is Mr. *Bell*ingham, madam."

She had intentionally called him by the wrong surname. Lily wanted to humble him, yes. But she also wanted to distract him. The more, the better.

"Mr. *Bell*ingham," she repeated, stressing the same syllable he had. "Do forgive me. Are you the son of Mr. Bellingham, then?"

In truth, Lily knew a great deal about Tarquin Bellingham. She had made it her business to know as much about him as possible. Aside from his general lack of compassion. Or soul, for that matter. He was the bastard son of a duke. He had built Bellingham and Co. with partners he had paid to part ways with, leaving him the sole owner of Bellingham and Co.

"I am the *only* Mr. Bellingham," he said coldly.

"Indeed?" She fluttered her lashes, feigning more surprise. "Are you the owner of this fine establishment?"

He raised a dark brow, his countenance forbidding. "Yes."

"How lovely," she said, as if she hadn't a thought in her head.

Lily was no novice. Subterfuge was part of the game.

"Enough," he snapped, his voice turning harsh. "I am not fooled by you, Miss Sutton. Come with me at once."

He took her hand in his, forcing it into his crooked elbow, and unceremoniously began pulling her from the furs and fans department.

*Rantum scantum.*

She'd been caught.

~

THE PROBLEM WAS ABOUT to be solved.

Tarquin should feel a deep and abiding sense of calm. The irritation which had been a constant, nettling presence, agitating him more with each new day and additional revelation of lost inventory, ought to begin easing.

And yet, as he led Miss Lily Sutton to the office he kept at the rear of Bellingham and Co.'s vast shop, he knew not a modicum of relief. He felt, instead, a far more vexing and unwanted sensation residing deep within him. Sharp and strong and undeniable. Sinful and wrong, yet resisting his every attempt to banish it, nonetheless.

But he was nothing if not restrained. Control had become the guiding principle of his life.

At his side, Miss Sutton looked as if she were poised for flight. He wondered if she would run. Lord knew he would not do anything as vulgar as chase after her before all his customers. Which was why he had men stationed at the front and rear of the shop, should the cunning minx make any such attempts. He had chosen not to involve the magistrate or a Runner, for inviting the law would only produce unwanted gossip. The reputation of Bellingham and Co, in the eyes of its patrons, was paramount.

Miss Sutton held his arm in a light grip that suggested she may break free at any moment.

And curse the woman, but even through the layers of his coat and shirt, that touch of hers made sinful, scorching heat curl through him. His reaction to her was wholly unacceptable. If only his body possessed such a response to Lady Clementia. However, regardless of how much he had tried to foster carnal enthusiasm for the woman who would be his bride, he could not. Instead, and very much to his eternal shame, he had spent the last few weeks simmering in a pitiful stew of desire for the criminal on his arm.

"I do not suppose why you should think I am attempting to fool you, sir," Miss Sutton said then, *sotto voce*.

Tarquin ground his molars. "Do you think me an imbecile, madam?"

"Not precisely," she said.

*By God.*

He slanted a glare in her direction, trying not to take note of the luminosity in her gaze. Those eyes of hers were a rare combination of color, gray and green and blue and brown blended together. It was breathtaking. Pity such beauty was wasted upon a common rookeries-born thief.

"Not precisely," he repeated, scarcely able to keep the tremor of fury from his voice.

The sheer impudence of the brazen baggage.

A display before his customers would be unseemly. He needed to remember that. He could give the wench the tongue lashing she so richly deserved in the privacy of his office.

"How am I to judge, based upon the merit of a single conversation alone?" she asked brightly at his side, as if he had not recently witnessed her stuffing a Bellingham and Co. fan down her bodice.

But then, perhaps she did not realize he had been watching her, waiting for her to grow so comfortable in her thievery that she made a mistake. Boldness was ever a criminal's downfall. Even one as skilled as Miss Lily Sutton, a woman who used every wile and tactic available to her to steal. It occurred to him then that she was remarkably well-spoken for a thief. Educated, perhaps. Still, her true nature shone through, like tarnish on silver.

"How indeed," he drawled.

A lady he recognized as the Marchioness of Searle was observing them closely, accompanied by a maid. Tarquin affected a smile for her benefit, pretending as if nothing were amiss. The patrons of Bellingham and Co. were of the utmost import. Without them, he had nothing. One false step, and his castle would come crumbling down.

He bowed to the marchioness in passing. "My lady. Thank you for dignifying our establishment with your presence."

Tarquin carried on, reaching the paneled door which concealed the rear of the shop not a moment too soon. He flicked the latch, keeping it in place, and pulled Miss Sutton over the threshold with him, amazed at her lack of struggle. Either it was pretense, or she truly had no notion he now had undeniable proof of her pilfering. The fan was between her breasts, for God's sake. Try as he might, he could not keep his wicked mind from returning to that sole, depraved detail.

Would he have to remove it?

Heat crept up his throat.

No, he would ask her to retrieve the stolen fan herself. He would turn his back and give her the privacy necessary to dislodge the contraband.

"Where are you taking me, Mr. Burningham?" Miss Sutton demanded, calling him by the wrong name again.

He was sure her error was intentional.

"To a place where you might enjoy considerably more privacy than the furs and fans department whilst you remove the fan secreted in your bodice," he said coldly as they entered his office.

The door slammed ominously shut behind them.

The room seemed suddenly small.

And warm.

He extricated his arm from her grasp and took two steps away, putting some respectable distance between them.

"I haven't a fan in my bodice," she said, indignation in her countenance and her voice. "If you have brought me here to make such an insulting accusation, I can assure you I will no longer be patronizing this establishment."

She was either exceedingly brave or exceedingly stupid. Tarquin was inclined to believe the former rather than the latter. After all, it had taken him weeks of watching her to finally garner the proof with his own eyes that confirmed his suspicions.

"I have no doubt you will not be patronizing Bellingham and Co. in future," he returned, clasping his hands behind his back.

Against his will, his gaze dipped to her bodice. Her breasts were full and high beneath her pelisse, effectively concealing any evidence. He swallowed hard, willing his body to remain impervious.

Miss Sutton's lips compressed, the only evidence of her displeasure. "Sir, I imagine that since you are aware of my name, you must be familiar with my brothers."

He knew of the Sutton family, yes. They owned a notorious gaming hell. They were apparently marrying their way

How could he want a woman so desperately when she was everything he despised?

"You want my pelisse off, Mr. Bellingham?" Her fingers went to the closures on her pelisse. "I shall take it off."

The fact that she had called him by the correct surname of her own volition brought him a pleasure that was quickly obliterated by a bolt of appalling lust as she began plucking each button from its moorings. One shrug of her shoulders, and the garment fell to his office floor.

His mouth went dry.

There was nothing exceptional about her gown. He had seen finer raiment on any number of ladies. Most of the textiles in his shop were far superior. And yet, the way her gown clung to her breasts... The shape of her flared hips evident beneath the skirt...

Lily Sutton was nothing short of temptation incarnate. And Tarquin very much could not afford to be tempted.

"What else shall I take off for you, sir?" she asked, her voice cheery and pleasant, more suited to the drawing room than the East End, it was true. "My gloves, first. It is easier to disrobe without their encumbrance."

She tugged at the wrists of first one glove, and then another, removing them with ease. Her fingers were pale and elegant. They were not the reddened, chapped hands of a woman who worked in service. He found himself wondering just what tasks she performed at The Sinner's Palace before recalling that it hardly mattered. What she did was none of his concern, provided that she conducted her business far from Bellingham and Co.

He blinked. Her bare fingers were on the line bisecting her bodice. More buttons, Tarquin realized. To his horror, she began to undo them.

*Dear God*, she intended to remove *all* her attire.

And for a fleeting second, the devil in him was desperately enticed to allow her to do just that. To stand here in his office and watch her draw that sinful gown over her head, and next her stays and petticoats and chemise. Every bit of fabric until she was gloriously naked...

"Stop," he bit out, panic assailing him.

He could not allow her to do it. And, like the calculating minx she was, Lily Sutton knew that.

She paused, tilting her head, considering him with that vivid gaze. "Stop, Mr. Bellingham?"

He clenched his jaw, the throbbing in his temples growing to a stunning crescendo.

She had bested him, the cunning jade. He had watched her slide his merchandise between those magnificent breasts of hers, and he had no means of proving she had done so. No recourse, save the one she had already demonstrated. It was perilous at best and ruinous at worst. He had intended for her to remove her pelisse, for the evidence of her guilt to be outlined by her sinfully snug bodice. And yet, it had not been. And she, meanwhile, had held firm to her lies, threatening to strip herself bare.

If word were to travel in polite circles that he had forced a lady—albeit one of such questionable lineage as Miss Lily Sutton—to go nude before him, Lady Clementia would have no choice but to refuse his suit. And if she refused him, he would fall out of favor with his father. The duke had made it clear that Tarquin must wed Lady Clementia or suffer the consequences.

"You have proven your point, Miss Sutton," he ground out. "I cannot, as a gentleman of honor, require you to offer me the proof we both know is hiding within your gown at this very moment. Therefore, I am willing to be merciful and show you leniency. You will remove yourself from my shop, and you will never return. In exchange, I will not turn you over to the law as you so richly deserve."

Those nimble fingers were already at work, refastening buttons, and the wickedest part of Tarquin mourned the flesh she hid from his avid gaze.

"I maintain my innocence," she said quietly.

*Sincerely.*

Had he not seen her slide the fan inside her gown with his own eyes, he would have been tempted to believe her. However, he *had*. And Lily Sutton was a damned liar.

"I will have your promise you will not return to Bellingham and Co.," he countered, giving no quarter.

"Of course, Mr. Bellingham." She pulled on her gloves, then bent to retrieve her discarded pelisse, hastening to don it. "Good day to you, sir."

With an abbreviated curtsy, she turned and took her leave from his office. Not with a harried, humiliated gait, as a lady in her position might be expected to possess. But rather with languid, elegant strides. She moved as if she were in no hurry and his threats were hardly cause for alarm.

She moved as if she were a queen and he her lowly vassal. As if *she* had dismissed *him*. The sheer arrogance. And her hips were swaying. Taunting him, he was sure of it.

Tarquin shook himself from the lustful stupor that threatened to overwhelm his wits.

"Good day, Miss—" The door to his office slammed closed. "Sutton," he growled, glaring at the door, fury warring with unadulterated desire.

Belatedly, it occurred to him that he should not have simply allowed her to roam free in the private labyrinth of the shop, a place that was devoted to his salesmen, his inventory, and his own office. Gritting out a curse, he stalked from the office, searching for her.

But Miss Sutton had already vanished, like a wraith.

He could only hope she remained gone, and that he never saw her again.

## CHAPTER 2

Marianne was missing.

Again.

Lily tried to control the worry tying her stomach in knots as her carriage swayed over all-too-familiar roads. Thank heavens Gertrude had sent word to her at The Sinner's Palace. Hopefully, Lily could find the girl and return her to the foundling hospital before anyone noticed she had disappeared.

For if she did not...

No, Lily would not consider failure. Not now. As she had on every occasion upon which the headstrong girl had vanished from the foundling hospital before, landing in one scrape or another, Lily would find her. Yes, she would find her, issue a stern admonishment, remind Marianne why she must not displease the head matron, and return the far-too-daring child to the relative safety of the foundling hospital.

Fortunately, Lily suspected she knew where Marianne had gone.

Unfortunately, it was the very last place Lily was supposed to be: Bellingham and Co.

The frigid, supercilious, arsehole of a proprietor had forbidden her from returning.

Perched on the edge of the bench seat, Lily kept her face pressed to the window, fingers keeping the Venetian blinds spread to facilitate her outside view. Not enough to allow anyone on the streets to see in, however. Just as she preferred. As the carriage swayed toward the familiar façade bearing Bellingham and Co., Lily rapped on the roof of the carriage to let Sly Jack know he was to stop.

The carriage slowed.

One of the lads opened the door, and Lily descended, emerging into the gray, grim rains of the day.

"At Bellingham and Co., miss?" Sly Jack called down to her, his tone skeptical. "Are ye certain?"

For he knew she had been sent away from Bellingham and Co. in haste and shame, breathless, a fan dropping to the cobblestones at her feet just before she had managed to enter the carriage. Being Sly Jack, he'd said nary a word to her, and nor to any of her siblings either. But he *understood*.

"Quite certain," she confirmed. "Wait for me in the rear of the shop as usual, please."

It had been a week since she had last ventured within. A week since she had retreated from Tarquin Bellingham's office after just narrowly besting him at his own game. He had shown her mercy then. But she knew the man was sharp as a fresh blade. He would not be fooled by her twice.

"And ye're going *inside* the shop," Sly Jack pressed, fatherly concern etched on his countenance.

"Inside," she repeated with a firm nod that suggested far more confidence than she felt. "Yes."

"Miss Sutton," he began.

"Sly," she interrupted firmly. "Marianne may be within."

The coachman whistled through his uneven teeth. "Bloody 'ell, not again."

She trusted Sly Jack as she trusted few others; his loyalty was to all the Suttons, but he had an innate ability to keep secrets. And that was why she had told him about Marianne, her favorite charge at the foundling hospital. It was also why he had accompanied Lily here on previous shopping excursions. When one was engaging in a precarious business such as she had been at Bellingham and Co., one needed the ability to flee with haste and the assistance of a coachman who was more than happy to turn a blind eye to what she was about.

"Yes," she agreed wearily. "Again."

It seemed the poor dear would not surrender the grudge she held against Mr. Bellingham. And whilst Lily could hardly blame Marianne, she had already committed a great deal of sins on the girl's behalf. Stealing from the rich to aid the poor had never seemed wrong to Lily. Indeed, when she had been within Bellingham and Co., knowing what she did about the shop's owner, it had seemed not just frightfully easy, but right.

Necessary, really.

Until Mr. Bellingham had nearly caught her, that was.

"Ye'd best be going inside to find the lass, then," Sly Jack said with a weary sigh, shaking his head.

If Marianne had stolen inside to make trouble, and if Tarquin Bellingham discovered her…

Lily wouldn't think on that now. Instead, she turned and marched into Bellingham and Co., head held high, as if she had not recently been banished from its hallowed walls by Tarquin Bellingham himself. Gertrude had said Marianne told her she was going to Bellingham's in the hope she could filch a fancy fur. Lily should have known that her lack of spoils could lead the girl to return to pickpocketing and thievery.

She slipped inside the shop as she had so many times

before, hoping and praying that neither Mr. Bellingham nor Mr. Smythe would see her and that Marianne would be easily found. The sooner the girl was returned to the foundling hospital, the better.

Lily moved with haste, fretting as she passed through the haberdashery department. The last time she had found Marianne within Bellingham and Co., the imp had absconded two reticules, a pocket watch, and half a dozen fans.

"You."

The low growl at her back was as familiar as it was frigid as she passed into the jewelry department.

Her heart pounded faster, and not just with the rush of knowing she'd been seen. But also because she was going to have to face *him* again.

Lily turned to find Tarquin Bellingham towering over her, his haughty countenance as harsh as if it had been etched from stone.

She pinned her brightest smile to her lips, feigning pleasure to see him. "Mr. Bellingham."

His lip curled. "Madam, you were warned."

Yes, she had been. But she was not afraid of him. Well, not entirely afraid of him. His ire on their last meeting had been formidable, and she knew he was a wealthy and powerful man. But the Sutton family was not without means. They had been steadily growing their businesses and their influence. Her siblings would fight every way they could to protect her, of that she had no doubt.

"I can explain, sir," she offered.

"Do not bother," he snapped, his icy gaze narrowing on her, his voice like the crack of a whip.

"I am looking for someone," Lily said anyway, worry for Marianne trumping all else. "A young girl with dark hair and blue eyes."

*Who looks frightfully similar to you,* she added silently. The heartless oaf who had abandoned his half sister would not care who Marianne was anyway. He had already refused to offer her care, despite his obvious wealth. Moreover, Lily did not trust Bellingham not to embroil Marianne in trouble with the dreadful head matron at the foundling hospital, Mrs. Frost.

His stare was sharp and searching. "An apprentice of yours, Miss Sutton? One you have trained in the finer art of thievery?"

*Oh dear.* It would seem that he had perhaps indeed spied Marianne.

"I am not a thief," she denied coolly. "Have you seen her?"

"If you are referring to the scurrilous little waif who was chased away by Mr. Smythe a quarter hour ago, I regret to inform you that she is no longer haunting my establishment," he drawled. "By God, madam, you are low, forcing a child to do your insidious bidding."

*Good heavens*, now he believed she had enlisted Marianne to aid her in stealing from Bellingham and Co.

"I can assure you, I did not," she said quickly. "The girl is a bit wayward, but she is harmless enough. Understandable, since her family has abandoned her to the foundling hospital."

The moment the accusation had fled her lips, Lily wished she could recall it.

"Harmless does not attempt to purloin the reticule of the ladies frequenting my shop," he said, keeping his voice low and measured, though it remained tight with irritation. "We are drawing undue attention, Miss Sutton. Come with me to my office."

Being alone with him was the last thing she could afford to do.

"I must find my charge," she said.

After all, since Marianne's own brother had not a care for her, *someone* had to.

Again, Lily was careful to keep that to herself. Further drawing Mr. Bellingham's ire would not do Marianne any good. And the girl was currently on the street, running about on her own. Lily shuddered to think what could happen, even in this relatively safe part of London. Hopefully she would return to the foundling hospital on her own.

"We will find her together," he countered grimly. "The miscreant must be made to atone for her sins."

"She is a child," Lily said, wondering what punishments he would see inflicted upon Marianne should he realize who she was.

He had already done enough harm to the poor girl in doing nothing to provide her a home. If he spoke with Mrs. Frost, there was no telling what the woman would do to Marianne. It was possible that she could turn her out.

"Children must be taught the difference between right and wrong, Miss Sutton. I gather you were never educated thusly, which begs the question of why someone of your dubious influence has been allowed to attend foundlings."

Something inside Lily broke.

"The difference between right and wrong," she repeated, her voice trembling with her suppressed outrage. "Surely you do not mean to suggest *you* have learned it, sir."

He scoffed. "You dare to imply I am lacking in moral fortitude when you are a common thief?"

A dowager moved past them, her gaze hawkish as she drank in the sight they undoubtedly presented—the august, perfectly proper Mr. Bellingham conducting a bitter argument with one of his female customers. And Bellingham took note, if his suddenly stiffened posture was any indication.

"For God's sake, Miss Sutton, let us move this discussion elsewhere," he bit out, his expression thunderous.

"I have no intention of being alone with you in your office again, sir," she returned primly.

And not just because Marianne needed to be found, either. Rather, because she could not trust her body's reaction to Mr. Bellingham. Even knowing what a dreadful, heartless scoundrel he was.

"Then I shall accompany you," he said smoothly.

There was no good way to extricate herself from this situation, it seemed, save agreeing with the stubborn cove.

"Very well," she allowed reluctantly. "But we will take my carriage."

With Sly Jack to protect her, she needn't fear, Lily knew.

He inclined his head. "We will leave through the rear of the shop and enter the carriage separately. I cannot afford to be seen alone in a conveyance with you."

That rather stung Lily's pride. But then, if Bellingham thought himself too high in the instep to be seen with a Sutton, to the devil with him. His opinion meant nothing to her, much like the man himself.

"As yournabs wishes," she said, unable to keep the edge of bitterness from her voice. "I'd 'ate to sully your virtue, I would."

Deliberately, she dropped her *h* and strengthened the accent she had spent her formative years doing her utmost to rectify.

But Bellingham simply continued to pin her with his frigid glare, as if she were the offal stuck to his shoe. "None of your sharp tongue, madam. I warned you there would be consequences."

TARQUIN EXTRACTED his pocket watch and consulted it for the fourth time in the last quarter hour.

"If you need to return to your shop, Sly Jack would be more than happy to take you back to Bellingham and Co.," Miss Sutton said pointedly.

Naturally, the wench did not miss a single action. She was meant to be watching for the missing thief she claimed was her charge. They had been driving in circles for the last two hours, and he was becoming increasingly convinced the imp they were looking for was already back at the safe haven of the foundling hospital. If indeed that was truly where she resided. For all he knew, she made her home at the infamous Sutton gaming hell. The frantic search for the girl was, he suspected, another of Miss Lily Sutton's ruses.

And why was he not surprised that her coachman ought to have a dubious name such as *Sly Jack?* The hulking Scotsman with the patch over one eye was likely a partner to the Queen of Thieves herself.

He tucked his pocket watch inside his waistcoat. "My time is valuable, Miss Sutton. Far more so than the objects lining the shelves in my shop. I suspect that is why you are intent upon stealing it as well as my fans and furs."

When Smythe had informed him that a young girl had been attempting to steal the Duchess of Whitley's reticule, Tarquin had been horrified. His establishment's popularity with the ladies of the polite society was not guaranteed. He had to work to maintain their trust, to continually prove Bellingham and Co. could provide them with luxurious goods at the best prices, and further, that a shop featuring a wide array of selections in four departments—the first of its kind—was not just reputable but also revered.

And he could not accomplish any of those feats with thieves infiltrating his shop, particularly when they began turning their efforts upon his customers.

"If you will but recall," Miss Sutton was countering smoothly, "you are the reason for your presence in my carriage, Mr. Bellingham. I intended to find Marianne on my own, without your aid."

He considered her sternly. "Yes, but you have not found her, have you?"

Intentionally, he had no doubt.

"Not yet," Miss Sutton allowed, her tone steeped in reluctance. "There is a possibility she has returned to the foundling hospital of her own volition."

"Then we ought to go there next," he decided, nearly out of his skin after having to share the small confines of the carriage with the woman.

She smelled of lavender.

He had never found the scent to be alluring previously. But it was driving him to distraction. As was her proximity. The pelisse and gown she wore today were even more tempting than those she had worn on the previous occasion their paths had crossed, even if they were a trifle plainer. The color was a pale blue that verged on green. It heightened the gray in her eyes.

Miss Sutton sighed softly in defeat. "Perhaps we should go to the foundling hospital. If she is already safely returned, there is little reason for us to continue this interminable voyage together."

*She* thought it interminable? She was not the one lusting after a thief who had robbed him of an inestimable amount of goods before setting an orphan upon his customers' reticules.

He scowled at her. "By all means, madam. Let us go to the foundling hospital. I am certain the brat will be awaiting you."

But finding the scamp would not solve the problem of what he was to do with Miss Sutton. It seemed she was a plague, and he was forever doomed to be visited by her. Tempted. Tormented.

Miss Sutton rapped on the carriage roof. "To the foundling hospital, if you please, Sly," she called to the coachman.

"As ye wish, Miss Sutton," came the gruff reply from the box.

He could not help but to take note of her abbreviated use of the man's name. *Sly*. Did that denote an intimacy between the two of them? And why should the thought send a sharp spear of jealousy straight through him?

Stupidity, he was sure.

His wits had abandoned him.

Nothing remained of ration and reason; all he had was a raging cockstand that was growing increasingly difficult to shield from that roaming, knowing hazel gaze of hers.

He hated himself for wanting her. Hated *her* for making him want her. For sitting there so primly, a bonnet perched on her head as if she were a true lady. For smelling like flowers and possessing such magnificent breasts and sweet, feminine curves. For having a mouth he would die to kiss…

*Cease this, Tarquin*, he scolded himself inwardly. *Cease all such veins of thought at once.*

There was nothing between them save silence and the familiar sounds of the road; tack, hooves, the crush of traffic beyond their carriage.

He became aware that Miss Sutton was twisting her gloved fingers in her lap. Almost as if she truly were fretting over the little scoundrel who had been so intent upon pilfering reticules earlier in the day. Not for the first time, he wondered at the connection between the two, Miss Sutton and the girl. He had not witnessed the child himself, but from Smythe's description, it sounded as if she were eight years of age. Perhaps even ten. Miss Sutton was far too young to be the child's mother.

Why, then, did she burden herself with such a child? Was it solely to use the girl for her own gain? Teaching her to steal? But he hardly thought a foundling hospital would keep such a child or allow a woman like Lily Sutton to befriend her and lead her down the path to evil.

As the carriage turned in a new direction, swaying over pitted roads, his patience surrendered to his curiosity.

"Who is she to you?" he asked Miss Sutton. "The miscreant so intent upon stealing the reticules of my customers today. Smythe tells me it is not the first occasion upon which he has seen her haunting my establishment. It was, however, the first time she was caught in the act of filching."

"She is a child," Miss Sutton repeated her earlier defense of the girl's inexcusable thievery.

"Not your child, surely?" he pressed before he could stop himself. "One of your brothers' bastards, perhaps?"

Her nostrils flared, and her chin went up, a pose he recognized. He had angered her.

"My brothers care for their children, Mr. Bellingham. We hold family sacred. None of us would ever abandon our blood, unlike others."

Why did he feel as if she were somehow intending to pay him insult with her pointed words?

He was feeling beastly, so he responded in kind. "How nice for you, Miss Sutton. 'Tis a pity none of you hold the law sacred. I gather you do understand stealing is a crime, do you not?"

Her lips pinched into a thin line. "We are a respectable family."

He raised a brow, watching her closely. "Quite respectable indeed, stuffing fans down your stays, all the better to steal them. To say nothing of using innocent children in your campaign of thievery. And then there is your family's gaming hell. A more amoral paradise for sinners, I have no doubt, there isn't to be found. One can only imagine the games within are weighted heavily in favor of the Sutton family. Woe to any unsuspecting fool who should be witless enough to think he might have a lucky roll of the dice."

Perhaps he had been too cutting. He did not miss the way Miss Sutton flinched as he settled into his diatribe. But curse her, she had cheated him, stolen from him. She was the one in the wrong, not Tarquin.

"At least we have never abandoned our sisters to foundling hospitals whilst we surround ourselves with riches and pretend to be faultless," Miss Sutton snapped. "Have you any notion of the misery of such places? The children there are left behind, loved by no one, forced to learn trades and take in needlework to pay for the wretched food in their bellies."

He blinked, trying to comprehend the first half of her intended insult. He hadn't a sister. He was a lone bastard, who had been abandoned and forgotten, left to forge his own path in the world.

"I haven't any sisters to abandon," he forced himself to say. "And the only riches I surround myself with are the ones I sell to others."

"Convenient lies you tell yourself, no doubt," Miss Sutton said harshly. "Perhaps it quells the guilt, keeping it from eating you alive. I do not know how you sleep, sir."

Once more, he was taken aback by the vitriol in her tone, in her speech.

*He* was the injured party. He was the one who had been robbed, for heaven's sake. And repeatedly. Thoroughly. By *her*.

"I sleep like a babe, Miss Sutton," he told her coldly. "The only guilt eating at me is in relation to the mercy I showed you on our last meeting. If I could go back to that day, I would never give you the chance to set a thieving orphan upon me. I would demand the price you owe me instead."

"Oh?" She raised a golden brow in defiance. "And what would that be? What is the price you suppose I owe you, Mr. Bellingham?"

For a moment, he was mesmerized by the sunlight catching in the burnished-blonde curls peeping from beneath her bonnet. There were hints of red threading through the strands. He was besieged by an image of those curls draped over his pillow, spilling over his hands. Of touching them. They would be soft and silken to the touch, he knew.

His lust astounded him, as did the sudden realization accompanying it. The price he wanted to collect was sinful and wrong. He, who prided himself on his ability to abstain from the moral failing which had produced his miserable entrée into the world, wanted a woman in his bed. And not just any woman, but this thieving, cunning jade. The woman who had, without compunction, stolen from him repeatedly. There would be only one way to purge her from his blood.

And yet, he could not make the proposition. The lovers he had known were very much in his past. He intended to offer for Lady Clementia soon. He would not succumb to base lust. He was not a merciless rogue. He was a businessman. A gentleman. The son of a duke, if never the heir.

"You owe me a small fortune for the goods you have stolen from me," he informed Miss Sutton, shaking himself from the heavy weight of his thoughts. "I will be repaid, and there will be no more urchins invading my shop."

The carriage rolled to a halt.

They had reached the foundling hospital.

Miss Sutton's chin tipped up in defiance, a flash of something he could not define in her hazel eyes. "And if I refuse?"

"Then I will extract payment from you however I must." The thinly veiled threat left him before he could think better of it.

But once the words were spoken, he could not recall them. And there *were* means of extracting payment from her. Delicious, forbidden means. He loathed himself for even thinking of them, for the hastening in his pulse, the longing tightening in his gut.

"I dare you to try it, Mr. Bellingham," she said, brazen as ever. "Now, if you will excuse me, I must go inside and see to my charge. Sly Jack can return you to your shop."

Tarquin wasn't about to go anywhere alone with the ruffian.

He raised a brow. "I'll wait, madam."

Her lips tightened. "As it pleases you."

Tarquin could think of many things which would please him more, but for the moment, he would accept remaining in the carriage. For this discussion of theirs was far from over.

## CHAPTER 3

*L*ily found Marianne in the kitchen of the Foundling Hospital for Abandoned Girls, cleaning crockery alongside a handful of fellow orphan girls. Fortunately, the dreadful head matron, Mrs. Frost, was preoccupied with overseeing a new group of charges who would need to be acclimated to their surroundings. Part of the mission of the foundling hospital was to prepare orphaned children for productive lives. The girls took turns caring for the hospital itself, helping with all manners of its daily operations, from laundry to cooking and scrubbing and dusting.

From the guilty expression on Marianne's little face, it was apparent the girl knew the reason for Lily's visit.

"I didn't take nothing, Miss Sutton," she blurted. "I swear it."

"Come with me, if you please," she told the girl quietly, relief mingling with irritation that the child had deliberately gone against her wishes.

She had told Marianne to stay away from her brother's shop.

And the girl had promised she would.

"I'm to be helping with the crockery," Marianne protested, eyes wide.

"And help you shall in just a few minutes," she said calmly. "I have Mrs. Frost's permission to speak with you."

The matron did not like favoritism of any sort, and particularly not when it came to Marianne. Mrs. Frost had precious little patience and tolerance for the girl's antics. On more than one occasion, she had threatened to send Marianne to the workhouse. That Lily had secured the dour elder woman's permission to seek out Marianne and take her from her chore for a few moments was owed to Mrs. Frost's distraction alone.

Most definitely not to any leniency or a softening heart.

Marianne nodded, looking uncharacteristically glum as she followed Lily to a corner of the dank kitchen where they could speak privately.

When they were beyond earshot of the other curious girls, Lily frowned down at Marianne. She had charmed her ever since Lily had first visited the foundling hospital. But her penchant for making trouble for herself and others could well prove dangerous if Lily did not seek to address it.

"You went to Bellingham and Co. today," she said softly, not mincing words. "Gertrude sent word to me."

Marianne hung her head. "Yes, Miss Sutton." She then mumbled something beneath her breath that sounded suspiciously like *stupid Gertrude*.

"Marianne, you promised you would not do so again. You are not to be leaving the foundling hospital and wandering about Town alone." Lily was careful to keep her tone low as she chastised the girl.

If any of the other orphans were to carry the tale to Mrs. Frost, Lily had no doubt the matron would make good on her threat of banishing Marianne to the workhouse. And as an unwed woman without much of her own means, there would be nothing Lily could do to stop her.

"The fans fetch a good price," Marianne said with a pout. "I haven't any more of them to sell."

When Lily had first discovered Marianne's game—selling filched goods for unscrupulous merchants to resell—she had initially been shocked. But she had also admired her pluck. At Mrs. Frost's direction, the girls took in needlework, which they were then charged with delivering on a weekly schedule. When it was Marianne's turn to make the deliveries, she cleverly took her pilfered items with her and stopped along the way to earn her coin. Lily had caught the girl quite by accident when she had been leaving the foundling hospital with her loaded cart of mending and it had overturned in the alley.

A sobbing Marianne had revealed all to her, from the perilous story of her abandonment at the foundling hospital, to the confession that London's wealthiest shopkeeper was her brother. It had dashed Lily's heart to bits to learn of Bellingham's refusal to acknowledge his own sister or to aid in her care. She had been furious on Marianne's behalf, and she had vowed to aid her in her cause. The outrage—a rich cove like him leaving his own flesh and blood to the foundling hospital.

Lily herself had been a dab hand at pickpocketing in her youth. And she could admit, if only to herself, that there had been an element of adventure that had appealed to her. That, coupled with the knowledge she was helping to right a wrong, had led her to abscond with an untold number of items from Bellingham and Co. over the last few weeks.

"I told you that I would gather the fans," she reminded Marianne now, careful to keep a stern edge in her words. "Have you any idea the trouble you could have found yourself in?"

Marianne was only eight years old. She had much to learn about the world. But if Lily had any say in it, she would protect her from the very worst of its evils, however she could.

The girl crossed her arms, her countenance turning mulish. "I didn't get into trouble."

"Only by sheer luck." She shook her head. "You are fortunate indeed that Mr. Bellingham or one of his shop assistants did not catch you. To say nothing of what could have happened on the streets. I have been searching for you everywhere, Marianne."

Marianne bit her lip, some of her bravado fading. "You were?"

"Of course I was."

Marianne shuffled her feet, looking crestfallen. "I didn't mean to worry you."

"You broke your promise," she reminded the girl.

Lily saw so much of herself in young Marianne. Perhaps that was the reason she had been drawn to take the girl under her wing. But she also knew that coddling Marianne would only make her bolder. She could not continue to sneak away from the foundling hospital. The next time could well prove her last.

"I'm sorry," Marianne said, her eyes welling with unshed tears. "Will you stop coming to visit me now?"

The girl had been abandoned by her father, mother, and brother, and whatever other family she may have had. It came as no surprise to Lily that she would instantly suspect the same of her.

"Of course not," she said gently, patting Marianne's thin shoulder. "You mustn't be upset now, dearest. But you must promise me you will not sneak away from here again. It is far too dangerous, and Mr. Bellingham is very displeased that you have been causing trouble in his establishment. He says you attempted to steal a reticule from one of the grand ladies. A duchess, no less."

Marianne looked down. "Only cares about his customers and his money, he does."

Sadness pierced Lily's heart on the girl's behalf. She may have been born in the rookeries, but her siblings were loyal and loved her. She had always felt protected and cared for. How dare Tarquin Bellingham, that arrogant, supercilious oaf, abandon his own sister?

"Never mind him," she told the girl firmly. "I care about you, and I want to see you safe. Eventually, Mrs. Frost will catch you if you continue to slip out, and if she were to discover what you've been about..."

She allowed her words to trail off, for they both knew.

As difficult as life was in the foundling hospital, and as terrible a dragon as Mrs. Frost was, the workhouse was a far worse fate.

"I won't do it again, Miss Sutton," Marianne said quietly.

"Do I have your promise?" she prodded.

The girl sighed. "I promise I'll not leave the foundling hospital on my own again."

She raised a brow. "And you will cease pickpocketing as well, yes?"

Marianne frowned. "If I must."

"You must," Lily confirmed, frowning. "I am doing everything I can to help you, Marianne, but you must do your part as well."

"Very well." The girl nodded. "I shan't pickpocket."

"Good." At least that was settled. "I shall return tomorrow, at the usual time. Until then, try to keep yourself out of trouble, my dear."

"Yes, Miss Sutton." Marianne curtseyed and then dutifully returned to her task with the other girls.

With a heavy sigh, Lily took her leave, knowing that

Tarquin Bellingham awaited her in her carriage. His threat to extract payment from her loomed. She had funds, of course. But she had no wish to pay him for that which she had taken. It was, she believed, what was owed to poor Marianne.

Perhaps she ought to tell him so, now that she had made certain the girl was safe.

However, she did not wish to make additional trouble for her. There was no telling if Bellingham was a spiteful man. There was the possibility that he could demand Marianne be sent to the workhouse or worse as a punishment. And if he realized the impish pickpocket who had been thieving reticules in his shop was the sister he had abandoned to the founding hospital, it was entirely possible he would exact stinging retribution. Bellingham did not strike Lily as the sort of man who showed mercy unless he had no other choice.

It was raining by the time she reached the street. A sound deluge that the brim of her bonnet did little to defend her against. The door to her carriage opened, and to her shock, Bellingham emerged, holding his coat over his head.

"Come, Miss Sutton," he shouted above the sudden din. "It isn't a rain umbrella, but hopefully it will shield you from the worst of it."

He was…being kind?

It seemed horridly at odds with everything she had come to know of the man thus far. Lily faltered in her step and nearly tripped over her hems in her startlement. Bellingham caught her by the elbow in a sure and steady grip, guiding her over the wet cobblestones to the carriage. He helped her inside whilst holding his now-sodden coat over her head, rain pouring over his hat, slicking the dark hair peeping beneath it.

Sodden and surprised, she fell onto the squabs, Bellingham following after her, the door to the carriage snapping closed. He settled himself on the seat opposite her, his crisp, white shirt and waistcoat soaked through, his sharp cheekbones and long nose wet with the sheen of rain.

Their gazes met and held, a simmer of something strange and momentous passing between them, just for a flash. Rather like a bolt of lightning.

"Where will ye be traveling now, Miss Sutton?" Sly Jack called down.

"To The Sinner's Palace," Bellingham said.

At the same time, Lily answered, "Back to Bellingham and Co., please."

She blinked, frowning at the other occupant of the carriage. "You are not accompanying me to my family's gaming hell, sir. My brothers will eat your liver for breakfast."

He appeared unimpressed. "For being gentleman enough to escort you back to your home? I hardly think the Suttons will be as bloodthirsty as that."

Perhaps not. But they were protective, fiercely so. And word traveled faster than the wind about The Sinner's Palace. If any of her brothers were to learn she had been traveling about alone with a man, she would have much to answer for.

"You wish to escort me," she repeated, wary.

"Yes."

His simple, one-word response was troubling. He should be wishing to return to his shop immediately. What did he want from her?

"I cannot think it wise, Mr. Bellingham," she said crisply, shifting her damp skirts so that she could look away from his compelling face.

In his shirtsleeves, he was even more handsome. The carriage seemed impossibly small. And stifling. His long legs were nearly brushing against hers.

"As we have established, you owe me, Miss Sutton," he countered. "I trust your charge was within, else you would have emerged long before now."

"Mari—" she began before stopping herself, realizing who she was speaking to. "She was, yes."

"It is simple," he said, leaning forward, bracing his elbows on his knees as he held her pinned by his bright-blue stare. "Either you tell the highwayman masquerading as a coachman to take us to The Sinner's Palace, or I will go inside and find that waif of yours."

He was threatening Marianne. That could not stand.

"Miss Lily?" Sly Jack prodded from the box-seat.

Bellingham held her in that steely regard, watching. Waiting.

She swallowed hard. "To The Sinner's Palace, Sly."

"Wise choice," Bellingham said softly.

She glared at him, trying to tamp down her own awareness of his proximity.

Was it the rain, the damp smell of him infiltrating the carriage? His scent was more pronounced now. The sharp freshness of rain mingled with the earthiness of musk and a hint of bay. Heat unfurled low in her belly, and she clamped her thighs together to ward off the sensation.

The carriage lurched into motion. Poor Sly was likely getting soaked to the bone, but there was no help for it. They could not remain here in this carriage indefinitely. His greatcoat would have to serve him.

"The thief was unharmed?" Bellingham asked into the silence that had fallen between them.

"She was," she confirmed.

"And you have warned her against future expeditions to my shop, I trust?" he prodded.

"Naturally," she bit out.

Rain dripped from the brim of her bonnet, landing on her

gloved hands and reminding her that she likely presented a bedraggled mess. Not that she should be concerned with how she must look.

Bellingham presented her with a damp handkerchief.

She hesitated to accept the offering.

"Take it," he ordered. "Your nose is dripping."

*Good heavens.*

Heat crept up her cheeks. A bedraggled mess indeed. She took the handkerchief and dabbed as discreetly as possible at the end of her nose.

The handkerchief smelled even more of him. Pleasant. Far too pleasant. Hastily, she finished blotting the rain from her cheeks and attempted to pass it back to him.

"Keep it." His tone was wry. "You seem to have an affinity for items that belong to me, Miss Sutton."

Ah, so they were returned to the icy chill which had fallen around them before she had gone inside the foundling hospital. It was just as well. Barbs and insults were far easier for her to endure than kindness.

She crumpled the handkerchief in her fist. "Why do you wish to accompany me to The Sinner's Palace?"

"I have been thinking about repayment." He smiled then, and the result was devastating. "It seems only right that we ought to reach an agreement."

He had never smiled before, at least not that she had seen. Her heart pounded faster. That inconvenient attraction to him, never far from the periphery of her thoughts, returned with a pang. It was criminal, longing for such a rotten man.

She ran her tongue over her suddenly dry lips, forcing herself to think of Marianne sobbing in her arms, telling her about the heartless scoundrel of a brother who had refused to welcome her into his home after her mother's abandonment. "What manner of agreement do you have in mind, Mr. Bellingham?"

The smile faded, his gaze burning into hers. "A mutually agreeable one."

Lily did not like the sound of that. He was looking at her differently. The very air within the carriage had changed. But another part of her liked it. Liked it far too much.

"Please elaborate, Mr. Bellingham."

"The goods you stole from me were very fine, Miss Sutton. And then you invited ruin upon my establishment by encouraging your orphan imp to accost my customers." He paused, watching her from beneath a hooded gaze, his expression impenetrable. "You must recompense me in a manner suiting to the great harm you have caused."

"Are you propositioning me, sir?" she asked, astounded—and, to her shame—thrilled at the prospect.

A small, wicked smile curved his lips, the very air in the carriage changing. "Do you *want* me to proposition you, Miss Sutton?"

Was he teasing her? He appeared serious. Intent. Heat blossomed within her, a fire she could not control, chasing the coolness of the rain and the damp of her sodden gown.

She eyed him warily. "I do not think we would suit."

"Why not?"

He appeared amused. Did he enjoy toying with her? She had to admit that it was possible. And that, equally so, she found some small measure of pleasure in their sparring. It was the height of foolishness, she knew. As was her inability to keep from finding him handsome. To wonder what it would feel like to have those expertly molded lips pressed to hers.

But no, she must not think on any of that just now.

"Because I do not like you, Mr. Bellingham," she dared.

"Just as I do not like you," he drawled wryly. "However, liking one another has naught to do with such matters."

She swallowed against a sudden rush of desire, for it was

wrong. How could her body and her mind be so thoroughly at odds? She knew he was an odious villain who had refused to care for his own sister and instead had heartlessly cast her upon the mercy of the foundling hospital, leaving Marianne to her miserable fate. And yet, that knowledge somehow did nothing to abate the desire burning brightly to life within Lily.

"I am equally certain it does," she countered, despising herself for the thickness in her voice.

His gaze dipped for a moment to her lips. "Shall we put your theory to the test, Miss Sutton?"

Something inside her lurched.

Warmed.

Glowed.

*Burned.*

"How?" she asked stupidly.

"With a kiss," he said.

~

TARQUIN WATCHED as Lily Sutton's mysterious neither-blue-nor-green-nor-gray eyes flared with awareness. Deepened to a murky gray-blue. He did not think he was wrong to detect passion in their brilliant depths. The rains had made her pelisse and gown stick to her feminine curves. Her creamy skin was wet and glistening. And he could not stop thinking about having her every way—and everywhere—he could.

A moral failure of the greatest magnitude, to be sure.

"A kiss," she repeated, the huskiness of her voice revealing herself to him.

She was not unaffected, just as he thought. The attraction between them was burning too hot and true to deny.

"If you are too afraid, I understand," he demurred, knowing his words would spur her pride.

"If you want to kiss me, then do so, but it shan't change my mind about the two of us suiting," she said coolly.

How wrong she was. He would show her.

As if he had not spent these last years living the life of a monk, Tarquin felt the seducer coming to life. He had forgotten how thrilling it was—the newness of a lover. Learning her. Pleasing her. *By God*, how had he waited this long? His fall seemed inevitable now.

Or perhaps not inevitable, but stirred by one woman alone. There was something ridiculously intoxicating about Lily Sutton. He could not resist her.

Tarquin slid forward on the squabs slowly, giving her time to retreat if she chose. Giving her the chance to adjust. She did not move away. Instead, she watched him. Watched him with that minx's gaze framed by lush lashes. She could have made her fortune as a courtesan; he did not doubt that any man in London would have given every last ha'penny to his name to have her in his bed.

His hands settled on her waist and he pulled her neatly between his thighs.

"Do you object?" he asked her.

Her eyes lowered to his mouth. "Kiss me if you like. I can promise I will remain impervious."

Ha! He could promise her otherwise, but a demonstration would prove far more preferable.

He slid a hand up her spine, taking his time, holding her gaze. He did not think he had lost his ability to woo a woman. The heat and femininity of her, even through her sodden layers, secretly thrilled him. He thought in that moment that he could touch her forever and never have enough.

He ought to be disgusted with himself for this indulgence, for desiring another woman when he had sworn to himself that his next lover would be his wife. But he could not summon even a crumb of self-loathing just now, with his heart galloping in his chest and the fiery heat of his longing for Lily Sutton careening through him.

"Come closer," he urged her, wanting her to meet him halfway.

She obeyed, sliding nearer, her bottom resting perilously on the edge of the bench, her knees just barely grazing his groin.

It was the most erotic position he had found himself in for as long as he could recall. His hand swept higher, finding the ribbons of her bonnet and pulling them free. He deposited the hat on the squabs at her side and studied her. The rain had dampened her blonde hair, and little curls had worked free of her coiffure to frame her face.

She was stunning. He took a moment to admire her. To forget who she was and why they had been thrown together, ignoring everything but Miss Sutton herself.

"You are prolonging this," she accused without heat.

"Yes," he agreed simply. "And why should I not? These matters take time, if done properly. If not done properly, well, they are not worth doing."

"Oh."

She inhaled deeply, her breasts rising and falling. The darkening of her eyes, the wideness of her pupils, told him how affected she was. And just like that, he was the seducer. Breaking every rule he had set when he had determined to fashion himself into a gentleman worthy of his father's praise.

Tarquin caught the forefinger of his glove between his teeth and tugged, removing it. He had to feel her smooth skin, no barriers between them.

"You have been kissed before, have you not, Miss Sutton?" he asked, cupping her cheek lightly, stroking his thumb over the creamy softness of her jaw.

Her flesh was warm and slightly damp from the rain. He could not resist gliding his hand lower, finding her neck, his fingers dipping into the upsweep of her hair. For a wild moment, he imagined plucking all the pins free, letting those golden tendrils fall around her. But there wasn't sufficient time for that. He had to satisfy himself with her lips.

Not such a hardship.

"Of course I have," she said, pink rising in her cheeks. "It is nothing extraordinary. Do hurry up."

Nothing extraordinary?

Ah, then she had never been *truly* kissed.

He smiled, pleased by the revelation. "If you are in such haste, Miss Sutton, perhaps you should take action."

He was testing her mettle. He did not think she would be bold enough to command the situation, to kiss him first. But then, she proved him wrong.

"Very well," she announced with grim determination.

Awkwardly, she placed a hand on his chest, just over his madly thumping heart, and leaned forward, eyes closed. She pressed her lips to his quickly. Chastely.

Nothing but a warm, fleeting pressure and then gone. But the connection—sparks to his soul, a flame burning to life—was there.

She leaned back abruptly, as if he had scorched her, eyes fluttering open, lips parted. Her hand was still on his chest, and when she would have removed it, he caught her wrist in a gentle grasp and held it there.

"That was not a kiss," he told her.

"Of course it was," she protested.

"Not enough to decide if we'll suit." He leaned across the space separating them, until his mouth was perilously near to hers.

"We won't." Her voice was stubborn and prim.

He'd prove her wrong. Slowly. Deliciously.

Tarquin kissed the corner of her lips first, lingering there, relishing the spark that roared to life. He brushed the backs of his fingers over her throat in the barest hint of a caress, absorbing the frantic flutters of her pulse. And then he kissed the other corner of her lips in the same fashion, breathing in her scent. She smelled of flowers and soap. Lavender with a new hint of rose, he thought. And rain and woman.

He moved to the fullness of her lower lip next, brushing against it lightly to tantalize them both. Her lashes lowered, hiding her reaction from him. But he could feel it in the shiver that coursed through her, the hot kiss of her breath on his lips as she exhaled, the way her body curved toward his, seeking connection, her fingers curling into his shirt to hold him there.

He kissed her fully then, pressing his mouth to hers, coaxing her to respond. She held still for but a moment, and then she came to life. Lips moving, opening. She sighed into the kiss, and his tongue dipped inside for just a taste of her. And *God*, she was sweet, like the finest of confections. She made a wordless sound low in her throat, her arms winding around his neck. He deepened the kiss, stroking her tongue, nipping at her lips, and wondered how he had managed to exist without this thrilling rush of need.

How had he forgotten the joy of kissing a lover? How had the art of passion fled him? Why had he let it go?

Duty, reminded an old voice within. Acceptance. The Duke of Hampton had appeared in his life, offering the promise of benediction. For fear of losing everything he had worked to build, he had abandoned the reckless desires of his youth. He had told himself he did not require passion in his life.

He had been wrong.

The carriage suddenly rocked over a bump, jolting him from the kiss and his musings both. He and Lily Sutton careened to the floor together, a jumbled heap of limbs and skirts. Breathless and panting, but not in the way he would have preferred. Still, his point had been made, and he could read it in her eyes.

"It seems we suit after all, Miss Sutton," he drawled.

"What do you want from me?" she asked.

It was a valid question, and one he was not sure he knew the answer to now. Not after those kisses.

He helped her to reposition herself on the squabs and rose once more to the bench opposite her as the carriage rolled to a stop before The Sinner's Palace. "I will come to you tomorrow evening at half past ten. Be ready."

# CHAPTER 4

*L*ily left her attic room at The Sinner's Palace bearing gowns, slippers, and petticoats. Her brother Hart had come to her earlier, asking that she share some of her gowns and other necessary items with a particular *friend* of his who was in need of proper attire. She hadn't pried; Hart was not the most forthcoming of her siblings, and if he wanted to keep a secret, he bloody well kept it. Besides, word had been spreading about the gaming hell that he'd brought home a rum doxy from The Garden of Flora. She reckoned she knew what manner of friend she was going to clothe.

Lily didn't mind. Nor would she judge. For she was relieved for the opportunity to distract herself from all inconvenient thoughts of Tarquin Bellingham. His words of the day before echoed in her mind with each step she took.

*I will come to you tomorrow evening at half past ten. Be ready.*

Bellingham could order her about all he liked, but that did not mean she had to comply. She had no intention of repaying him in any fashion, and most especially not by playing at rantum scantum with him, if that was what he intended.

Even if his kisses had been—

No, she would *not* think of his kisses.

Lily reached the door to Hart's room and delivered a sound knock. As far as she knew, it was Hart's turn for floor duty this evening, watching the coves who kept their gaming hell so flush in funds for any hints of cheating. But if he were within, making the beast with two backs with his ladybird, Lily had no wish to witness it. Once, she'd unintentionally walked in on one of the guards shagging a moll, and the memory of Hugh's furry arse thrusting wildly would forever haunt her.

She paused, listening, but heard nothing within.

Balancing the garments loaded in her arms, she delivered another loud rap.

"Come," called a feminine voice from within.

Lily sighed with relief and opened the door, spying Hart's *friend* immediately. She was undeniably lovely, and she was also nearly naked. Bare feet, long, blonde hair unbound, breasts on display, a slit in the skirt of her gown to reveal a shocking expanse of bare skin...

Lily had seen her fair share of doxies. Some frequented The Sinner's Palace. She had been born and raised in the rookeries. Ladybirds were a part of the territory. But her brothers did not ordinarily bring them to their private rooms above the hell.

This one must be somehow different.

"May I?" she asked when the woman stared at her, looking rather lost.

"Please," she responded softly, gesturing for her to enter. "I am Emma."

Her voice was well-modulated. Her accent that of a lady.

*Hmm.*

"I am Lily," she said, crossing the threshold and then kicking the door closed at her back, lest any of the guards wander by and catch a glimpse of Hart's *friend* with her bubbies in the wind. "Hart said you need some new rigging and I was to lend you some of mine while you're staying on with us."

"Yes," Emma said, rubbing her hands over her bare arms, as if she were uncomfortable in her scandalous gown. "Some new...rigging would be most appreciated, Lily. Thank you."

Lily drew nearer, eyeing the mysterious woman who had apparently captured Hart's interest so thoroughly. "You look as if you've come straight from The Garden of Flora."

Best to be blunt, she reasoned. Hart could keep his secrets, but he couldn't expect Lily not to be curious. Especially not when he asked for her help. And the longer she lingered here, chatting with his mysterious friend, the less opportunity she would have to fret over the looming appearance of Bellingham this evening, and what it would mean for her.

"That is because I have," Emma said quietly, her composure cracking for a brief moment before she appeared to regain control of her emotions.

*Interesting.*

"If you don't mind my asking, what are you doing here at The Sinner's Palace?" she couldn't resist querying next.

Emma frowned. "Did your brother not tell you?"

She wondered just how well this golden-haired beauty knew Hart.

"I'm afraid not." Lily shook her head. "He ain't particularly leaky when it comes to his secrets."

"Ah," was all Emma said.

"Are you one of Madame Laurent's ladies?" Lily wondered.

"No," Hart's friend said simply. "I am not."

Not a ladybird then, and yet dressed as one? The revelations grew more confusing by the moment.

Lily crossed the room and deposited the burden in her arms on Hart's bed. "Then what are you? You speak like a nob."

"I am…" Emma's words trailed off behind her before she tried again. "I am your brother's guest."

More vague explanations. It seemed Emma was as reluctant to reveal the true nature of her relationship with Hart as he was. But then, she supposed it didn't truly concern her, and she had most certainly been keeping secrets of her own.

"It's all plummy." Lily turned back to Emma, smiling with what she hoped was reassurance. "Hart loves his secrets, so I might as well know he'd have one of his own." She flipped through the pile of gowns and removed one of her night rails, holding it up for Emma's inspection. "It's late, so I expect you'll be wanting this one first. I've more if you need them, depending on how long you're thinking to stay."

"Not long," Emma said shyly, flushing. "One week's time, is all."

"Here you are then." Lily offered the simple white cotton gown to her. "You look tired, if you don't mind my saying."

"I *am* tired," Emma said, a tinge of sadness in her voice. "Thank you for your generosity. I can only hope one day I will be able to return it."

A kind gesture, to be sure. There was something about Hart's friend that Lily liked. She had a feeling they would be friends.

"No need," she told Emma. "With my sisters gone, I'm pleased to have some feminine companionship aside from the maids and the washerwoman. Agnes is a dear, but she's busy and she hasn't time for me."

Pen and Caro had married wonderful husbands and were happily in love. Lily had thrown herself into the foundling hospital in their absence, putting as much of her time into it, Marianne, and her jaunts to Bellingham and Co. as possible.

Which reminded her. The hour was growing ever closer to half past ten.

What would Bellingham do if she defied him? Lily supposed she would find out.

Emma shivered and rubbed her arms then, and Lily took that as her cue to depart.

"Forgive me, Emma," she said. "I'll leave you to your privacy now. I expect you'll be wanting to change into something that affords you more warmth."

"Yes," Emma agreed, sounding relieved. "It was a pleasure to meet you, Lily."

"And you." Lily took her leave, more perplexed by the other woman's presence at The Sinner's Palace—and who she truly was—than ever.

But as she ventured into the hall, all thoughts of the mysterious Emma and her brother vanished at the sight of Randall, one of the most fearsome and trusted of the gaming hell's guards, approaching her with a grim expression.

"Miss Lily," he said. "A cove's downstairs asking for you."

A cove?

There could only be one man who would ask for her directly, and curse him for doing so. If her brothers learned of Bellingham's presence, it would cause her no end of strife.

"Do my brothers know, Randall?" she asked, hoping the answer would be no.

"Not as yet, miss." Randall gave her a brotherly glower. "What's this nob wanting with you?"

"He is from the foundling hospital," she lied, offering the first explanation that arrived in her mind, and the most innocuous.

Randall's eyes narrowed. "At this hour?"

"Yes." Her chin went up, and she held his gaze, daring him to argue.

"At a gaming 'ell?" Randall prodded.

"Where else am I to be found?" she countered neatly. "Now where is he, if you please?"

"In the family parlor."

"Thank you, Randall," she said, skirting around his towering frame and starting down the hall, her mind whirling with the possibilities of what she might do with the man awaiting her below. Halfway down the hall, she paused and looked over her shoulder. "Oh, and Randall?"

"Aye, Miss Lily?" He was rubbing his jaw, scowling at her.

"Don't tell my brothers."

He muttered a curse. She didn't wait to hear further arguments. Randall was loyal to them all, but she knew he would heed her wishes. At least, for as long as he could stave off her brothers, should any of them get word that a man was awaiting her in the parlor.

Tarquin Bellingham had come calling to collect his debt.

What was she going to do?

∼

TARQUIN PACED the length of the room, feeling like a large beast which had been caged inside a menagerie.

The parlor of The Sinner's Palace was surprisingly elegant.

Tarquin hadn't known what to expect from the private rooms of an East End gaming hell. But it was clean. No half-naked doxies were roaming about. The mountainous fellow who had grudgingly squired him to the parlor had been *almost* polite.

Still, it had aggrieved him mightily to have to abandon the private confines of his carriage and venture inside this den of vice. The duke would not tolerate even a whiff of scandal. And neither would Lady Clementia's father.

Which begged the question of why he was here.

It was one hell of a risk to take, when he could least afford to take it.

The door to the parlor opened as he was mid-stride, and he was instantly reminded of the reason for his presence in The Sinner's Palace at this late hour. The reason for the incredible, stupid gamble he was taking.

The sight of Lily Sutton hit him like a blow to the chest.

She was beautiful. But it wasn't her lovely features that drew him the most. It was something indefinable about her very presence. The lithe fluidity of her movements. The brazen way she carried herself, as if she did not give a damn about what anyone watching thought of her. She exuded complete and utter confidence. She was bold and unusual.

An original.

And she called to a deep and primitive part of him. One that he had thought long dead and buried. She was dangerous.

Yet, here he was, offering her a courtly bow as she closed the door behind her in complete lack of deference for propriety. Compared to the staid, quarter-hour calls he paid upon Lady Clementia beneath the strict supervision of her marriage-minded mama, this was the height of unseemliness.

"Miss Sutton," he greeted her, allowing the grim awareness that was never far when she was near to seep into his voice.

She did not curtsy in return. Had he expected her to? If he had, he was to be disappointed, for Lily Sutton was completely lacking in artifice this evening.

"What are you doing here?" she demanded, glaring at him as if he were the criminal between the two of them.

As if *he* had somehow wronged *her*.

"I told you I would come this evening," he reminded her. "To collect the debt you owe."

In truth, he had not known if he would show. He had spent the entirety of the night before and all day long in a haze of indecision, part of him yearning quite desperately to follow through with his threat. Part of him knowing doing so was the height of foolishness. She owed him, yes. But he had far more to lose than the goods she had thieved from his shop.

She crossed her arms over her generous breasts in a defensive gesture. "Whilst I told you that I owe you nothing."

And just like that, her bravado lured him in once more.

"You are a brave woman, Miss Sutton," he observed, drawing nearer to her because he could not help himself. "Brave and exceedingly foolish."

He was reasonably sure that, of the two of them, he was the most foolish of all. However, he refused to make such an admission aloud.

She cocked her head, sweeping him from head to toe with that gray-green-blue stare that he felt as viscerally as if it had been a touch. "If you ask me, you're the brave one of the two of us, coming into the den of the lions thinking they won't bite you."

He chuckled, prowling around her in a circle. "My dear, do you not realize who is the true lion here among us? I am not afraid of the Sutton family, if that is what you suggest. My reach far exceeds yours."

"Perhaps we should test that assertion," Miss Sutton told him, shoulders straightening as if she were a warrior preparing to do battle.

He stopped before her, in such proximity that he could take her into his arms with ease, her floral scent curling around him. "Do you recall what happened the last time we tested a theory?"

Her lips parted, and he suspected she was remembering the kisses they had shared in her carriage the day before. They had not been far from his thoughts. The warm softness of her lips, the sweet sounds of surrender she had made. He had kissed many times before, but he knew to his marrow that he would never forget those first kisses with Lily Sutton as the carriage carried them over congested, pockmarked London roads.

"That addlepated nonsense won't be happening today," she told him crisply.

He noted the way she took her time to form her words, affecting the accent of someone far above her station as best as she could. Here and there, the strains of her true upbringing slipped through. And even that lack of polish, that hint of the raw, real part of her, was somehow irritatingly enchanting.

If only he could summon even a modicum of similar interest for Lady Clementia.

Instead, he was lusting after the most unsuitable woman in London. A woman who could never be his wife. A woman who had stolen from him, repeatedly. Who had driven him to the edge of reason with a delirious combination of fury and desire.

And she thought there would be no more kissing today.

He hadn't traveled here, against every sense of self-preservation he possessed, to exchange barbs with her, entertaining though it was.

"I've told you there is a price to be paid for your thievery," he reminded her calmly, keeping his tone deliberately light.

"And I've told you I'm no thief," she countered, displaying an enviable sangfroid.

He stepped nearer, drawn to her as ever, loathing himself. Longing for her. She was everything he should never want. And *dear Lord in heaven*, how he had thought he had banished these indefensible weaknesses, these parts of himself that were unworthy and wicked. Only to discover he was wrong.

He lowered his head. Not touching her. She was quite a bit shorter than he was. His neck ached from the angle. But it was worth it, for the manner in which her eyes widened, their mysterious depths darkening. Longing for her lodged inside him, deep and painful as a splinter.

"You forget," he said softly, his gaze dipping to the lush, pink lips he had so thoroughly plundered the day before. The lips he could not seem to stop wanting beneath his again. "I witnessed you slipping a fan into your bodice. You kept some of the buttons of your pelisse undone, the better to aid your nefarious efforts. It was clever, I will own. You took great care to make certain none of my men were watching. But you could not have known I was observing you from within a hidden chamber, the door slightly ajar."

Some of the fight fled her. He had surprised her, it would seem. It occurred to Tarquin that he had been in such a state that day in his office when she had begun to disrobe, he'd had no choice but to send her away before he could present his case.

"A hidden chamber?" she repeated. "Where?"

"Within the shelves behind the counter," he answered smoothly. "I watched you, Miss Sutton. There is no question. And later, when you realized you had been caught and could no longer haunt my shop yourself, you sent that wretched little imp into my midst—"

"Stop!" Her voice rose. "She ain't wretched. She's an innocent. One that's been betrayed and left by everyone who ought to 'ave shown her love."

In the frenzy of her emotional response, Miss Sutton's carefully cultivated accent had slipped.

He wondered how much care she took with her words, how difficult it was for her to pretend to be someone else.

And for a moment, he felt a kindred sense of understanding. All his life, he had been pretending to be someone he was not. One-and-thirty years old, and he was still walking this earth, trying to please everyone else instead of himself.

"She's a thief," he said quietly. "Just as you are."

"You're a coldhearted bastard," Miss Sutton accused, shocking him with the fervent pitch of her voice, the tremor.

"Because I dislike having the business I have worked so painstakingly to build robbed beneath my nose by a pair of deceitful criminals?" he asked sharply.

"No, because you don't give a bloody goddamn about that child," she bit out.

Her language was coarse. As was her background, of course. For the first time in their brief acquaintance, Miss Lily Sutton sounded as if she were from the rookeries. And still, she stood, bold and determined, facing him without shame. Nary a blush. She was ferocious, like a little dog with a vicious bite. And damn her, she was incredible to behold.

He had to calm the fierce pang of need for her, rising and threatening to vanquish his control.

Tarquin shrugged. "And why should I, Miss Sutton? Do you suppose Bellingham and Co. is a charity? There are hundreds, if not thousands, of orphans in London. Why should one filching beggar inspire me toward sympathy or mercy?"

"Oh," she breathed, inhaling with so much force that her entire being moved.

And then in the next moment, her palms landed flat on his chest in twin, stinging blows, pushing.

She took him by surprise, both with her strength and her actions.

He stumbled backward, regaining his footing before he went sprawling onto his back.

"You!" she exclaimed, striding forward, chasing him, fire

in her eyes. "You scoundrel! You cold, heartless, frigid...monster!"

On the last accusation, she shoved him again.

But this time, Tarquin was prepared. He caught her wrists in his hands and held her to him, because if he was felled, she was accompanying him. He stumbled backward as her forward momentum made the both of them struggle to stay standing. But it was a hopeless effort. They tumbled backward, and he knew there was no point in attempting to correct their fall. They were going down.

*Together.*

He landed with a jarring thud, flat on his back, Lily Sutton atop him as his head struck the carpeted floor. Her hands were still on his chest, doing little to prevent her forehead from striking his nose when they fell.

Pain shot through his skull at the connection, bringing scalding tears to his eyes in a natural reaction. He blinked them away, holding her to him, glad he had cushioned the blow of their fall with his own body. Hoping she had not injured herself even as he wondered if his damned nose was broken.

It hurt like bloody hell.

"Damn," he muttered, his thoughts going to her despite his own injury. "Are you hurt, Miss Sutton?"

"Your nose," she said on a gasp.

"Indeed," he gritted, raising a hand to gingerly assess the damage.

Warm wetness coated his fingers.

"You're bleeding!" she exclaimed, wriggling against him in a way that made him remember, for a fleeting moment, that he had a cock and forget that he had sharp, stinging agony radiating from his battered beak to the roots of his hair.

Until he breathed and the pain came rushing back.

"Your head," he managed, attempting to explain. "I believe it connected quite firmly with my nose."

This was decidedly not how he had intended the evening to transpire.

Seduction, yes. Accusations and a possibly broken nose, absolutely not.

"I had my back up, I did," she said, sounding fretful. "Never intended to knock you in the bowsprit."

He struggled to make sense of her words. She was once again descending to the rookeries, her accent slipping, her language losing its luster. And she remained atop him, a warm and welcome weight even as he pinched the bridge of his nose to control the flow of blood.

"Indeed," was all he managed, a grim acknowledgment of her apology—he was rather busy at the moment, one hand attempting to find his handkerchief and the other holding firmly to his injured appendage.

"Is it broken?" she asked, her voice high, trembling.

Apparently, the sight of blood was all that was required for the indomitable Lily Sutton to turn missish.

And the realization was...oddly endearing. A reaction likely owed to the aching in his nose and the loss of blood both.

"I suspect not," he said, finally pulling his handkerchief free and pressing it to his nose to blot up the blood. "Noses are sensitive to blows."

"Oh," she said, her stare pinned to him, her pallor growing alarming. "I..." she paused, seeming to lose the course of her words before resuming. "That is rather a lot of blood."

"It will stop," he assured her, even though he had no notion of whether or not it would.

It had to, did it not? Tarquin had been engaged in bouts of fisticuffs before, though he had never been dealt a blow to the nose. A first for every occasion, he supposed. And how fitting that it should have been Miss Sutton to deliver it.

"What if it doesn't?"

Her low, horrified question confused him for a moment.

"It will," he repeated.

"I didn't intend to maim you," she said, sounding contrite. "Although you deserved it."

He bit back a bark of laughter from behind the blood-soaked handkerchief. "You are damned troublesome, Miss Sutton."

The Problem that had been plaguing him had a face and a name, but she was still haunting him. Tempting him. Making him want her, making him bleed.

And yet, despite her outrageous refusal to admit the wrongs she had committed, despite her stubborn lack of contrition over the damage she had done his nose, as Tarquin lay there on the carpet of a gaming hell's parlor, a river of blood gushing from his nose, he desired her more than he had ever longed for another woman.

He was mad. That was the only reasonable explanation for the unwanted thoughts, the scurrilous sensations careening through him as wildly as a runaway carriage.

"I will own that trouble seems to be a faithful companion of mine, but you are the one who has been following me about," she countered, still firmly atop him.

He wondered if she had forgotten their positions.

He was not inclined to remind her, for he liked her just where she was, and the flow of blood from his nose seemed to be slowing.

"I have been following you about because you have been stealing from me," he pointed out, tentatively withdrawing the handkerchief to test whether or not the bleeding had stopped.

"You look as if you've received a sound drubbing," she

observed wryly instead of responding to his charge, shifting on him in a way that produced a bolt of pure, unadulterated lust.

She was all but riding his thigh, nothing but a few flimsy layers of fabric to keep the heat of her cunny from him.

"I feel as if I have." He winced at the aching in his nose, which was only surpassed by the aching in his groin.

Two different kinds of pain.

"I believe the worst of the bleeding is over," she said, her gaze searching his countenance as she paused for a moment, catching her lower lip in her teeth. "I am sorry."

"An apology at last. Are you feeling well, Miss Sutton?" he could not resist taunting.

She nibbled at her lip some more. "As well as to be expected when a haughty shop owner storms into my family's gaming hell, demanding to see me."

"I told you I would come at half past ten," he reminded her.

"And I told you I'll not be paying you in any fashion," she returned. "Is it not enough that I have agreed that neither I nor the girl will ever venture into your shop again?"

"No," he told her simply, tucking his bloodied handkerchief away.

Because if Lily Sutton never came to his shop, he would not see her again. And Tarquin very stupidly, very foolishly, very recklessly, wanted to see her again.

And again.

She huffed a small sigh, her displeasure evident as she rolled to her side at last, removing her tempting weight from him. Gracefully, she rose to her feet whilst he attempted a sitting position.

Miss Sutton extended an ungloved hand. "You're still quite claret-faced, Mr. Bellingham. Come with me and we will see you cleaned up."

"Your consideration warms my heart," he said drolly, accepting her hand but not because he required the assistance.

Rather, because he wanted to touch her.

Their hands clasped, the warmth of her making awareness slide over him as he stood.

## CHAPTER 5

Lily was taking Tarquin Bellingham to her attic room.

It was a risk. A very big one she could ill afford. And yet, she felt guilty for the damage she had unintentionally inflicted upon his poor, perfectly formed nose. She hoped she hadn't broken it. He had deserved it with his callous attitude toward Marianne, just as she had told him. But Lily had a soft heart, and the sight of his handsome, arrogant face spattered in blood had been too much.

As had the feeling of his tall, masculine body beneath hers.

She had become astoundingly aware of him, each place their bodies connected humming with the fierce flare of desire. His thigh had been between her legs, pressing against the ache there, and she had just scarcely resisted the urge to move like a cat in the gutters searching for her mate.

"Where are you taking me?" Bellingham asked at her side, a note of suspicion entering his voice.

Likely, he thought she was going to take him somewhere to fleece him. The notion of tying him up did hold some wicked appeal to her, she could not lie. But she knew that she alone could not overtake a man of his size.

"To my room," she answered softly, taking care to watch the hall for any signs of her siblings.

If Hart was on the floor, that meant Wolf was likely in the office. Since Jasper had married Lady Octavia, he spent his evenings at home with his wife and daughters. The same could be said of Rafe and Lady Persephone. At this time of night, the guards would be in position at the doors and on the periphery of The Sinner's Palace. But there was no telling who might be wandering about in the busy bowels of the gaming hell by chance, and Lily didn't want anyone to see her slipping a cove into her private chamber.

She had committed a great deal of sneaking in recent years, but none of it had involved bringing gentlemen to her room. She had never been so inclined. In the last year, she had taken an interest in kissing, it was true. But any more than a buss on the lips with a handsome cull was where she drew the line. Well, that and the threats her brothers made concerning the Biblical portion of a man's anatomy, should he be found within her private quarters...

With a wince she returned her gaze to Mr. Bellingham's handsome, blood-spattered profile. Aye, if he were to be found within her room, there was no telling what would become of him if any of the Sutton men were involved. She would not think of it now.

Bellingham slanted her a sideways glance as they moved together, approaching the narrow attic stairs at last. "Do I look that dreadful, then? You are wincing at me as if I look like the very devil himself."

It was not possible for the man to look dreadful, she was sure of it. Even after the unintentional injury to his nose, he was the epitome of a fine, handsome gentleman. For a moment, she recalled how he had looked the day before, rushing to her rescue in the rain with his coat held over both their heads.

And then she reminded herself of his cruelty concerning his sister. His utter lack of regard for Marianne's welfare. A wealthy, successful man, and he had relegated the girl to the foundling hospital, where she would be trained into service and then sent off to work herself to death in a few years' time.

It was that recollection which made her tone sharp when she responded, "I was just thinking of what will become of your Man Thomas if any of my brothers discover you've been here with me."

She started up the stairs before him, not caring how unseemly it was if she flashed him a bit of ankle along the way. He was a coldhearted arsehole. She did not care what Tarquin Bellingham thought of her.

"My Man Thomas?" he asked behind her, sounding perplexed.

"Your whore pipe," she clarified, deliberately being as vulgar as possible.

The more horrified he was by her, the easier it would be to keep him at bay.

"My... Good sweet God," he muttered. "You are a blasphemous wench, are you not?"

"I pride myself upon it," she told him lightly.

They reached the top stair and she bit her lip to keep from grinning as she lit the way with her taper. Fortunately, she had tidied her rooms that morning. There would be no evidence of her sins to be found within. She reached for the latch of the door and swept inside, knowing by heart just where the brace of candles awaited her. She tilted the flame of her taper toward them, setting each wick alight until the spacious, low-ceilinged room was dancing with the candles' soft glow.

"There we are now." With her task complete, she turned toward her unexpected guest. "Take care with the rafters, now. The roof is slanted, and it—"

Her warning was abruptly cut short by the solid *thunk* of Bellingham's head connecting with a massive beam.

"Bloody hell," he growled, rubbing at his forehead as he pinned her with a glare. "You might have warned me a moment sooner, Miss Sutton."

She bit her lip to suppress a sudden burst of laughter. It was almost comical, the manner in which his injuries continued to mount.

"You planned that," he accused.

"I did not," she denied, leaving her taper with the brace of candles she had lit and moving toward him. "Did you hit your head very hard?"

It would serve him right if he had, she told herself sternly.

This man was not to be pitied, regardless of how quickly he made her heart beat or how wonderfully he kissed.

"I expect I shall survive." He raised a brow, studying her in the low light. "But I begin to wonder if you are an assassin as well as a thief."

She stopped just short of him, taking note of how odd it looked, him bent forward. He was taller than she had realized. Or perhaps, her stature was just so petite that she had failed to note just how slanted and low the roof was.

"I told you, I'm not a thief," she said. "Let me see if you've a lump."

"You are a thief. Telling me you are not one won't make the lie true, Miss Sutton." Dutifully, he removed his hand, showing her the patch of angry red skin on his forehead.

It wasn't bruised, at least, but it did look as if it pained him.

"I'd make a poor assassin," she observed. "You'll live."

He cocked his head, considering her with that bright-blue

stare that made her feel as if he could reach deep into a part of her she hadn't known she possessed. "You make a poor thief as well."

Again with the thief nonsense. She'd had a perfectly good reason to pilfer his damned shop. She was righting the wrong he had paid his own flesh and blood.

Her chin tipped up. "Have you ever heard of Robin Hood, Mr. Bellingham?"

"A foolish legend, Miss Sutton. Nothing more. A means of justifying thievery for centuries."

Of course he would think so.

For a moment, she forgot her reason for bringing him to her room. Instead, she allowed her frustration to spill over.

"Sometimes," she told him pointedly, "it is necessary to take from the wealthy and give to the poor. Particularly when the wealthy have no inclination of helping the poor."

"Do not tell me you fancy yourself a Robin Hood."

That was exactly what she fancied herself. At least, in a small measure.

She glared at him. "Someone must help those who are abandoned and left behind, betrayed by everyone who ought to have loved them."

He rubbed his jaw. "And you mean to suggest stealing my fans and encouraging an orphan to become a criminal herself makes you a hero of some sort? Forgive me, Miss Sutton. But thievery makes you a thief. There is nothing heroic in it."

He was a scoundrel. She hated the weakness in her that allowed her to forget that for small spaces of time. Hated the effect he had on her. It was as if her body possessed a mind of its own, and one that was easily swayed by the undeniable good looks of the heartless Mr. Bellingham. Why could she not have been this drawn to someone else?

*Enough*, she told herself. She had to carry on with her reason for bringing Bellingham to her room. Oh, why was it so difficult to maintain her common sense in this man's presence? She did not even like him, and yet, whenever he was near, he made her want to forget everything but his lips and the way they had felt moving tenderly over hers, the possessive slide of his tongue inside her mouth.

No, she must not think of that either.

"Come," she said, taking his hand in hers and pulling him toward the pitcher and basin across the room. "Let me wash your face so you can carry on with your evening."

"My evening involves nothing more than collecting the debt you owe." Bellingham followed her, his fingers tangling in hers.

And she liked it, curse her to her very soul.

She *liked* the way his big hand felt on hers, around hers. Strong and warm, the fingers long. So much heat burning into her.

They reached the basin and she withdrew, severing the connection.

*Think of Marianne*, she sternly reminded herself.

Lily poured water into the basin and reached for a clean cloth, dipping it into the cool depths. It was chilled far more than usual. The attic was cold in the evenings, especially at this dreary time of the year, and ordinarily she had heated bricks carried up from the kitchens, along with hot water. But she had not dared to call for anything with Bellingham here.

"The water is cold," she warned him, wringing the excess from her cloth before turning back to find him in far closer proximity than she had imagined.

She attempted to take a step in retreat, but the table holding the pitcher and basin stopped her, biting into her rump. There was nowhere to go.

"I don't mind," he said, his gaze finding hers.

There was an unexpected warmth in those blue depths.

She had to swallow against a rush of longing and offer him the cloth. "There it is, then."

He shook his head slowly. "I cannot see the extent of the damage. You do it for me, Miss Sutton."

Tending to him felt far too intimate. Wrong. Tempting.

"Mr. Bellingham," she began, only for him to stay her protest with a forefinger laid tenderly across her lips.

"You did the damage."

She had. She could hardly argue the point. But she did not want to touch him, because as much as she hated what he had done to Marianne, the rest of her was a disloyal wretch. And all she wanted was to be as close to him as possible.

More kisses. Touches.

"You can do it well enough," she said hastily.

"I want you to do it. Please."

His voice was low and silken. It slid over her skin in a caress all its own. Making her forget all the reasons why she should never indulge his request. Why she should fling the wet cloth at him and make her escape. Leave him to the wrath of her brothers.

Instead, she found herself trapped in the blue sea of his eyes.

"Very well." Reaching for him, she gently traced the line of his cheek, cleaning the dried blood from his skin. Lower, along the blade of his jaw. Beneath his proud chin.

She did her utmost to remain impervious. To keep her gaze free of his. To remember she was performing a task, the same as many others. Just as she dealt with broken crockery, the chef, the washerwoman. Just as she balanced the ledgers, a task which had recently been falling upon her on occasion.

Yes, this was nothing more than a simple job to be finished. She felt nothing.

Nothing at all.

Pleased with herself for her fortitude, she turned back to

the pitcher and bowl, rinsing the cloth before wringing the water from it once more. He remained silent and still as she worked at cleansing the rest of the blood from his face. Unfortunately for Lily, she saved his philtrum for last. By the time she reached the blood-bedecked skin above his lip, his breath was coasting hot over her fingertips. The scent of him was infiltrating her senses. What a liar she was.

She felt *everything*.

Lily wiped the last speck from his skin, swallowing hard again, her fingers lingering. "There you are. All clean."

He kissed her fingertips, a soft brush of his mouth against her eager flesh. "Thank you."

She forced herself to study his nose, searching for a sign it had been broken. There was no knot on the bridge, and the blood had long since ceased spurting forth. Nothing remained save a hint of redness where her head had struck him.

"You will live," she pronounced, as if it were a miracle.

"An unsuccessful assassin," he said, smiling.

And the beauty of his smile made something inside her seize, as if a blow had landed in her chest.

It was almost painful, her body's reaction to that rarity. He was exuding warmth, his icy-blue stare glistening with amusement, as if the two of them were sharing some manner of private joke. How intimate it felt. How intoxicating. How thrilling.

The cloth fell to the floor, and she scarcely paid it any heed. Her reason for bringing Bellingham to her room faded. So, too, her deep-seated anger toward him. She was remembering the delicious tenderness of those stolen kisses in the carriage. Of how they had moved her, showing her the full extent of what a kiss could—and *should*—be.

It was as if her body had a will all its own.

One moment, she was standing before him, hand on his

jaw. And the next, she was grabbing a fistful of his cravat and pulling his stern lips down to hers.

∾

HER SUDDEN MOVEMENT STARTLED HIM. He had the notion she was going to shove him, that he had somehow run afoul of her temper yet again. But her lips on his proved otherwise. She was taking control, and he liked it.

Tarquin could scarcely tamp down the growl rising in his throat as her mouth moved over his, ardently, hungrily. The tug of her hand on his cravat was ridiculously rousing. Even after he had suffered a bloodied nose and a knock to the head on the rafters, his cock went instantly hard.

It occurred to him the quality he admired about her most, the one that had drawn him to her despite his every intention otherwise, was her boldness. She was a fearless woman, and how he envied her that bravery, the ability to carry on as she wished, with a complete disregard for how she was perceived by others. His entire life had been founded upon the perception of others. He had been born a bastard, after all.

But Lily Sutton's lips were warm and smooth and everything he could not seem to get enough of, and Tarquin could no longer be bothered with heavy thoughts. Instead, he slid his arms around her, pulling her more firmly against him, angling his head, his lips answering hers in kind. She kissed much the way she performed all other tasks: wholeheartedly. He could not resist the feeling she was giving something far more to him than her mouth, revealing herself, showing some vulnerability where previously there had been none.

His hands were on her lower back, anchoring their bodies together, the womanly heat of her searing him as surely as any flame. Her hold on his cravat remained, but with her other hand, she threaded her fingers through his hair, exploring him as if he were a marvel. When her tongue tentatively swept over his lower lip, requesting entrance, he groaned. And she rightly perceived it as an invitation, her tongue slipping boldly inside to tangle with his.

Yes, this was what he wanted. The price he had not been able to reconcile with either himself or with her. She had stolen from him repeatedly. And now he wanted something from her in kind. *This.* This was what he wanted, her mouth soft and pliant, her fist curled in his cravat, demanding and seductive as hell. He wanted her to want him, to know the ache that had been his constant companion from the instant he had first spied her parading about his shop with the airs of a damned queen.

Queen of the East End, perhaps.

Queen of Thieves, certainly.

It didn't matter what she was, who she was. Did not signify that he was being deliriously reckless even now, lingering in a gaming hell and risking the wrath of his father the duke. That he was endangering the future he had fought to build.

Here he was, kissing Lily Sutton, wanting her more than he wanted to live another day.

She moved against him, sinuous as a cat, her belly brushing over his rigid cockstand once, then twice. The thin thread of his control snapped. He caught her waist in his hands and lifted her to the washstand, settling her atop it. The pitcher and bowl rattled and splashed. His hand was wet. He didn't give a damn.

He caught the skirt of her gown in his fists and pulled it higher, stepping into her parted thighs without breaking the kiss. This seduction was unlike the others he had conducted. It had been years since he had last touched a woman with the intent of bringing her pleasure. Perhaps it was the intervention of time which had rendered him rusty, much like a piece of equipment gone out of use and no longer functional. He ought to be taking greater care with her. Moving with torpor and grace, teasing and tempting her, stoking the flames higher into an out-of-control fire.

All his former skills, however, seemed to have abandoned him.

He dragged his mouth to her neck, where she smelled so fragrantly floral, and kissed her there. The shape of her waist beneath her stays mesmerized him. His hands traveled without elegance or purpose, simply loving the way she felt. Needing more of her. Everything she had to give.

There was some inherent charm in the moment. The rafters around them. Brace of candles casting a warm glow and soft shadows through the spacious confines of her room. It was shabby yet comforting, and it smelled of her.

One of her legs hooked around his waist, drawing him in tightly. His hands fled her waist with reluctance, winding up in her hair and on her upper thigh. Beneath her petticoats and chemise, above her stockings, he found skin. Delicious, sensuous, *soft*. He gripped her thigh, grinding his cock against her center in a parody of what he would do to her had he the ability. Making them both mindless and boneless. And as he did so, he sucked on her neck, knowing he would make his mark and not caring. He wanted her to see her reflection in the looking glass and think of him. To think of how well they fit together.

To long for him the way he longed for her. He cupped one of her breasts. She made a sound low in her throat. A breathy half gasp. The protrusion of her hard nipple kissed his palm through the layers separating them. He found his way to her ear, kissing her there, catching the fleshy lobe in his teeth and nipping.

"Bellingham," she said, clutching him tightly, holding him to her. "You are... What are you... *Oh.*"

He licked the hollow behind her ear and simultaneously found that pointed peak of her breast, catching it between his thumb and forefinger and tugging. Her response was gratifying. Pleasing. Made him hunger for more. And more.

"My given name is Tarquin," he told her, for he disliked hearing her refer to him by his surname.

The time for formality between them was done. Even though he knew it was forbidden, this affair he was embarking on. He had no business here, alone with her. No business seducing her when he would be asking Lady Clementia to marry him soon. But none of those facts stayed him.

"I know your name," she said.

And he was not surprised. Naturally, the brazen baggage would have made it her business to learn everything there was to know about him. He somehow, instinctively, understood her.

He kissed her throat. "Then use it."

"If I don't?"

Always testing him, was she not? Drawing him to the end of reason and then beyond.

Tarquin kissed a path back to her jaw, his lips lingering in that sacred space between her mouth and her ear. He brushed a kiss over her soft skin once. Twice.

"If you don't, I..." He allowed his words to trail off as he kissed his way back down her throat, forgetting what he had been about to say because her breast was filling his palm, and lust was dancing through his blood, wreaking havoc with his sensibilities.

"You?" she repeated, her voice throaty and breathless.

"Damn it," he muttered against her throat. "You make me forget myself."

An understatement, that. She banished his ability to possess coherent thought.

"I should not be doing this with you," she murmured, still clutching him tightly.

"And I most definitely should not be doing this with you," he agreed grimly, before returning to her mouth for another kiss.

This one was slower and sweeter.

He allowed himself to savor every sensation, breathing deeply of her scent. Feathering his lips over hers. Yes, this was what they both needed. What they wanted...

A steady knocking on the attic room door intruded, along with a gruff male voice.

"Miss Lily? You're needed below."

Lily stiffened, the hands which had been holding him near suddenly changing to flattened palms, pushing him away.

"Randall?" she called, hopping down from the washstand and straightening her skirts. "Is that you?"

"Aye, Miss Lily. It is," came the voice.

Randall? His pulse still pounding, the thick pulse of need roaring through him, Tarquin looked from Lily to the closed door, his sluggish brain attempting to make sense of the interruption and its source.

"Who the devil is Randall?" he asked.

Did she have a lover?

And why did the very thought make his blood go cold?

"He is one of our guards," she whispered to him. "Hush. He mustn't know you're within."

"Or what?" Tarquin asked.

"I've already told you, my brothers will give you a basting," she answered in a low voice before raising it for the benefit of Randall at the door. "I'll be out in a moment." She turned back to Tarquin, looking frantic. "You'll have to leave after we're gone. Take care not to allow anyone to see you."

She was dismissing him?

The woman had stolen from him, vexed him at every turn, bloodied his nose, and now she was telling him he must flee the gaming hell as if *he* were the criminal amongst the two of them.

"I haven't any notion of how to find my way out of here," he protested quietly. "Tell your guard to go to the devil."

Lily gave him a look of admonishment. "You'll have to try," she returned. "Take the stairs. *After* I've gone with Randall. Oh, and take care not to hit your head again."

With that final directive, she turned and fled the chamber, leaving him to watch her go. He hoped Randall-the-guard would take note of her kiss-bruised lips and the marks he had left on her throat.

Because Lily Sutton was *his*.

# CHAPTER 6

"The Duke of Hampton to see you, Mr. Bellingham."

Tarquin glanced up from the ledgers he was reviewing, surprised to hear his father had deigned to pay him an afternoon call at his place of business. But then, perhaps the visit would be a welcome diversion from the unwanted thoughts of one East End minx still haunting him. From the time he had watched her lush, feminine form vanishing over the threshold to her attic room until now, she had never been far, driving him to distraction with what could have been. With what may yet be to come.

Tarquin rose, straightening his coat and cuffs in an instinctive gesture.

"Thank you, Mr. Maier." A discreet glance down at his hands revealed an indelicate smear of ink on his right pinky, but there was no help for it. He was going to have to conduct his interview with the duke with a sullied hand. "See him in, if you please."

Mr. Maier dutifully disappeared, giving Tarquin a moment to tidy his desk. The Duke of Hampton stringently disliked a lack of order. And ever since his father had offered an olive branch to Tarquin, he had been living in the duke's shadow, striving to please him. Obeying his edicts, playing the puppet.

Tarquin finished aligning his inkwell with the ledger from the furs and fans department and straightened just in time to see his father entering the office, walking stick in hand.

He bowed to the duke. "Your Grace, good day."

"Mr. Bellingham," greeted the familiar, cool voice of the duke.

Boundaries were always to be observed. Tarquin was not permitted to refer to Hampton as *Father*. And likewise, the duke referred to him formally.

"To what do I owe the honor of your presence?" he asked.

The man who had fathered him crossed the carpets, leaning more heavily upon his walking stick than he ordinarily did. He was favoring his left leg, the sole sign that the Duke of Hampton was mortal rather than some manner of mythical god. He was tall like Tarquin, and his dark hair had long since turned gray. They shared the same blue eyes, long nose, and wide jaw. A portrait of the duke in his youth which graced the salon of his town house bore a distinct resemblance to Tarquin; there was no denying the blood connection.

"I am in need of a gift for Lady Dalrymple," Hampton said, referencing the lady twenty years his junior who was the duke's current mistress.

Tarquin tamped down a surge of disappointment at the purpose of his father's call. Of course it would not be a mere visit to Tarquin himself which would be enough of a lure.

"Fur or jewels?" he asked, slipping into his role as shopkeeper.

"Both, I should think." Instead of sitting in one of the

overstuffed armchairs arranged in a small seating area, the duke thumped to the fireplace, where Tarquin had recently seen a painting hung. "Sapphires are her preference. Perhaps a stole or a pelerine as well."

He cocked his head, considering the picture, his back to Tarquin.

"I will send a man over with some selections for Your Grace," he said, for he knew that was his father's preferred mode of shopping.

"Thank you. This painting is perfectly dreadful."

Tarquin tamped down a defensive retort about the duke preferring styles of a previous age.

"I admire it," he said mildly instead.

"Lady Clementia will help to furnish the town house, I trust," the duke drawled, his disapproval of Tarquin's taste apparent. "It would appear you have inherited some of your mother's proclivity for the gaudy. But then, she was born to a doxy and a drunkard. It was to be expected, I suppose."

"Undoubtedly." At his sides, Tarquin's hands balled into fists.

Not so much at the insult paid his mother. God knew that woman deserved every ill word spoken about her and then some. Rather, it was the reminder of Tarquin's illegitimacy. The duke liked to remind him of how beholden Tarquin was to him for everything. And he was not entirely wrong, much as it pained him to admit.

Hampton slowly pivoted, still favoring his leg, his blue stare hard and assessing. "You are fortunate Lady Clementia is amenable to your suit."

"Yes," he agreed, nails biting into his palms. "I am."

Marrying the witless Lady Clementia held all the appeal of plucking out his own toenails before bed.

The duke thumped nearer, his walking stick making a pronounced rhythm on the carpet that was almost ominous. "You might show your gratitude, Mr. Bellingham."

"I am grateful," he forced himself to say, feigning enthusiasm.

Trying not to think of a lifetime of conversing with a wife who possessed the faculties of a chicken. Trying not to think of someone else, someone whose brazen audacity called to him in a way he had never known. Just being in Lily Sutton's presence was secretly thrilling.

*Damn her.*

The duke stopped before him, his countenance impassive. "If you are grateful, then why have I heard from Brownley that you have been neglecting Lady Clementia? No calls paid in the last week, from what I understand. The girl is growing quite despondent over your lack of affection."

How to explain that he had spent his time caught up in Lily Sutton instead? No, best to keep that to himself. Although the duke had kept a mistress practically since he had been in leading strings, there was one set of moral conduct for Hampton to abide by and quite another for his amoral bastard son. Tarquin knew it. Accepted it because he had no other choice. But that did not mean he liked it.

"I have been busy," he hedged, forcing a smile. "I last saw her at Rivendale's not long ago. Surely not a week has passed."

"Hmm." The duke's eyes narrowed in assessing fashion. "And yet you have the time to carouse at an infamous gaming hell in the rookeries."

Apparently, in his attempts to remove himself from the labyrinth of The Sinner's Palace, someone had seen him. And word had already traveled back to his father.

Had they seen him with Lily? He thought not, though if it was that damned guard Randall who had somehow wagged his tongue, Tarquin had an idea or two of what he might do to even the score on the next occasion when their paths crossed.

"I am not a frequenter of such dens," he said slowly. "However, on the occasion, it is true that I may visit."

"You are not a young buck about town," the duke said sharply, his disapproval clear and stinging. "Nor are you a legitimate son of mine. If you lower yourself to the gutter, you cannot fault others for noting you came from it."

It was a cruel blow. One Tarquin was accustomed to. His entire life had been marked by the circumstance of his birth.

"Gentlemen of distinction frequent the establishment," he defended himself quietly, as he longed to rail against the duke for his narrow view of the world.

For his narrow, hateful view of Tarquin himself.

"You know my expectations, Mr. Bellingham," the duke countered coolly. "Have you forgotten the funds I provided you for this grand establishment? To say nothing of the fine lords and ladies I have sent your way. The approval of the Duke of Hampton is second only to that of the king."

There it was again, the loan.

Tarquin was beginning to think that selling his soul to the man who had sired him was a sin far greater than any other he had ever committed.

"I have not forgotten your generosity, Your Grace," he said with quiet humility. "I am indebted to you for the loan necessary to buy out my partners here at Bellingham and Co."

When Tarquin had first happened upon what was now Bellingham and Co., it had been known as Mason, Whitley, Lodge and Co. The original partners, all at least thirty years Tarquin's senior, had begun on Pall Mall with highly stylized chintzes and calicoes. Their business had begun failing, however, and by the time Tarquin had invested with every shilling he had spent years painstakingly saving, he'd had a dream of broadening the offerings of the shop that went beyond the comprehension of his older, far-more-conservative partners.

He had struggled to implement necessary changes, such as offering a host of shops within one destination. Mason and Whitley had been opposed to offering furs, fans, and haberdashery. Lodge had been adamantly against the notion of jewels being on offer. The war with France had made the importation of certain luxury goods damned difficult, if not impossible. But Tarquin had means. He also had determination. Still, it had not been until the influx of funds from his father that he had been able to truly realize his ambition in the newly renamed Bellingham and Co.

There was not another shop of its kind to be found in all London.

By design.

It had been his intention, from the moment he had first spied Mason, Whitley, Lodge and Co., to become a part of it. To grow it into the sort of shop London, England had yet to see. He wanted Bellingham and Co. to be the most exclusive, desired establishment in the world. He may have been born to the gutters through no fault of his own, but he was ambitious.

He had never been afraid to work for what he wanted. To give every part of himself in the furthering of his goals. But he could admit to himself, in moments such as these, that accepting the aid of the Duke of Hampton had likely been a misstep.

A terrible one.

"You are indeed indebted to me, sir," the duke reminded him, raising an august, white brow. "I have nothing short of a fortune invested in this shop. A fortune which I am willing to forgive."

Tarquin nodded, swallowing down a rising lump of resentment. "I am aware, Your Grace."

"Are you?" The duke thumped his stick on the floor for emphasis, his nostrils flaring. "It dashed well does not seem like it. Not when you are neglecting your future wife and running to sow your wild oats about gaming hells in the rookeries."

Tarquin loathed being spoken to in this fashion, as if he were a child too simple of mind to understand the complexities before him. Hated the way he had allowed the duke to essentially buy him—to purchase his future, his decisions, his very wife!

"Forgive me," he bit out, forcing the words, the sentiment. In truth, his contrition was frightfully lacking.

Why should he apologize? For being a man in search of his own happiness? For wishing to marry a woman with wits between her ears instead of airy clouds? For wanting to be responsible for his future, his destiny?

"You have yet to offer for Lady Clementia," the duke observed.

He had been delaying, it was true.

Distracted by a golden-haired, thieving East End beauty.

"I was not aware there was a time limitation affixed to my duty," he told his father calmly, for that much was true.

When their agreement had first been reached, there had been no immediacy in the Duke of Hampton's plans for him.

"Too much time has elapsed since you first began courting her," the duke snapped. "Lord Brownley has three other daughters who will need to secure matches of their own. His lordship is growing weary of the wait, just as I am. Just as Lady Clementia herself is. There will be no further delay. You will offer for her, so that we may proceed with the calling of the banns."

A thread inside Tarquin snapped. He could not quite

define or explain his reaction, but there was something about the arrogant air of command in his father, the absolute belief that he could order Tarquin to do his bidding.

Because he could, he realized. He had paid for the right.

But damn if that knowledge didn't chafe, like a cravat knotted too tightly, making him feel as if he were about to choke.

"And if I refuse?" he asked suddenly, challenging Hampton for the first time.

He sensed that his question took Hampton by surprise. And well it should, for Tarquin had never previously opposed him.

The duke's shoulders straightened, his features settling into a chilling line of hauteur. "If you refuse, I will have no choice but to call in the debt you owe me. Immediately."

There it was then, the proof that the duke's desire for him to wed Lady Clementia and do his bidding was the true motivator in his offer of the loan. It had not been to help Tarquin achieve his dream of growing Bellingham and Co. into London's finest shop. Rather, it had been for himself, much like every other action the Duke of Hampton had committed in his life.

The realization ought not to have surprised or disappointed Tarquin, and yet it sent a spear of acute anguish through him as old betrayals he had thought long healed proved to be very much capable of festering.

He nodded. "Understood, Your Grace. I will do as you wish."

And hate himself for doing it.

∼

"What's this I hear about you spending time with a gentleman caller, eh, sister?"

Lily, attempting to make sense of the number of wine bottles The Sinner's Palace had purchased in the last month from the rum dropper—and to keep her mind from the dangerous territory where Tarquin Bellingham's masterful kisses dwelled—jumped at the voice of her eldest brother, Jasper. She had not heard him enter the office that had been his former lair but which, given his more recent transition to a man with a family and a lovely Mayfair house, was now in use by all the siblings whenever it was empty.

She held her brother's familiar hazel gaze, wondering who had squeaked. "I couldn't say unless I know what you've heard."

Jasper raised a dark brow as he sauntered forward, his countenance forbidding and laden with brotherly concern. "Randall said you'd a tall, rum-togged cove awaiting you in the family parlor yesterday. Wouldn't take no for an answer until he'd 'ad an audience with you."

*Rantum scantum.*

She obviously needed to have a stern word with Randall.

Lily affected a carefree smile and returned her quill pen to the well before rising from the massive desk. "I had a caller, aye. That is true."

"A gentleman one," Jasper pressed. "Randall said the cull's cravat was knotted as if by the hand of God."

Bellingham did have perfectly executed cravat knots, all snowy-white perfection. Had he never dribbled a speck of wine on them, she'd wondered? Some broth? A bit of sauce? Heaven knew she often wore her dinner on her bodice. It was one of her greatest faults, much to the dismay of the washerwoman.

"I've never known Randall to admire a cove's duds," she said, avoiding the implicit question in Jasper's observations.

Because she hadn't an inkling of how to explain Tarquin Bellingham to her elder brother. Not the means by which she had found herself entangled with him, not her confounding reaction to his kisses, and not the man himself. She could not even explain any of that to herself.

"Clever attempt to distract me from the true matter, sister." Jasper stopped before her.

He was dressed the part of a gentleman himself today. To look at him, no one would ever suppose he was a rookeries-born gaming hell owner. He looked more like a lord. Although, his cravat knots could not compare to Bellingham's; there was no equal she had ever seen.

She decided to take the offensive. "Am I not permitted callers, then? Hart has a lady in his room from The Garden of Flora, and I'm not to allow a gentleman to pay me a call?"

"Damn. This ain't about you versus Hart. He'll have to answer for his own bad behavior too." Jasper shook his head. "I move to Mayfair and the whole bloody family goes to the devil."

She crossed her arms, eying him, feeling stubborn. "And how do you know my behavior was bad?"

"You're a Sutton, girl." Jasper shook his head, grinning ruefully. "Being bad is in our blood."

Well, she supposed she could not argue that particular point.

"You've settled down now," she pointed out instead. "You've a family and a wife."

"In spite of myself," he agreed, stroking his chin thoughtfully. "As the eldest, it's my responsibility to make certain none of you are doing anything fat 'eaded. Such as allowing a fancy cove to be alone with you so he can…"

"So he can?" she prompted her brother, daring him to answer with what he had been about to say.

Jasper flushed in a rare show of embarrassment. "Christ, Lil. You know what I'm saying."

"No," she lied brightly. "I don't. Perhaps you could tell me."

Jasper squirmed. "Damn it, just give me the bastard's name so I can 'ave a little patter with him myself."

Jasper, have a talk with Tarquin Bellingham?

Absolutely not, and for so many reasons, not the least of which was that it was entirely possible that Bellingham would tell her brother she had been stealing from his shop, or that Jasper would threaten to cut off Bellingham's tally-wags and feed them to his dogs...

She was spared from responding by the office door crashing in, admitting their brother Rafe.

His gold curls were in wild disarray, and he was out of breath, as if he had run from wherever he had been. "Dead body," he said.

Lily's heart leapt to her throat. Surely not... *Good heavens*, she had set Tarquin Bellingham free the night before with nary a backward glance. What if something ill had befallen him in the dark of night? A well-dressed, wealthy cove such as he, meandering about in the darkness would have been far too tempting for a pickpocket. She would never forgive herself if something ill had befallen him.

"Quite the greeting, brother," Jasper said grimly, cutting through Lily's wildly careening thoughts. Unlike her, he was apparently unaffected by the pronouncement. "Where is it, then?"

*It*, her brother had said.

*Dear God, Tarquin.*

"In the alley," Rafe said.

Would Bellingham have gone to the alley when he left? "What is 'e wearing?" she managed to bite out past the worry clogging her throat.

She had lost the *h* in her speech in her upset, but feigning fancy airs was the least of her concerns just now.

Rafe gave her a searching look. "You in the business of hushing culls these days?"

"Of course not," she bit out, feeling frantic. "Was he wearing a neatly knotted cravat? A dark-blue coat and light trousers, very fine leather shoes? A greatcoat trimmed with fur and an elegant pocket watch…"

Undoubtedly, if he had truly been robbed and killed, those luxurious pieces of clothing which proclaimed him a man of means would have long since been filched. Her stomach clenched, churning in a violent sea of despair at the notion.

"Didn't stop to 'ave tea with it, Lil," Rafe said.

"Oh dear God," she said, doubling over.

"Fucking hell," Jasper muttered, the looseness with which he had carried himself instantly disappearing. He was like a warrior, prepared to do battle. "Calm yourself, Lil. I'm sure it ain't your fancy cove. Rafe, I'll have to call the charleys. Is the body one of ours?"

"Wolf doesn't think so," Rafe offered. "He's gone to shake Hart loose from his lady's bed so we can take a closer look."

Jasper raked his fingers through his hair. "Damn it all."

"What if it's Bellingham?" Lily wondered aloud. "I need to come with you and see the man."

Had she sent him to be murdered? She had been so worried about her brothers discovering she was secreting a male caller that she hadn't given proper thought to whether or not Bellingham could fend for himself.

"Bellingham is it?" Jasper's eyes narrowed. "That the name of your caller, perchance?"

"I'm coming with you," she insisted rather than answering her brother's probing question.

"No you're not," Jasper and Rafe said simultaneously.

"It could be dangerous, and that ain't something for a lady to see," Jasper added, softening his tone.

"But..." The room swirled around her as tears welled in her eyes. "You must let me."

Rafe swept forward, settling a calming hand on her shoulder. "We'll come to you after we see what's 'appened. You stay where you are until then."

"Please," she said, feeling desperate, responsible.

Terrified.

"No," Jasper's denial was firm, clipped.

And she knew she had no choice but to obey. Her eldest brother was the leader of their family, and his word was law.

She nodded. "Very well."

"I'll 'ave your promise," Jasper pushed.

"I promise I'll wait for you," Lily said reluctantly.

Jasper and Rafe looked to each other, seemingly sending an unspoken communication, and then they left the office.

Lily remained until she heard their receding boot steps. She gave it a few moments before venturing to the door and peering out into the corridor. No one was about. Guilt warred with the need to know whether or not the dead man was indeed Bellingham. She did not like to lie to her brothers, but then, she had only promised to wait for Jasper and Rafe. Not to wait *within* the office where they had left her.

The halls of The Sinner's Palace were oddly empty and quiet. It was not often that they were entirely bereft of guards and Suttons, rushing to perform their duties. The silence was eerie, as was the reason for it.

A dead man had been found in the alley.

Summoning her courage, Lily moved through the halls, making her way to the entrance to The Sinner's Palace. Her brothers and the guards would have used the rear entrance which led directly to the alley. No one was guarding the front door, which should have been a warning sign.

For when she opened the door and emerged, it was to the din of mayhem rising from the alley. Loud cries. Clashing and clanging, horses whinnying. If she had to venture a guess, she would say there was only one reason for the cry which had been raised: Bradleys.

The Bradley family had risen to become a fierce rival of the Suttons, attempting to harm The Sinner's Palace in whatever insidious means they could. Most recently, the unleashing of rats within their gaming hell. But this—war in the streets—was decidedly new.

Lily hastened toward the sound of the fighting, wondering what in heaven's name was happening, but when she ducked into the covered alleyway separating The Sinner's Palace from the building next door, she collided with a familiar tall, masculine form.

"Bellingham!" she cried out, throwing her arms around him. "You aren't dead!"

## CHAPTER 7

One moment, Tarquin was hurrying down the darkened alleyway alongside The Sinner's Palace, and the next, a woman was crushed up against him, her arms ringed tightly around his neck.

"Bellingham! You aren't dead!"

Of all the ways Tarquin had imagined Lily Sutton would greet him when next their paths crossed, it most certainly had not been using those last three words. But judging from the fight brewing around the corner, he thought he knew why she may have suspected he had met his early end.

A battle was unfolding in the alley behind him, one involving fists and knives and God knew what else. Of all the days he had decided to be discreet, it would seem he had chosen the worst. But following the duke's disapproving call, and even knowing he should stay as far from Lily as possible, he had not been able to resist. In deference to the visit, he had deemed it wise to have his coachman drop him off at a respectable distance.

He held Lily to him tightly, disliking just how good she felt in his arms.

A bloodthirsty cry rose up from the skirmish behind them.

"I am indeed quite alive, but how much longer I remain so depends upon the length of time we can stave off the marauders behind your family's gaming hell."

"Yes of course. How silly I am." She released him, taking his hand in hers, and he was astonished to see the brilliant sparkle of tears in her eyes. "Come with me."

Tears? Lily Sutton? He would have supposed her as hard as an anvil.

But he allowed her to tug him to the entrance of The Sinner's Palace just the same. The door was thankfully ajar, as there was no man stationed there, and they slid inside, Lily bolting the door at their backs.

"Just what the devil is happening out there?" he demanded, wondering how safe they were, bolted door or no.

This was the price he paid to chase after an East End minx who had stolen from him. What else had he expected? Stilted drawing room conversation? Oh, no. It was blades and fisticuffs and blood for the Sutton family.

"There was a dead cove," she said fretfully, wringing her hands in her agitation. "And my brothers went to investigate. But now it seems the family from our greatest rival has descended upon us."

A dead cove. *By God.*

"And you supposed it was me?" he guessed grimly.

"Yes!" She nodded vociferously, then swiped at a stray tear with the back of her hand before laughing. "I am happy you are not dead, is all."

He would have laughed as well were there not a band of murderous miscreants waging war beyond the bolted door.

"Please, Miss Sutton," he drawled. "Do not offer me such praise, lest it go to my head."

She clapped a hand to her mouth, eyes going wide. "Oh, that was dreadful of me, was it not? I didn't mean it the way it sounded. That is to say, you *are* a selfish arsehole, but I like you far more than I ought."

She was rambling.

And insulting him yet again.

Tarquin had never seen her in such a state. Because of her fears for him, or because of the mayhem outside? He could not be certain. But he did know one thing without a doubt.

"You are a Bedlamite," he declared without heat. "A thieving minx who has been the bane of my every day from the moment I first realized how much inventory I was missing."

"And you are a maddening, supercilious, arrogant oaf," she returned.

"You vex me mightily, and yet I cannot stop thinking of you, seeking you out at every opportunity when God knows I should never lower myself to continually returning to this godforsaken gaming hell."

"The feeling is mutual, Mr. Bellingham! I cannot fathom why you insist upon plaguing me as you do."

They stared at each other, wordless and assessing, breathless with anticipation and the wild heights of their emotions both.

And then, in the next breath, she was back in his arms. He was holding her tight, and he could not be sure which of them had moved first, but all he did know was that her mouth was beneath his, hot and insistent and sweet. He had missed this. Had missed *her*.

And his presence in an East End gaming hell after he had been warned by his father and threatened with the calling in of his loan was proof of that. He never should have come here. It was the height of recklessness, jeopardizing everything he had worked for, and he had warned himself not to seek her out the entire ride from his shop.

A warning he had promptly ignored.

Because this—having her in his arms—felt more right than it did wrong.

Felt very right indeed.

The rightest thing he had ever done.

He backed them against a wall, pinning her there, and kissed her as he had longed to do every moment of every hour since he had seen her last. Had it only been the night before? It felt as if it had been a lifetime.

She clung to him tightly, making a soft mewl of acquiescence that heightened the rapidly rising tide of longing within him. He was ravenous. Desperate for her. The scent of her flooded his senses, her warm softness radiating into him. He parted her lips with his, and she opened for his tongue, hers meeting his in equal abandon.

Tarquin cupped her face, angling his head to deepen the kiss. She tasted so sweet, just as he remembered, and he could not get enough.

But then, she pushed at his shoulders, reminding him of where they were. He could not kiss her senseless in the entrance to The Sinner's Place, for God's sake. What had he been thinking?

Tarquin stepped away, his breathing harsh, and stroked a hand over his jaw, attempting to gather his wits and calm his wildly racing pulse. "Forgive me. I don't know what came over me."

"Nor do I," she said, blinking as if she were dazed.

And then she launched herself at him again, throwing her arms around his neck and nearly sending him toppling to his arse beneath the force of her enthusiasm. He caught her around the waist, holding her tight to him, lifting her shorter frame from the floor. The weight of her even felt perfect in his arms. Her lips demanded response from his, and he gave it, kissing her deeply, licking into her mouth.

He thought he could kiss her thus forever and never grow tired.

She withdrew again, head tilted back. And *God*, she was lovely, those green-blue-gray eyes sparkling up at him, her burnished curls slipping free of her coiffure to frame her face. Her lips were dark, berry-red from kissing him, and he liked that, too.

"My brothers are waging a battle in the alley," she said.

"I gathered," he told her dryly, forcing himself to return her feet to the floor and extricate himself from her embrace.

"I ought to see if there is any way I can be of help to them."

When she moved to skirt him and head for the door, he took a step to the side, blocking her path.

"The hell you will," he denied. "There was quite a melee as far as I could see. Fists and blades and all manner of fighting. I cannot imagine your brothers would be pleased to see you injured or worse at their sides."

She hesitated, catching her lower lip in her teeth as if she were contemplating his words with care. "I suppose you are correct. Unlike some men, my brothers care a great deal for their sisters."

He frowned down at her. "Why do I feel as if you are paying me some manner of insult I cannot comprehend?"

"Because I am, you lout!" She swatted at his arm as if he were a noisome smell she might dispel in the air. "Although why you should not comprehend it, I haven't an inkling. Abandoning poor dear Marianne to the foundling hospital as you did. You ought to be ashamed of yourself. And 'ere I am, having a smack at you just the same."

Confusion washed over him. There was quite a bit to unravel.

"Marianne," he repeated. "I know no Marianne."

Miss Sutton shook her head in apparent disbelief. "And now you dare to pretend as if you don't know her."

"That is because I *do not* know her, Miss Sutton," he said calmly. "Perhaps you'll inform me who she is. Before or after you tell me what *having a smack at me* means. The choice is yours."

Her brow furrowed as she searched his gaze. "What do you mean you do not know Marianne Bellingham? She is your sister."

Tarquin maintained his patience by the barest of threads. "I've told you before, Miss Sutton, I haven't a sister. Not a Marianne Bellingham. Nor a Mary Bellingham. None. No sisters. No brothers. A lone bastard."

He almost winced at the last revelation. It was common-enough knowledge, he supposed. But he did not like to air it about. All his life, being born on the wrong side of the blanket had been a merciless scourge, and it was one he continued to pay for daily.

"But that cannot be." Miss Sutton looked crestfallen. "Marianne told me herself."

Tarquin struggled to comprehend. "You mean to say you believed the word of an orphan? No doubt the thieving orphan who attempted to filch the Duchess of Whitley's reticule."

Miss Sutton bit her lip again, and he knew he had not missed his guess.

"What proof has this girl of her parentage?" he asked.

"When she was brought to the foundling hospital, the head matron told me that Marianne's brother had not wanted her. That her parents had both died, and she was left an orphan." Miss Sutton paused, frowning, her expression growing puzzled. "I don't suppose I ever learned of who her brother was until I caught the little scamp selling some wares she'd thieved from your shop…"

He thought he understood everything, and quite well, too. Miss Sutton had been bamboozled by a crafty orphan.

"And no doubt, Miss Marianne told you she was only stealing from Bellingham and Co. because her dastardly brother had refused to take her in, deciding instead to send her to the foundling hospital," he finished for her.

Miss Sutton's expression grew pinched. "I… I suppose that is somewhat how it went."

"My mother has been dead these last twenty years," he said gently.

What the devil was the matter with him that he felt sympathy for her, when she had believed the worst of him? And not only had she believed the worst, but she had proceeded to steal from him as if she were some manner of Robin Hood.

Miss Sutton's face fell. It was rather like kicking a kitten, watching her realize that she had been wrong. That she had been taken advantage of. That he was not the evil monster she believed him to be.

"Your mother is dead?" she asked slowly.

"Quite," he assured her. "Buried, gone. The world is a better place without her. So you see, Miss Sutton, your Marianne orphan cannot possibly be my sister."

"Oh." She pressed a hand to her lips, eyes going wide as the full implications of his revelation sank in. "*Oh.*"

He was about to offer a reply when the sound of booted feet and male voices interrupted the silence.

"That will be my brothers, I expect," she said. "You must hide!"

"Hide?" *By God*, he was not going to stow himself away like a criminal aboard a ship without passage.

"Yes." Her tone was urgent, her voice hushed. "Here!" She

grasped his shoulders and turned him around to face a door. "Wait for me."

"Miss Sutton," he protested.

"Please? I'll only be a moment," she whispered, sounding frantic.

And blast the woman, but she was tugging at his heartstrings once more. He lifted the latch to the door and stepped inside a darkened room. Nary a candle was lit within, and it was dark as a tomb and smelled of old boots. He turned about to ask her for some light, but she had already closed the door.

Grimly, Tarquin crossed his arms over his chest, willing his eyes to grow accustomed to the darkness, and waited for Miss Sutton to return.

∽

LILY RUSHED TO THE OFFICE, breathless and frantic, and managed to slip inside just before her brothers and the guards arrived. Her mind was whirling with the revelations Bellingham had just made to her. He was not a monster. Marianne had cozened her, the mischievous scamp! And she, who had reckoned herself inured to every ploy in the realm, had fallen neatly into the trap…

The door to the office burst open, revealing Jasper, Wolf, and Randall. They were battered and bruised, but alive, all of them. Except that some of them were missing. Her heart leapt into her throat yet again. She was not certain how many more shocks she could withstand in the span of one day.

"Where is Rafe?" she demanded. "And Hart?"

"Rafe is gone home to his lady wife," Jasper said. "Hart returned to his room."

"And Hugh and the rest?" she demanded, worrying over the guards, who were much like family to her.

"Safe. All is well, Lil," Wolf assured her. "A bit of trouble with the Bradleys, nothing more. We gave them the drubbing they asked for."

His fists were scraped and bloodied, but Lily had no doubt the poor man on the receiving end looked far worse. Wolf was a big, powerful beast of a man. Of course, his heart was soft and tender as a newborn babe's inside, but one would never suppose it to look upon him.

"A bit of trouble," she repeated. "Because of the dead cull, you mean?"

"Aye," Jasper said. "The dead cull is one of theirs. It'll be sorted. No need to worry." He turned to Randall. "You'll be on the floor for the evening. I need to return to my wife and daughters for a bit, or my lady will 'ave my bleeding 'ide. Any further trouble, send for me immediately. The rest of the lads are at the doors."

Randall nodded and tugged at his forelock. "Aye, sir."

With a bow, he quit the room.

"You are certain none of you are injured?" Lily pressed.

Jasper made a fanciful pose that only served to accentuate his dirtied, bloodied person. "And do we look injured to you, sister?"

"You should see the Bradleys," Wolf added with a smug grin.

Lily shook her head, thinking of Bellingham trapped in the room used for cleaning the boots of the men who worked at The Sinner's Palace. Nothing worse than muddied boots, was Jasper's credo. He expected everyone to look top of the mode for the lords and wealthy men who came to gamble their coin.

"I am relieved you are all unharmed," she told her brothers as she turned to fetch the ledgers she had been reviewing earlier. "I'll be taking these to my room to fret over this evening."

"Fair enough," Jasper allowed. "But we still need that patter about this cove of yours. But it'll wait for another day, I reckon."

Hearing Bellingham referred to as hers sent a visceral reaction through Lily, and for more than one reason. She did not often dissemble to her siblings directly. Her deceptions were more of a lack of full disclosure. But she was hiding the very man they were speaking of in the boot room just down the hall, and the knowledge made guilt creep up her spine and heat seep into her cheeks.

"He ain't mine," she denied sharply. Perhaps too sharply. Her brothers both stared at her strangely. She clutched the ledger before her as if it were a shield. "I'll bid you both good evening, then."

"Good evening, sister," Jasper said, offering an exaggerated bow.

"What's this?" Wolf was asking as she swept hastily past.

"I'll tell you later," she heard her eldest brother saying as she snapped the door closed.

There was not a moment to waste.

Making certain no one was lingering about in the hall, she rushed to the closet, yanking open the door.

Bellingham stepped over the threshold, blinking at the light coming from the sconces. "I thought you had banished me to perdition—"

"Hush!" Lily pressed a finger to his lips, heart beating faster than the wings of a bird. "Follow me and make haste!"

Bellingham was not accustomed to taking orders from anyone. His displeasure was written all over his handsome, perfect face.

"My brothers," she reminded him through gritted teeth.

He raised a supercilious brow. "See here, Miss Sutton. Let it be known that I am not afraid of your brothers."

"You ought to be," she whispered furiously. "They'll eat your—"

"Liver for breakfast, etcetera," he finished wryly. "Yes, yes. I've heard this before. Carry on, then. But only because I intend to have the full truth from you this evening, and not for any other reason."

Was it his manly pride at stake? Lily had been blessed with five brothers. She knew how hardheaded, stubborn, and foolish they could be. But then, she supposed she and her sisters were hardly any different, and this was certainly no time to quibble over details. If Wolf and Jasper emerged, she would be caught with Bellingham. And for the evening, one explanation was all her frayed composure could manage.

"Of course," she muttered in agreement, grasping Bellingham's arm and giving him an unceremonious tug. "Follow me."

Lily had expected a struggle. But to her surprise, he followed without further protestation. They moved hastily through the hall, up the private stairs to the family's quarters. From there, it was a gamble whether or not Hart or his lady would emerge. She held her breath to the narrow attic stairs, feeling Bellingham's stare on her back as acutely as if it were a touch.

It was only when they had reached her private rooms, the door closed behind them, that she breathed easily. It was gloomy despite the hour, only a hint of gray sun sprinkling through the eaves to light the way.

"Stay here while I light some candles," she told him. "I'll not have you knocking your knowledge box on the rafters again."

"I am not a dullard, Miss Sutton," he said at her back. "I

recall the slant of the ceiling in this queer little rafters room of yours. Amongst many other relevant details."

She ignored his barb, moving forward toward the table which housed her tinderbox and spills. Ordinarily, she brought a candle from below for it involved far less fuss. However, she had been in a damned hurry to bring Bellingham to where he would not be seen. Thank heavens it was not the height of busyness for The Sinner's Palace. The doors had yet to open for customers, and it was just as well, for had customers arrived to find a melee with the Bradleys unfolding, it would have been deuced bad for business.

Lily took up her tinderbox and attempted to strike a spark.

Bellingham touched her wrist, just below the cuff of her gown, his bare hand on her skin sending a jolt straight through her. "Allow me?"

He was asking rather than demanding, and it was a surprising and unexpected concession from him. She told herself it was the conciliatory nature of his request rather than the reaction his touch caused that made her relinquish the tinderbox wordlessly.

She watched while he made short work of lighting a spill and then used it upon the brace of candles atop the table. When had he removed his gloves? And why was he being so solicitous?

His task complete, he turned to her, the glow of the candles illuminating the hollows and planes of his face in all the best ways. She wanted to kiss him. But she also felt horridly guilty for wronging him. And, if what he had told her earlier was true, she had indeed wronged him. Vastly.

And Marianne had wronged the both of them. Also vastly.

"At least we can see one another properly now," he said, his low voice velvet and silk to her senses.

Like the wares he sold in his beautiful shop, Tarquin Bellingham's voice was exquisite. Something delicious and special and...*rare*. For the first time, she wondered if it was an affectation or if his voice was naturally so buttery rich.

"You've always seen me well enough, I reckon," she told him coolly, determined to understand everything that had transpired. Just how thoroughly she had been bobbed.

"To the contrary." Bellingham's tone was thoughtful, his gaze assessing. "I think I've only seen you for the first time today, Lily Sutton."

*Lily Sutton.*

The way he said her name—*oh*. Was it wrong of her to feel a quiver all the way to the soles of her boots?

*Yes*, said her conscience.

*Absolutely not*, said the Sutton within her.

She raised her chin, meeting and holding that brutally blue gaze of his. "Indeed? And how do you suppose that?"

"I thought you a simple thief before," he said softly. "Not simple. Perhaps that is the wrong choice of words. But a thief, nonetheless. Now I understand what you were truly about. It never made sense to me. Why would a woman from a family rising in wealth and prominence, attempting to gain acceptance from the quality, so lower herself to thieving? Surely you would have plenty for yourself, what with the Sutton family and your thriving gaming hell. You *do* have plenty, do you not, Miss Sutton?"

His assessment was not wrong. She *did* have plenty. The Sutton family worked together to provide for each other. To look after each other. And look after each other they had, until they had lost one of their own... But no, she would not think of Logan now.

"I do," she agreed evenly. "And you've the same, as I understand it, Mr. Bellingham."

He inclined his head. "I've plenty. I'll not lie. Or at least, I did until a certain thieving orphan, accompanied by yourself, stole from me repeatedly."

She swallowed against a rush of shame. "We never took enough for it to hurt you."

"Oh," he drawled, stepping forward, closing the polite distance between them, his hands clasped behind his back. "You never stole enough to render me destitute, is that your defense?"

Lily frowned. "A fan here, a fur there, a pocket watch, some gloves or fabric…"

"A price on all of them," Bellingham said. "You, more than any other, ought to understand the price of conducting business. Should you not?"

She did know. She understood. But somehow, in her righteous manner of thinking, her quest to right a wrong, she had not paid attention to anything else. All her thoughts had been for Marianne. None had been for Tarquin Bellingham, a wealthy business owner. The man who reigned over London's greatest shop. Surely, such a cove had nothing to lose.

At least, she had once supposed so, until she had come to know him.

*Know him.*

Did she, truly?

Lily knew the comforting certainty in his hands, guiding and steadying her. In his embrace, pulling her close. In his lips, firm and tender and coaxing.

Was it enough?

"Miss Sutton?" he queried, tearing her from her wildly vacillating ruminations with his stinging question. "Should you not, as part of this fantastical business your family has cultivated and grown, understand the price of conducting business? More specifically, the price of *stealing* from a business?"

She hadn't the answer. She *had* stolen. From *him*. But only because she had supposed it would benefit Marianne. And it had. The child likely had at least ten pounds sewn into the bottom of her mattress by now. All booty, as if the girl were a pirate plundering a wealthy merchant ship.

And indeed, in hindsight, that had been precisely what the child had been doing.

"I…" she began, only to pause. Her thoughts were running wilder than a spooked horse. "I never intended any 'arm. Not to you, nor to your shop. I was only aiming to aid Marianne."

There she went, losing her polish, her firm grasp on her control. But how was it to be helped in a moment such as now, Tarquin Bellingham temptingly near, his sharp gaze pinning her in place, his mellifluous voice asking her pointed questions she did not wish to answer?

"I know," he said, shocking her with his words as much as the tenderness in his expression.

Tenderness? For her? He was regarding her strangely. Warmly. And something low in her belly shifted. Tightened.

"You know?" she repeated stupidly.

He stepped nearer, bringing with him the enticing scent of musk and bay and leather. "Lily?"

He was calling her by her given name. The air between them hung suddenly thick with desire. Their earlier, frantic kisses returned to her, along with the same feeling of longing and relief that he had not been harmed. Was it possible that she had somehow come to care for this man?

*Dear heavens.* She had never supposed it possible.

"Yes?" she asked, her voice betraying her confusion.

"I am going to kiss you." He closed the last of the distance between them, holding her gaze. "If you object, now is the time to tell me."

She didn't object, and that was a problem. Her heart lurched. He was methodically removing his outerwear. He placed his hat on the table. His greatcoat came next, shrugged from his broad shoulders with ease. It would seem Bellingham intended to stay for a while.

"Last chance," he warned. "You are frightfully quiet. I daresay I've never witnessed you bereft of words before now."

She licked lips which had gone dry. "I don't object."

A smug smile curved his lips. "I didn't reckon you would."

Of course he would be arrogant about his ability to woo a woman, just as he was with everything else. Lily might have told him what she thought of his pride, but in the next moment, he had taken her neatly into his arms, aligning her body with his.

His heat radiated into her, his hard strength feeling better than it ever had. Her hands found their home upon his chest, her fingers digging into the expensive cut of his superfine coat, holding him to her. She rolled to her tiptoes as his head descended, meeting him halfway. His mouth settled softly over hers, familiar by now, coaxing and slow at first and then moving with greater urgency.

And this kiss...

It eclipsed every kiss which had come before.

Including his.

Because this kiss was molten. *Exciting.* It changed something inside her. Brought her to life. It was as if the wings of a hundred butterflies were simultaneously catching flight inside her. She felt exhilarated. Awakened. As if she had found some part of herself which she had failed to notice missing until now.

A realization.

That was what this was.

She pressed nearer, seeking...something. Could not keep herself from making a small sound of need as her breasts crushed against his chest and the evidence of his desire prodded her lower belly.

His cock.

Wickedness intruded. She had kissed coves before, but she'd never been so intrigued by the male anatomy. So tempted to touch. Perhaps because, unlike Tarquin Bellingham, the men she'd kissed before had all been friends. Guards at the gaming hell. Once, a handsome young lord. None of them had inspired the blazing fire inside her that he did.

As Bellingham expertly guided her lips apart, his tongue slipping inside to tease hers, she slid her hand down his chest. Didn't stop until her fingers boldly coasted over the fall of his trousers where the thick, rigid length of him was kept from her by only a few scant layers of fabric. His hips jerked forward into her touch, thrusting his hardness into her palm, and oh how she liked it. Liked it very much.

But just then, he tore his mouth from hers, raising his head to stare down at her, his breathing as ragged as hers.

"Christ," he hissed.

It was the first time, she realized, that she had ever heard Tarquin Bellingham take the Lord's name in vain. She didn't remove her hand, however. He felt far too lovely to abandon. Far too intriguing. She was touching him. And he was allowing it. Not just allowing it, but enjoying it, if the harsh set of his jaw and the way his hips continued to tip toward her were any indication.

"Is something wrong, Mr. Bellingham?" she asked softly, boldly giving his cock a stroke.

She may have never touched a man's arbor vitae before, but she was not ignorant as what was to be done with them. She'd heard talking. Had befriended some of the molls who came into The Sinner's Palace to sing whilst the men played at the tables or otherwise plied their wares.

"Tarquin," he bit out. "Call me Tarquin."

"Am I doing it properly, Tarquin?" she asked, liking his name on her lips as she tentatively stroked him again. He seemed to be growing larger beneath her hand.

A sure sign she was indeed carrying on in proper fashion.

However, some affirmation from the implacable man himself would be appreciated.

"God yes," he said. "That is to say, you must stop before you unman me."

She didn't stop, because unmanning him sounded…interesting. Making this cool, composed, high in the instep man lose control held infinite appeal, in fact. Instead, her fingers found the buttons on the fall, plucked one undone.

"Lily," he muttered darkly.

"Tarquin," she repeated, smiling back at him as she located another button and undid it as well.

He closed his eyes, as if he struggled with himself. "You do things to me. I can't control myself in your presence. This was not my intention in coming here today."

"It was not my intention in bringing you to my room, either," she conceded, biting her lip as the last button was pulled free of its moorings and her hand smoothed over the cotton of his drawers.

Oh, the absence of one layer. And what an interesting discovery, a slit. She slid her hand inside it and met with hot, silken male flesh. Nothing could have prepared her for the sleek feel of him, so firm and yet so soft. The shape was perfect for curling her fingers around his rigid length.

So she did.

"Minx," he said without bite, his hips rolling into her touch.

His eyes had opened once more, and they were burning into hers, fiercely and brightly. She could not look away. Did not dare, for fear she would miss something. How incredibly powerful she felt in this moment, how bold, how fearless. He was deliciously formed, and she found the opportunity to explore him nothing short of thrilling.

"Damn it," he growled then, cursing once more as he gently grasped her wrist in his hand, his fingers circling all the way around, stilling her further investigation. "I never intended to go this far."

She had been rather enjoying her discoveries, and his reaction to them. Disappointment mingled with shame as she released him.

"Forgive me for displeasing you," she murmured, hoping she had not disgusted him with her forward actions. She had simply been unable to control herself.

"No." With his other hand, he tenderly caressed her cheek. "You have not displeased me, Lily. Quite the opposite, in fact. But I should not have begun this now."

"Why?" she asked, confused. "There has never seemed a better moment. We are alone. No one knows you are here."

He groaned, leaning his forehead down to rest against hers. "*I* know I am here."

"Tell yourself you are somewhere else," she suggested, restless and aching and wanting something more than what had transpired between them. Wanting the elusive, the unknown, the reckless, the dangerous. What everyone whispered about. "You can fret over it later."

This was new to her, this need from her body. This desire, deep in her core. It was alarming and demanding, and she was not entirely certain what she was meant to do with it. All she did know was that she wanted to finish this—*whatever it was*—with Tarquin Bellingham. Here and now.

"You tempt me unmercifully," he said, voice low and harsh. Not accusatory. But not pleased, either. Rather, he sounded as if he were in pain.

And she was too, in a sense. She wondered if their aches

were kindred. She was persuaded they were, and that he longed for her every bit as much as she yearned for him. It was his outmoded sense of honor, or perhaps even his disapproval of her, which prevented him from seizing what he wanted, wholeheartedly. But she wanted it too, and if her brother could be wooing the sweet and kind Emma in his rooms even now, then why should Lily not seize what she wanted as well?

The answer was clear. Apparent. She *should.*

"*You* tempt *me*," she countered, her gaze never wavering from his. Their mouths were close enough that their breaths mingled, coasting over each other's lips. "I suppose we might consider ourselves even."

"I am going to marry soon," he said abruptly.

Everything stopped. Her lungs. Her very heart, it seemed, as it shriveled and collapsed inward on itself. The hope of the evening died like a waning fire.

Lily's desire experienced a swift and sudden death, too.

She retreated, withdrawing from his embrace, from the charmed sphere of his proximity. From longing and yearning and this desperate desire.

"You are to marry," she repeated hoarsely, hoping she had misheard.

Bellingham was correcting his trousers. Tucking himself discreetly away. Looking shamefaced. She wanted to plant him a facer. To bury her fist in his jaw and feel the stinging bite of the punch in her knuckles. But she also wanted him gone with equal fervor. Wanted to crawl beneath the coverlets on her bed and hide away until she forgot Tarquin Bellingham's beautiful face and duplicitous kisses.

He nodded now, wincing. "Unfortunately, I am bound to marry a lady of my father's choosing. I thought I could... Bloody, flaming hell, I do not know what I thought. What I was thinking. All I wanted was to see you again. You are an infection in my blood, going to my head, making me take risks I never thought to take."

Lily crossed her arms over her chest, confused and hurt, though not entirely certain why. It was not as if he had declared his love for her, and nor had she for him. He was handsome and she was curious.

"You are marrying another woman," she said.

"I have not married her yet."

"But you will," she prodded.

He inclined his head. "I must. The choice is not my own."

She struggled to comprehend the words, such a shock after their raw, unbridled intimacy. Her hand had been on his cock!

"I don't understand." Lily shook her head, still inwardly vacillating between outrage and confusion and shock. "What do you mean when you say the choice is not your own?"

"I mean that I am a bastard," he said baldly. "My father is a duke, and one of vast wealth. He has contributed a significant amount of his funds to the building of Bellingham and Co. In return, he requires me to take the wife of his choosing."

*Dear God.* Lily began to understand. It sounded positively primitive.

"Your father the duke has bought you, then," she concluded. "And in return, you must be a good lad and marry whomever he wishes."

His jaw tensed, his lips thinning. "I suppose so."

She felt ill. "You kissed me, knowing you are to marry another."

His head lowered, his eyes closing once more. "I never should have done so. My sole defense is that I cannot control myself when I am in your presence. You are…intoxicating to me."

On any other day, she would have been proud to hear

Tarquin Bellingham admit she had such an effect upon him. But after she had just learned that he would be marrying someone of his father the duke's choosing, no longer. The sensual spell which had held her firmly in its thrall from the moment he had appeared before her earlier in the streets had shattered.

She moved away from him. "Then you ought to save such enthusiasm for your wife, Mr. Bellingham. If you fear I shall return to your shop, you needn't. You have my promise that neither myself nor Marianne shall trouble you again."

"Lily, it is not so simple." He reached for her, but Lily danced away, avoiding his touch.

She knew that if he touched her, making him go would be that much more difficult. And asking him to leave was for the best, for both their sakes. She had not been thinking properly when she had kissed him and undone the fall of his trousers. Instead, she had been carried away by the upheaval of the day. Moved by relief that he was well, as much as misplaced desire for him. But Lily wasn't going to be any cove's ugly secret.

"Send word of what I owe you," she told him. "I shall gladly repay it, along with every debt Marianne has as well. Then you will be free to go into your new wife's arms, and I'll be free as well."

"And what shall you do?" he asked, a muscle in his jaw twitching as he took up his gloves and hat, followed by his greatcoat.

She held his gaze because she had to, willing away the bitter sting of tears that suddenly yearned to make themselves known. "I'll do whatever pleases me, with whomever pleases me. Good day, Mr. Bellingham."

"Lily—"

She held up a staying hand. "Enough. Go now. Please."

"Of course." He nodded jerkily, looking proper and harsh once more. "As you wish, Miss Sutton. I'll take my leave."

It was not as she wished. But as she watched Tarquin Bellingham retreat from her attic rooms, Lily hoped it would be the last time she watched his broad back walking away. She did not think her fragile, foolish heart could withstand another.

# CHAPTER 8

*L*ily needed two things: distraction and to seek out Marianne so she could uncover the truth. And that was why she was awaiting Hart's lady in the hall outside his private room. She had crossed paths with Emma earlier that morning when the other woman had been in search of the kitchens, and she had issued the invitation on the spur of the moment.

Lily had spent the night alternately plotting curses and potions which might make Tarquin Bellingham's lovely Man Thomas fall off, ransacking her room for all pilfered Bellingham and Co. inventory that remained so she might have a better notion of how much money to send him, and humiliating herself by weeping. A more unpleasant passage of time was not to be had this side of London. Fans, furs, and all manner of fripperies were strewn everywhere. It looked as if her attic room had been infiltrated by a band of thieving Bradleys.

But by now, it was afternoon. Her primary concern of the day had been to send a banknote totaling more than she could fathom to Bellingham and Co., along with a terse note explaining he should consider her debts now absolved.

She had subsequently occupied herself by all manner of tasks about the gaming hell. Cobwebs in the corner? Lily broomed them all away. A scrubbing of the boot room floor? She took brush in hand. More wine to be ordered? She arranged it.

A wounded brother?

Aye, Wolf had stitched up Hart the night before without her the wiser. But she'd learned that apparently Hart had been stuck by a Bradley blade. And so, Lily had fussed over him, mocking Wolf's jagged stitches, and proceeded to sing a lusty afternoon song for the men in the gaming rooms. And then another. And another before her brothers had beckoned her from the floor.

She had promptly made it to the significantly better-smelling boot room and burst into tears. Lily Sutton did not indulge in waterworks. She had dried her eyes, calmed herself, admonished herself, and now she was set to have an accompaniment for her trip to the foundling hospital.

Diversion was what she required.

That, and forgetting Tarquin Bellingham existed.

Distracting her from the grim musings torturing her mind, Hart's Emma appeared, looking angelic and far too much like a lady torn from Mayfair for a walk to the foundling hospital. Sly Jack was otherwise occupied today, meaning they'd have to travel by foot. Just as well, if you asked Lily. The open air was always a welcomed jolt to the senses, even if it was infiltrated by fog and filth. And heaven knew she needed all the jolts and distractions she could beg, borrow, or steal.

Lily's gaze dipped to Emma's slippers. "You'll be needing some boots."

Emma glanced down at the footwear peeping from

beneath her hem. "I do not suppose you have a pair I might borrow?"

"Fortunately for you, I do," she said, thinking of the disaster in her rooms and then deciding it hardly signified. "Follow me."

She turned on her heel, striding down the hall as Emma trailed in her wake.

"The ceiling is a bit lower up here," she called over her shoulder as they began taking the stairs, thinking of Tarquin and the knock he had taken to the head, and then cursing herself for allowing her mind to drift to him at all. "I don't reckon you'll have to duck since you're short as I am. My brothers being the tall coves they are didn't wish for these rooms. But I prefer it for the quiet it brings me. Being surrounded by so many culls makes a lady positively touched in the upper works."

As they reached the door, Lily thought for a moment of the excited passion with which she had crossed this same threshold with Bellingham just the day before. And then she sternly banished all such thoughts.

To the devil with Tarquin Bellingham. *May he hit his head on more rafters.*

"How many brothers do you have?" Emma asked her at her back.

Daylight coming in the eaves was enough to illume the mess Lily had left that morning. Dresses, undergarments, shoes, fans, reticules, and other items had been flung across the room without regard for where they may land. She winced at the disarray, evidence of just how upset she had been.

Still was, curse the man.

"I've four now," she answered, crossing the room to a pile of slippers and boots near her bed.

"Now?" Emma asked, following behind.

*Logan.* Her heart gave a pang for the brother she'd lost.

"One of my brothers is dead," she explained, her voice hitching on the painful words as she shuffled through the pile of boots and slippers. "He disappeared over a year ago. None of us knows what became of him, only that he's gone."

"How terrible," Emma said softly. "I cannot imagine not knowing what has become of someone you love."

It *was* terrible. The agony of not knowing what had happened to their brother haunted them all in various ways.

"It's broken our hearts," Lily said solemnly as she straightened, a pair of boots in hand which she offered to the other woman, trying valiantly to keep her mind from thoughts of Loge. "You may fit in these."

Emma took them from her, and then removed her stockinged foot from her slipper, sliding the boot on. They pattered on for a few more minutes, with Lily deciding she truly did like Emma. She hoped they could be friends and that Hart would make an honest woman of her. But then, it wasn't her place to pry.

Not yet. She'd leave that for another day.

They made their way to the foundling hospital, without trouble, taking with them a basket of honey cakes, bread, and other sundries from The Sinner's Palace kitchens for the girls. At the door, they were greeted by a grim, red-faced Mrs. Frost.

"Miss Sutton, I was not expecting you today," the head matron announced coolly, an air of disapproval edging her voice.

Lily offered her basket and gestured for Emma to do the same, for she knew honey cakes were a preferred treat for Mrs. Frost as well. It was rather akin to a sacrifice for the gods. If one was to bring anything lovely to the foundling hospital, it had to also be something the dreaded Mrs. Frost enjoyed, and there had to be plenty for her. The woman's chief concern was herself rather than her charges.

"We've some spare honey cakes and thought they might be appreciated," Lily said.

"Honey cakes." Mrs. Frost made a low sound, pulling up the cloth covering the basket to inspect its contents. "May as well come inside, then."

"Thank you." Lily pinned a falsely bright smile to her lips. "I've brought another set of hands to assist me today. How might we be of use?"

"The eldest girls are working on their sewing," Mrs. Frost said, taking Emma's basket in her other arm. "I'll deliver these to the kitchens. You might aid them if you've the skills."

The belittling tone of her voice suggested that the head matron strongly believed neither Lily nor Emma would possess the requisite sewing abilities. Lily could sew just fine. Her stitches weren't particularly straight, but they did their job. She couldn't say the same for Emma, but if she were a wagering woman, she'd bet her last ha'penny that Emma could stitch her way around Mrs. Frost.

"Thank you, Mrs. Frost," Lily said, stifling the retort that longed to free itself.

The head matron disappeared with her bounty, leaving Lily and Emma free to seek out the girls in the room they used for sewing.

"What is it we are meant to do?" Emma asked quietly, sounding uncertain.

"Give the girls a hand," Lily answered. "There is one girl in particular I must speak with, but just carry on as you like. They adore having someone about who isn't as harsh as Mrs. Frost."

"I can well imagine," Emma said at her side. "She seems quite the dragon."

Lily raised a brow. "That's an insult to dragons."

Emma emitted a startled chuckle as they crossed into the room where the girls were all busy sewing beneath the guidance of one of the eldest orphans, Gertrude, who would be soon moving on from the foundling hospital. Lily wasted no time in finding the dark-haired imp she was seeking. Marianne's head was bent over her sewing as Lily approached, but it was plain to her that the girl was not making stitches as she was meant to be doing.

She could not lie. Marianne quite reminded her of herself. Lily was terrible at doing what she ought. Instead, she'd always found so much more satisfaction in doing whatever intrigued or moved her at the moment. And that was how she'd always found herself mired in all the trouble she had thus far found.

"Miss Sutton!" Marianne greeted her brightly, abandoning all pretense of the needlework in her lap.

The girl's impish demeanor was infectious; she was missing two teeth, which certainly added to her rascal's air. That and her deceptions.

Lily struggled to keep her countenance devoid of emotion, stern and serious. "Marianne, there's something we must speak about. Come with me, if you please."

The girl's face fell. "Something else?"

"It's about Mr. Bellingham," Lily said.

"Oh?" Marianne held her gaze, as if nothing were amiss.

Waiting to gauge her reaction based on what Lily revealed to her, no doubt.

She guided the girl a safe distance away from the others, where they could speak privately.

"Mr. Bellingham isn't your brother," Lily offered quietly, frowning at the girl.

Marianne blinked. "He ain't?"

"Marianne," she chastised quietly.

The girl hung her head and shuffled her feet. "I know he ain't."

"And yet you allowed me to believe he was," Lily continued. "Allowed me to think him a vile person for abandoning his own flesh and blood to the foundling hospital, leaving you to the life of an orphan."

"I'm sorry, I am, Miss Sutton." Marianne was appropriately shamefaced. "I didn't think it would do any harm." She looked around to make certain none of the other girls were listening in, lowering her voice to a whisper. "I didn't want you to stop me. I'm trying to buy my way out of here, and filching is the only way to do it."

"Oh, Marianne," she said on a sigh. "You've no notion of the trouble you've caused me with your mischief."

Bellingham's handsome face and wicked kisses rose in her mind, but she viciously tamped them down.

"I hope you don't hate me now, Miss Sutton," Marianne said, her lower lip quivering.

Although Lily was sorely disappointed in the girl for lying to her and tricking her so thoroughly, her heart ached at the sight. She patted Marianne on the shoulder.

"No waterworks, my dear. I could never hate you, and you know that." Indeed, Lily had come to think of the girl like a member of her own family. "But you must know that what you did was wrong, and I'll have your promise—your *true* promise—that you'll not do it again."

Marianne nodded. "I promise, Miss Sutton."

What Lily *did* loathe was that Marianne was so unhappily mired at the foundling hospital. How Lily wished that she had her own situation, that she might help Marianne and girls like her—ambitious, intelligent, and far too independent for a life relegated to service. But then, perhaps there was something she could do. How unfair it was, all the girls sewing together in the room, working on piecemeal mending, the life events which had landed them here beyond their control.

She had been attempting to right the wrongs done Marianne, but she had only muddled everything far worse. All these girls needed someone to speak for them. And it was not going to be the odious Mrs. Frost, who was likely currently pleasing herself with a mouthful of honey cakes.

No indeed. It was going to be Lily Sutton. And assisting these girls in their futures was going to make her far happier than Tarquin Bellingham's kisses ever had.

That was what she told herself, anyway.

~

AT THIS VERY MOMENT, Tarquin was meant to be properly courting Lady Clementia. He had accepted an invitation to a soiree this evening, knowing she would be in attendance, the weight of duty a heavy mantle upon his shoulders. In truth, he did not want to see Lady Clementia. Did not wish to smile and eat dreadful food and sip tasteless drinks and pretend he was a lord instead of his father's puppet.

However, it had been the arrival of the banknote, and the concise correspondence essentially telling him to go to the devil, along with the money Lily owed him, which had brought him once more to The Sinner's Palace. He paced the confines of the parlor where he had yet again been directed to cool his heels and await Lily's presence.

The note was the prompting for his presence here, but that was not the sole motivating factor. Because ever since he had first set eyes upon Lily Sutton gliding about his shop as if she owned it, all he had been able to think about was *her*. And all he wanted to see was *more* of her. After those wild kisses they had shared and the way she had so boldly unbuttoned the fall of his trousers and…

*No*, he inwardly admonished himself. He would not think of *that* now.

But there was more to it than the mere physicality of his desire. He also hated the way things between them had ended last night. Hated the hurt he had seen in her countenance just before she had hidden it behind her customary bravado. Hated the way her voice had been strained. Hated that he had caused her pain.

The door to the parlor opened, but not to reveal Lily as he had hoped.

Rather, it was the overly large guard who had led him to the parlor. The same man Lily had rushed to join two nights before.

"She ain't going to be seeing you today."

Tarquin started forward, staring the man down despite his magnificent size; he was tall himself, but the fellow was a head taller and possessed fists the size of ham hocks. "Then Miss Sutton ought to come and tell me that herself. If she cannot, I will continue to wait."

Likely, she was being stubborn. But he could be stubborn, too.

"She ain't coming to tell you anything." The man shook his head, his countenance grim. "There's been a scuffle in the alley."

*Good God*, not like the one he had witnessed the day before?

His heart leapt.

"Has Miss Sutton been injured?" he demanded.

"She's shaken, is all. A buzman tried to snaffle 'er reticule."

Tarquin blinked, attempting to make sense of the information the other man had just imparted. "Do you mean to say Miss Sutton was set upon by a footpad?"

The man nodded. "Right."

He started forward again. "Then I must see her myself. I insist."

The wall of man crossed his arms over his chest, looking menacing. "Don't your wattles work, sir? I said she ain't going to see you."

Tarquin stopped short of the man impeding his movement. "And who has decreed this? You or the lady herself?"

"She's gone upstairs to 'er rooms."

Tarquin shrugged, a dark, hot coal residing in his belly at the way the guard was so protective over Lily. He tamped down the jealousy, the possessive urge.

"Take me to see her there, then," he suggested.

The guard shook his head, his countenance impassive. "Ain't proper."

Of course it wasn't proper to go attending an unwed lady alone in her chamber. However, this was not a Mayfair town house. And Lily Sutton was no lady.

"We are in a gaming hell," he pointed out.

The guard shrugged.

"I must see her," Tarquin growled, at last losing the thin control he had on his patience and shouldering past the man.

"Damn you, you can't 'ave your run of the private quarters," the guard growled, stalking after Tarquin. "Mr. Sutton'll darken my day lights if I allow coves to go sniffing about Miss Sutton's skirts."

"No one is sniffing about my skirts, Randall."

The familiar voice had Tarquin's full attention jerking in the opposite direction, where Lily Sutton herself was sauntering down the hall in a dirtied gown. Although her hem was coated in mud and she had a smear of dirt on her cheek, she was so damn beautiful, he ached just looking at her.

"Miss Sutton," he said formally, sketching a bow.

The guard issued an indelicate snort.

Tarquin turned back toward the man, fist clenched. "Have you something to say, you lumbering lout?"

"Mr. Bellingham," Lily chided, her voice frosty. "That will be enough."

"I've something to say, aye." The man grinned, cracking his knuckles. "Care to open your wattles wide enough to take a listen?"

That was it.

Tarquin held up his fists in challenge. "Perhaps I'll open *your* wattles instead."

He was not entirely certain what wattles were, but he gathered they were ears.

"Gentlemen!" Miss Sutton's voice rose sharp and high as she planted herself between the two of them. "There will be no opening of wattles or throwing of fists."

"The cove refuses to leave, Miss Sutton," the guard grumbled.

"You're damned right I do," Tarquin returned, the fire of fury in his blood. "I need to speak with you, Miss Sutton. But after I learned of your altercation, I was more concerned with seeing to your welfare."

Miss Sutton shook her head. "Like a pack of dogs fighting over an alley bone, you are." She addressed the guard first. "Randall, I'll speak with my guest in privacy."

The guard's eyes narrowed. "Your brothers ain't going to like it."

"My brothers don't need to know," she countered. "Now do carry on with your evening. I'm sure there is more important work to be done than hovering over me."

With a grudging air, the guard tugged at his forelock in a gesture of respect. "Aye, Miss Sutton."

With a glare in Tarquin's direction, which was met with a dagger-sharp glower in return, the guard left. When he was gone, Lily took Tarquin's arm and pulled him back into the parlor, closing the door at their backs.

"Well?" she demanded, her face an impenetrable mask.

"What happened?" he asked hoarsely, worry for her trumping all else. "Were you hurt?"

She pursed her lips. "I am perfectly well as you can see. A miscreant attempted to steal my reticule on the way back from the foundling hospital, and unfortunately for the cull, I keep a pistol in that very same reticule."

"Thank God," he breathed, his gut tightening at the thought that she went about the East End unchaperoned, walking on foot. "You must take better care, Miss Sutton. What of your coachman, Sly Jack? Where was he?"

"Busy, not that it's any of your concern." She planted her hands on her hips and eyed him balefully. "Why have you come, Mr. Bellingham?"

"To return your banknote." Tarquin reached into his coat and extracted the missive she had sent round earlier, holding it out for her. "Here you are."

She wrapped her arms around her waist, refusing to accept his offering. "It's yours. To settle the score between us. I reckon it's enough to cover Marianne's debt and mine, with some extra for you to buy a lovely betrothal gift for your wife."

There was a bitterness in her voice as she said the last that Tarquin did not miss, and regret settled in his heart, heavy as a stone.

"I do not require the debt to be paid," he said, his voice husky.

"You've been chasing me about, demanding I pay what is owed," she reminded him. "Why have you suddenly changed your mind? If it is because you have some misguided notion I'll become your mistress—"

"No," he interrupted her, hating that she believed him

such a scoundrel. "I would neither ask nor demand that of you."

But then, what had he done thus far to earn her trust, to make her see him as a gentleman? He had kissed her at every opportunity, and while he did not regret knowing the smooth softness of her lips beneath his, he owned that he had not given her cause to hold him in high esteem.

She raised a brow, cocking her head to consider him with that mysterious gaze of hers. "What, then?"

Tarquin was going to have to explain himself. And that would be damned difficult since he was not certain he knew how. All he did know was that she had bewitched him, and he could not think of anyone else. It had been somehow easier before, when he had believed her a true thief. But now he knew she had been championing a child. And that knowledge warmed the icy cockles of his heart in a way nothing else had.

"You were trying to help the girl," he said. "Your method was questionable, but I have come to understand you differently. I may not possess as vast a wealth as my father, but I surely have enough to spare for one orphan child. Whatever you have taken, and whatever she has absconded with, it is hers to keep, the debt forgiven. There is one caveat, however, and that is the child must be told thieving is not the answer to her problems. If she carries on in this vein, she will only find herself in prison, or worse."

Miss Sutton nodded. "I already told her as much. She knows she was wrong to steal and to lie, and to cause all manner of troubles for the both of us. It is my dearest wish to take her in myself, but an unwed woman can hardly offer a proper situation for an orphaned child. I know Mrs. Frost would never allow it."

How good her heart was. Tarquin had misunderstood Lily Sutton quite desperately.

He could not keep himself from reaching for her then, taking one of her hands in his, and pressing the note into her palm. "Take your banknote. And please know how very sorry I am."

Her fingers were bare, and the jolt of awareness that skipped through him was stronger than ever. The desire was still there between them. Nothing could change that.

"You are apologizing?" Her brow furrowed as she searched his gaze, some of the ice melting from her voice and countenance.

"I did not intend to dishonor you," Tarquin elaborated with great difficulty, for it was no easy feat, admitting he had been wrong. "I was outraged when I discovered the thefts. But I'll not lie. From the moment I first saw you in my shop, it was no longer the stolen fans and other fripperies that concerned me. It was you."

Her fingers curled around his, staying them when he would have withdrawn. "Me?"

"You," he repeated softly, surveying her in all her glory. Her hair was mussed, wisps of dark-blonde curls framing her face. That smudge of dirt yet upon her cheek. Her gown was muddied and all but ruined. And she was the most beautiful sight he had ever beheld. "You're nothing short of captivating, though you vex me mightily and you are the last woman on God's earth I should long for."

And yet, he did.

He longed for her fiercely.

It was an ache in his lungs, a driving need forcing its way into his chest. A burning hunger simmering in his groin. A fever overtaking him.

"You must not say such things to me," she said, frowning at him.

"Why?" he could not resist asking, though he knew the inherent danger in doing so.

"Because it makes me want to kiss you, even when I know I should not," she murmured. "Just when I am persuaded you are the most arrogant, coldhearted scoundrel I've ever met, you show me a different side of yourself, and it makes me weak when I should be strong."

"You were strong enough to chase away the footpad earlier," he said, his voice thick with mangled, confused emotions. "Promise me you'll not go gadding about London on foot again. Something could have happened to you."

"Why should you care if it had?"

"Because." He paused, struggling to find the proper words, gritting his molars. "I care for you."

There it was, the full revelation. He, Tarquin Bellingham, who had prided himself upon his need for no one, his ruthless determination, his iron grip upon control, had somehow developed tender feelings for this dirt-bedecked minx from the East End. That was the true reason he had continued *chasing after her*, as she had called his pursuit. That was why she lived in his head, sleeping or awake. Why he walked through the department containing perfumes at his shop and thought none of the scents could compare to hers. Why he continued risking his father's wrath and the calling-in of his loan by seeking her out, again and again.

"You care for me," she repeated softly.

No sense in denying it, now that the humiliating confession had been uttered.

He gave a jerky nod. "I do."

Her fingers tangled in his, tightened. "Come with me."

# CHAPTER 9

They scarcely made it over the threshold of her attic room before Lily was in Tarquin's powerful arms. She was snug against his chest, the erratic thumping of his heart beating against her breast, his mouth hot and hungry on hers, their tongues mating. It was reckless. Unwise. Wrong. This man could never be hers. *But*, a little voice inside her said, *he can be mine for tonight.*

Yes, hers for tonight.

It could be enough.

It would *have* to be enough.

Something had happened to her in the parlor downstairs when this proud, unrelenting, handsome man had looked at her with raw, unfettered tenderness and declared he cared for her. Because she had realized she had come to care for him too. Despite his bombastic ways and his perfectly knotted cravats, and in spite of the sense of self-preservation that told her to keep him at a safe distance. There was far more to him than the cold, overbearing shop owner he pretended to be.

He was also the man who kissed her so sweetly, who

touched her body as if it were a wonder, who waited patiently for her in a stinking boot room. The man who refused repayment, who showed mercy to herself and Marianne both when in truth neither of them had deserved it. The man who apologized when Lily herself had been the one who had wronged him first.

That man, she could not help but to feel, was the true Tarquin Bellingham. The gem hiding beneath his unyielding, harsh exterior. And that man, she could love.

But love was not what these heart-wrecking kisses were about, and she must not allow her mind to linger overly long on such unwanted emotion.

These kisses were an invitation, and she was issuing it.

To him.

Her fingers delved into his thick, dark hair, finding it soft and lustrous. His lips angled over hers with sensual possession, giving as much as he took. She whimpered into the kiss, feeling so helplessly achy everywhere. But especially between her thighs. He seemed to know what she was feeling—perhaps he felt it, too.

For he was slowly guiding them across the chamber, leading them to the bed.

Thankfully, she had left a brace of candles burning when she had descended earlier, and they illuminated the spacious attic room perfectly. She had been seeking her brother Jasper when she had come upon Randall and Bellingham arguing by the parlor, and all thoughts of her brother had been forgotten. Shadows and the warm glow of candlelight flickered around them now, making it possible to find their way through the objects she had recklessly strewn about that morning.

When they had nearly reached the bed, they stopped, their frantic kisses paused as they stared at each other, breathlessly drinking each other in.

"I shouldn't be here," he said. "You know I cannot offer you marriage, that there are obligations I am duty-bound to fulfill."

Again with the betrothed he would soon have. Lily bit her inner cheek to stave off the wild burst of jealousy at the thought of the nameless, faceless lady who would be fortunate enough to become this gorgeous man's wife. She fought to maintain her calm, imperturbable demeanor.

"Don't recall asking you to marry me, Bellingham," she told him.

He smiled, and the sight was so rare, so beautiful, that it quite stole her breath. "Of course not. But I wished to be clear."

"Clear as a windowpane," she agreed. "And I'm not about to be your convenient, either. Lily Sutton ain't any man's mistress."

His smile faded. "Of course not. I wish my circumstances were different, Lily, and that—"

She stopped him from finishing his sentence, pressing a finger to his lips. "Hush. They aren't different. We have tonight."

He kissed her fingertip, and she felt that kiss all the way to her toes.

"Tonight," he echoed softly.

She swallowed hard against a rush of foreign emotion she was not equipped to deal with at the moment. Later, she would sort out the way this man made her feel, how he overwhelmed her in all the very best ways, decimating her defenses and bringing her to her knees.

For now, she lowered her hands to the intricate knot on his cravat and began dismantling it.

"You are always too proper and starched," she said softly, concentrating on the linen stock instead of his beautiful face.

It was far safer to look at his clothing than all of him.

"I was not always so proper and starched," he said, voice low. "I was quite wild in my youth."

"You, wild?" She frowned at the knot, which was stubborn.

Or perhaps it was that her fingers were trembling with a combination of eagerness and suppressed passion. Whatever the reason, the knot was only growing tighter rather than loosening as she intended.

"It wasn't until I saved enough funds to buy my way into Mason, Whitley, Lodge and Co., as it was then known, that I styled myself a gentleman. I had great dreams of becoming a shop owner, of showing my father what his bastard son had made of himself."

Her heart ached at the vulnerability in his words, his acknowledgment of who he was and where he had come from. She understood him now, better than she had before. It was as if all the tiny, rigid pieces of Tarquin Bellingham had assembled themselves before her. And suddenly, she had a true vision of him.

It was then that Lily knew, he was not just a man she could love.

He was a man she *loved*.

Somehow, the shift had already happened, his place in her heart secured.

Her hands rose to cup his face. "I want you to make me yours tonight."

"You don't mean that," he murmured.

"Yes, I do," she insisted.

For she did. She wanted him more than she could recall ever wanting anything. Their lives were destined to take different paths. But not here. Not tonight. He was so much more complex than she had previously understood. Beneath his veneer of starched gentleman, he was a man who had struggled and worked diligently just as Lily and her family had, fighting for a bigger piece of the pie than the meager one the world wanted to bestow upon them.

"Please," she added when he still hesitated, his countenance torn.

He swallowed hard; her palms absorbed the ripple in his jaw. "You are certain?"

"Certain," she repeated.

"My God." He heaved out a shuddering breath, as if overcome with emotion, and perhaps desire as well. "Have you ever..."

She shook her head. "Never."

"Lily." He turned his head, kissed her palm with a reverence that made her knees go quivery. "Your husband should be your first."

Lily did not give a damn about being proper. She measured her life in shoulds rather than shouldn'ts.

"I want it to be you," she told him. "I choose you."

He exhaled again, seemingly struggling with himself. Lily decided to take matters into her own hands. She recalled his reaction in his office that day which now felt as if it had been a lifetime ago, when she had pretended as if she were about to strip away her gown before him. But this time, her actions were not a ruse.

Her fingers went to the small line of buttons on her bodice, unfastening them one at a time whilst holding his gaze.

"Lily," he ground out.

She was not certain if he was offering protest or praise. Lily decided upon the latter, clasping handfuls of her gown, before hefting it over her head. The garment traveled to the floor in a mud-burdened heap, the hems still heavy where they had become mired in the muck. She'd quite forgotten about the cutpurse earlier in the alley, the altercation which had ensued. That was how deeply Tarquin Bellingham affected her.

Her petticoat came next, having fared better than her gown in terms of mud, though it too was fairly besmirched near the hem. She tossed it atop the pile she was creating before him, clad in her stays, chemise, stockings, and boots. Tarquin's stare grew heated, traveling over her, and he shucked his coat, tossing it to the floor.

She took a moment to admire him in his shirtsleeves, the raw intimacy of seeing him in her private space, the careful air he usually affected gone. In place of the proper gentleman was the raw, sensual frankness of a seducer.

And she wanted to be seduced.

Her fingers flew to her stays, finding knots and struggling to undo them. He moved forward, closing the distance between them.

"Allow me to help you."

She held still as he stood behind her, his fingers chasing hers away. His face dipped to the curve where her neck and shoulder met, bared by the removal of her gown, and placed a hot kiss there.

He inhaled. "You smell so damned good." Another kiss. "And your skin is so soft and silken." *Kiss.* "I have imagined this so many nights."

She was melting on the inside. The ache between her thighs was intense and acute, a rising conflagration which threatened to consume her.

"I have, too," she confessed on a sigh as her stays loosened.

He gently nibbled on her shoulder and she shivered, though the action had nothing to do with being cold. With calm, efficient movements, he helped her out of her stays before firm hands settled possessively on her waist, the sole barrier between them the linen of her chemise as he turned her to face him.

His head dipped, and he took her lips. Slowly and softly at first, feathering his mouth over hers in a decadent tease. One of his hands slid from her waist, traveling higher until he cupped her breast. Gently, he squeezed, molding and caressing, working his palm over her painfully sensitive nipple until she moaned into the kiss.

The moment her lips parted, his tongue swept inside, delving deeply. He tasted of tea and honey, sinful yet sweet, and she gasped as his clever fingers plucked and pulled at the hard peak of her breast. Fire and need bloomed from the delectable place where he pleasured her. From her lips, too. It slid languorously down her spine, seeping into her belly and between her thighs.

She felt as if she were too heavy for her own body, her mind floating with a dreamlike sensation. Not even in the privacy of the dark night, alone in her bed when she had touched herself, had she ever known such an exquisitely heightened desire. If she did not have more, she was sure she would shatter to pieces.

Lily was ravenous for him. She wrapped her arms around his neck, anchoring herself to Tarquin as she arched her back and thrust her breasts forward for more of his sensual teasing. Her tongue mated with his and she fought to control the kiss, to take command of his mouth as he had done to hers.

He growled low in his throat at her urgency, and she caught his lower lip in her teeth and tugged. But this was not enough, his reaction. She wanted him to be as mad for her as she was for him. So she tore her mouth from his and rose on her toes to deliver a string of kisses to his jaw, all the way to his ear.

"I want you," she whispered, before carrying on.

More kisses down his throat, to where she was impeded

by that blasted perfect cravat of his. She paused to tangle her fingers in it once more. "I want this gone."

"You are a demanding thing, aren't you?" he asked, but there was no bite in his voice, only approval and the thick velvet tones of a man adrift in a sea of lust.

"I'm a Sutton," she said by way of explanation, finally pulling the knot free and tugging his cravat away.

Her fingers fell next to the buttons on his shirt, plucking each one free of its moorings. She grasped handfuls of his shirt and stepped back to help him haul it over his head. Lily took a moment to appreciate the sight of him, all sharp masculine planes and corded muscle, his chest broad, his arms strong. How handsome he looked, standing before her in nothing more than his boots and trousers.

"Let me help you with your boots," he said, going down on his knees before her.

She liked the way he looked up at her, his blue stare drinking her in, traveling over her like a caress. Wordlessly, Lily extended her left foot first, balancing on her right.

He took the boot in hand, working the lacings free until it was loose, despite the mud and muck crusting the serviceable footwear. He placed it gently to the side and then held his hands out again. "The other?"

Balancing on her stocking-clad foot this time, she offered him the right boot, watching as he used efficient, graceful motions to remove it as well. He dusted his hands off on his trousers before taking up her foot once more, caressing the heel, the arch, rubbing the aches and pains she had not realized were present from her tired muscles.

"Oh," she said, a pleased sigh that fled her lips. "That feels so lovely."

"You walked too far today," he said, frowning at her. "You need to take better care with yourself."

"I could say the same of you," she countered. "Pushing

yourself as you do. You must keep late hours at your shop, to come and go at the times you have here."

And how she hated the thought of him, alone and unhappy, poring over ledgers or whatever it was that kept him busy. He was an island, Tarquin Bellingham, in the midst of a vast sea, no one near. Had it been by design, or was the lonely life he lived the one he had chosen for himself?

*He won't always be lonely*, an unwanted voice reminded her. *He will have a wife soon enough.*

Lily tamped down that thought, choosing to dwell in the moment instead of in the uncertainty of the future.

"I keep the hours my position requires of me," he told her calmly, those knowing fingers traveling up her ankle, massaging her calf, caressing the back of her knee before reaching the garter keeping her stocking in place on her thigh.

His fingers flirted with her bare skin, brushing and teasing, gently stroking. Lily wanted that hand higher. She lifted her foot upon a nearby stool, opening her legs for him, encouraging his exploration.

"You shall work yourself to death," she admonished thickly, fretting over him even as his hand drifted higher.

The combination of cool evening air on her flesh and the anticipation of knowing that at any moment, his fingers would coast over the bare folds of her quim was too much. She inhaled sharply when his fingertips brushed her intimate flesh, grazing the most sensitive part of her.

He did not respond with words to her rebuke. Instead, he held her stare as his fingers stroked the bud of her sex. His hand was beneath her chemise, her body still shielded from him, and the dichotomy of his intimate touch, the pleasure it sparked from her core and sent radiating outward, was deliciously sinful.

As if he had sensed the direction of her thoughts, he

leaned forward, pressing a kiss to her linen-covered hip. "Your chemise. Will you take it off for me? I want to see your beautiful body while I touch your sweet cunny."

He did not have to ask twice. Lily raised the shift over her head and discarded it with the rest of her layers. Cool air kissed her breasts, belly, and limbs. There was something unspeakably erotic about standing before him, naked save her stockings and garters. To gaze down at his hand between her legs, caressing slowly.

"I have to taste you," he growled, voice guttural with a suppressed need that matched her own.

And then he shocked her utterly by replacing his hand with his mouth.

~

SILKEN AND SMOOTH AND WARM, like the finest hothouse fruit, only better because she was Lily, and she was his.

Even if for tonight only.

Tarquin licked along her slit, gathering her wetness, his tongue flicking across her distended clitoris in a series of light flicks that had her hips jerking, a throaty whimper emerging from above. *God*, how he liked this position, on his knees before her. The hard wood of the attic floor bit into his knees, but the pain was almost pleasurable. He wanted her to writhe against him. To order him to lick her until she spent, and then to ride his face until she came again.

He wanted her to stake her claim on him. To unleash her wildest desires. To use him and have her pleasure and find her pinnacle a dozen times before she allowed him to find his. All the desires he had ruthlessly tamped down for years returned. He felt, for the first time in as long as he could recall, truly free. And it was the freedom, along with the fantasies he could no longer suppress, that made him groan into her cunny as he fed on her. His cock stiffened to painful awareness in his trousers.

He sucked on her pearl hard, and then rocked back on his knees, looking up at her.

What a sight she presented. His Queen of Thieves, naked and flushed with passion. She was more perfect than he could have imagined, a mouthwatering confection of feminine curves, creamy skin, and perfect pinks. Her nipples were tight, hard buds prodding upward, her lips were parted, her mysterious gaze glazed, her breathing ragged.

"Take what you want from me," he told her. "Tell me what you need."

She was on the edge just as he was, the musky scent of her desire a perfume that was as delicious as the sight of her in nothing but those stockings and garters.

"I want your mouth," she said thickly, before biting her lower lip, a tinge of pink washing into her cheeks.

Her words set his blood aflame.

He lowered his head and obeyed, giving her his tongue, too. Long, lusty swipes over her, stoking her desire as he reveled in the way she tasted. She made a guttural sound of surrender, hips pitching forward as if she were helpless but to do anything other than abandon herself to pleasure. He licked and sucked, feasting on her, gorging himself on her uninhibited reaction.

Her fingers sifted through his hair, holding him to her, and he purred his approval as his suckled on her pearl some more. How bold she was, how sweetly responsive. He loved it and he...

He loved *her*.

The realization was astounding. Unexpected. Unprecedented. And yet, it did nothing to dim the rampant need inside him. The need to bring her to her pinnacle. One more hard suck as he caressed the soft skin of her inner thighs, and she came with a cry, falling into him, her bud pulsing beneath his tongue from the force of her release. He remained, gentling his touch, until the last shudder went through her.

And then he tenderly rolled down her stockings, admiring the bare expanse of flesh he revealed. He could not resist chasing his progress with his lips, kissing the insides of her knees, down her calves to her shapely ankles.

When she was naked at last, he rocked back, still on the floor like a supplicant, to admire her. Her beauty far exceeded any of his feverish imaginings. This moment, this memory, would have to last for all his days. His heart gave a bitter pang at the realization, but he forced all thoughts of the future from his mind.

Tonight was about him and Lily. About reveling in their mutual pleasure. About finishing what they had begun.

He stood, his need so great that he swayed as he regained his feet, as if he were adrift on a tumultuous sea.

"How else can I please you?" he asked her, wanting selfishly to hear her say the words.

To tell him wicked things. To seize her own desire and follow it wherever it took her. Whatever she wanted—he would do it. And he would love the doing.

She licked her lips and lowered the foot which had been atop the stool to the floor. Her nakedness did not embarrass her, and he was glad for it. She made no effort to shield herself from him, simply stood there proud and nude and glorious.

"I want you naked, too," she said.

She didn't have to tell him twice.

Tarquin toed off his boots and shucked his trousers in almost one fluid motion. His own stockings came next, and then they were both naked. His cock jutted high and thick before him, but he made no effort to hide his body's natural reaction to her. He wanted her more than life itself, the taste of her lingering in his mouth and the sight of her, flushed and nude and ready, making his cock leak.

"Do I please my Queen of Thieves?" he asked, holding still beneath her intense regard.

"Oh yes," she said softly, those velvety, mysterious eyes traveling over him like a lover's touch. Making him yearn and burn for her. "What did you call me?"

"Queen of Thieves," he repeated, smiling as he recalled her sliding that fan inside her bodice. "And a clever one. You bring me to my knees with such ease. Make me want you more than I want anything else."

His need astounded him—if he had thought it strong before, how very wrong he had been.

"Then take me," she urged him.

"If you command it, my queen," he said, desire rising within.

"I do." This time, it was she who moved forward, one step, her palm on his chest. "Take me to bed."

There was an urgency in her voice, a tone that made a sharp ache of hunger bolt through him. He took her arm in a gentle grasp and tugged her the rest of the way to her bed, allowing her to settle herself comfortably there before joining her. Their bodies aligned in perfect harmony, his painfully hard cock nestling against her slick folds as he found his home between her parted thighs. Lowering himself on his forearms atop her, he relished her hard nipples grazing his chest.

He knew then, that in all his days, nothing would ever again feel as right as this, the woman he loved beneath him, her body ready to accept his. Anguish threatened to overwhelm him, but he forced it away, lowering his head to take Lily's lips in a long, drugging kiss. And then he kissed down her throat, finding her breasts and sucking a nipple into his mouth.

"Oh," she said softly, arching into him.

He released her nipple, blowing a hot stream of air over the turgid bud. "Do you like this?"

"I do," she breathed. "More, please."

He smiled against the curve of her breast as he drew the nipple of her other breast into his mouth as well. Her fingers were on his shoulders now, nails biting into his skin, and it was the purest form of sensual torture he had ever known. But he forced himself to take his time, to proceed slowly. To prolong every moment and draw it out to the very last.

She hooked a leg around his hip and rocked against him. "I want you inside me, Tarquin."

And *God*, the rush of need inside him was so forceful, it nearly split him in two.

"I am trying to seduce you slowly," he murmured against her breast, suppressing a moan as she writhed against him some more.

"Your queen doesn't want slow," she said, her nails dragging down his back.

The words were torture. Pure and utter.

On a groan, he returned to her mouth, taking her lips in a kiss that was hard and deep. He could not wait any longer. She had driven him to the edge. Reaching between their bodies, he gripped his cock, gliding himself in her folds, slicking her dew on his shaft to ease his entry. She was ready for him. He teased her opening, and she was soaked, moaning into their kiss, her tongue lapping at his as if she were as mindless as he was.

Just the tip of his cock eased into her cunny. And she was hot and wet. She was fire and he was going to be burned, and he would relish every damned second of it.

He tore his mouth from hers. "Last chance to change your mind."

She held his face in her hands, her gaze searing his. "Never."

The tenderness in her countenance, her touch. He would take it with him to his grave. He did not deserve her softness, her sweetness. Did not deserve the gift she was giving him. But he was selfish and he wanted this piece of her to forever be his, for it was all he could ever have.

He moved, thrusting forward, into her. She gasped, and he paused, his cock half-buried inside her channel, which gripped him like a vise, beckoning him onward.

"Have I hurt you?"

"No." She moved beneath him, shifting her hips, bringing him deeper. "You've…surprised me. It's so much more than I imagined, the way you feel."

Her frank confession was all the spur he required. Another thrust, and he was fully sheathed, his cock held in the hot, velvet grip of her cunny. It nearly sucked all the air from his lungs, the sheer bliss of that moment, her body pulsing around him, soft and pliant beneath him, her fingers threading through his hair as if he were the one who was new at this. As if he required consoling and a gentle touch.

But then, perhaps she knew him better than he understood himself.

For when she began whispering sweet words of encouragement to him, pressing kisses along his jaw and down his neck, it was exactly what he needed. He felt an old, brittle part of himself cracking apart and falling away. He was new again. Reborn in this moment, in the fiery transcendence of making love to his Lily.

He stroked her swollen bud with the hand that remained between them and began to move at last. Retreating, then plunging deep. Finding a rhythm that had them moving together, her body tightening on his as she reached her pinnacle again, her high, breathy cry echoing from the rafters. He did not even bother to muffle it with a kiss, because he was proud of her passion. Proud he had pleased her.

Let anyone find them now, he thought wildly. He would make her his wife and love her forever and to the devil with anyone who denied them their happiness. All things seemed possible in this wild place of passion and connection, their bodies joined, their desire becoming one.

In and out and he moved, their bodies working in unison toward a desired end. They were covered in a sheen of perspiration that belied the chill air of the attic room, moving together. Faster, harder, deeper.

"Oh, Tarquin," she said on a gasp as he found an angle she liked, and she clutched him to her as he rode out his bliss.

Held him as if he were her saving grace. He knew the feeling, because surely she was his as well.

He kissed her sweetly one more time before withdrawing at the last moment, just before he lost himself inside her. Clutching his throbbing cock, he spent into the bedclothes between her parted legs as wave after wave of breath-stealing pleasure slammed over him. Came so hard that sparks of gold shot behind his eyelids and his chest hurt with the force of it. Shot streams and streams of mettle into her sheets and coverlet.

When the last drop had been wrung from him, he collapsed at her side, still holding her close, his arm around her waist as if he feared someone would take her from him. He could not bear parting from her. Not now. Not ever. Thoughts flitted through his mind, transient yet weighty, of what he would do now, what the uncertain future should bring. Of how he must have her always. Marriage? Perhaps.

She was worth risking everything. Champion of orphans.

Modern day Robin Hood. His Queen of Thieves with a heart of pure gold.

Lily kissed his cheek, her arm around his shoulders, holding him too.

Their gazes met and held.

Words were not needed in this moment of beautiful stillness, their bodies sated and entwined. Being together was simply enough.

# CHAPTER 10

*A* familiar thumping shook Lily from sleep. She had heard it before, would recognize it anywhere. Bare, flat feet racing on the stairs.

Lily blinked, remembrance raining down on her as she realized the low-burning brace of candles that illuminated a slumbering Tarquin at her side. They had made love. He had made her his, just as she had asked. And oh, how exquisite it had been. How tender and wondrous. She would never be the same. And afterward, they had lain in each other's arms, simply savoring the moment until they had fallen into the abyss of slumber.

But she had only a moment to savor his presence here, the preciousness of it—just this once was all she dared—before a frenzy came over her. If they were discovered…

She shook Tarquin's shoulder. "Someone is coming," she told him frantically.

"Hmm?" He rolled onto his back, his body sliding from beneath the counterpane, and on tempting, sinful display.

His cock was partially erect, thick and long and rising as she watched. Lily could not help herself. Warmth slid through her, an answering stirring now that she knew what was to be done with that particular part of him. And just how incredibly good it felt. How she loved him. Loved him more, now that they had come together so intimately, as only lovers could.

But a knock sounded at the door, a hard, frantic rap.

*Dear heavens.*

"Who is it?" Lily called, praying it was not one of her brothers.

That it was the washerwoman, one of the guards, anyone but a Sutton.

"It is Emma," said the familiar voice, slightly muffled by the door. "Please, I need your help. Hart is with fever, and I fear his wound has become infected."

"Blast," she said, heart leaping into her throat at the same time she flew from the bed, naked-arsed and uncaring.

Infection could well prove deadly.

Her mouth went dry as she struggled hastily into her discarded gown. All the newfound feelings and sensations which had lulled her into a false sense of peace were hastily dashed. She had known she only had Tarquin for one night, but she had not expected that night to be cut so damned short. Nor for Hart to take ill. And if Hart had sent his woman to fetch Lily, it did not bode well for his condition.

"Who is Hart?" Tarquin was asking her quietly, awake now as he too rose from the bed.

"One of my brothers," she said, keeping her voice low in the hopes Lily wouldn't overhear. Now wasn't the time to fret over discovery. Hart came first. But if she could take care, she would. She waved her arm at Tarquin, who was pulling his trousers over his lean hips, gesturing for him to stay out of view.

Not wasting another moment more, she raced across the room and pulled open the door. Belatedly, she realized that

Tarquin had followed her, and he stood just behind her shoulder, wearing his trousers and not a stitch more.

There was no hope for it now.

"How bad is he?" Lily asked Emma, still more frantic about her brother's state than caring about keeping her secrets.

"He is not himself," Emma told her, sounding as fretful as she looked. "And the wound looks dreadful. I am afraid for him, Lily, but I do not know what to do."

If Hart was truly in as bad a condition as that, there was only one person Lily would entrust with him. And that was their sister Caro, the healer in the family. At least, she had been until she had married her husband. Now, she was only called for when the situation merited it. And this one undeniably did.

"We'll send for my sister Caro," Lily said, knowing they didn't have any time to waste. "She will know what to do."

Emma nodded. "I'll return to his side. I'm too afraid to leave him for long."

"I'll take care of the rest," Lily assured her, feeling grim.

With a quick, searching glance over Lily's shoulder at Tarquin, Emma turned and descended the stairs.

Lily waited until she had gone before turning to him. "I must see to my brother. I'll be fetching my sister, who's the healer among us, to help him."

"I shall accompany you," he said firmly.

"To fetch my sister? You mustn't. Someone will see you." Lily moved past him and swiftly set about finishing dressing.

She bent and began rolling on her stockings first. She was using as few undergarments as possible in the interest of reaching Caro at her home in as much haste as she might manage.

"How do you intend to fetch her at this hour of the night?" Tarquin asked, his voice low and concerned as he pulled his shirt over his head before stuffing it into the waistband of his trousers. "If you say you are walking alone after what happened to you before…"

"I'll take the carriage," she said. "Sly Jack will have to be roused from bed."

Tarquin's lips compressed into a thin line of disapproval as he shook his head. "My coachman is waiting in the mews. It will be quicker for us to travel that way."

"But you will still be accompanying me," she pointed out.

"It *is* my post-chaise," he countered, shrugging into his coat. "No one will be the wiser. It is enclosed."

She pulled on a sturdy pair of boots that would keep her feet warmer at this late, dark hour.

"Very well," she allowed. "You'll accompany me."

Tarquin took her hand in his, and together they descended from her attic room.

The gesture felt strangely comforting.

It was eerily right and reassuring to have him there, at her side.

*For tonight only*, she warned herself sternly. *This cannot be repeated.*

And how her heart ached at the reminder. After the closeness they had shared earlier, this knowledge was sharper than the blade of a knife. By the time they reached his post-chaise and startled his coachman awake, Lily was frightfully cold.

She shivered as they slid into the cool vehicle, the heated bricks within having long since had an opportunity to lose their potency. Tarquin asked for Caro's direction and gave it to his driver before settling at Lily's side, and then pulling her into his lap. She did not bother to argue, wrapping her arms around his neck as she basked in the warmth emanating from his strong, solid form. In this final, fleeting chance to be near to him.

"You feel good here," he murmured, his lips brushing over her temple as he spoke, his warm breath coasting along her skin in a tantalizing tease.

"I like it too much," she admitted before she could think better of it, even as she willed herself not to cling too heavily. To long for far more than she could be allowed.

Because while it felt as if something momentous had happened, as if everything would be forever changed, their circumstances had not altered. Tarquin would have to marry the wife of his father's choosing. Lily would carry on at The Sinner's Palace. The worlds they currently inhabited were far too disparate.

To her dismay, her teeth began chattering, partially from shock and partly from the cold and the realization that not only was her brother's life in danger, but that she would have to part from the man she loved within hours. And that she may never see him again.

Tarquin kissed her cheek, seeming to understand her inner turmoil. "Your brother will be well, Lily. Stay strong and calm."

His encouragement helped to quell some of the frantic worry swirling within her.

She took a deep breath, holding him tightly. "I pray you are right."

∼

Tarquin sat alone in the office of his shop as the sun rose.

How quiet it was, how still.

Soon, the men he employed would begin to diligently arrive and begin their day. But where once he had found not just joy, but a deep-seated sense of meaning in his role here, helming the vast ship of Bellingham and Co. as it traversed the seas of an ever-changing London, by the grim morning's light, all he felt was...

Indescribably hollow.

After seeing Lily and her sister Caro safely deposited at The Sinner's Palace, Tarquin had been obliged to leave. Lily's brother was in desperate straits and he would require all her time for the next few days. It was understandable. Tarquin himself had no hold on her, nothing to offer, caught as he was in this untenable circumstance where he was forced to obey his father's edicts. And so, he had returned to his town house by the dark of night, feeling like a usurper in his own home. His cursory ablutions and a change of clothes later—he had not even bothered to break his fast, for hunger was the least of his concerns—and he was returned to his shop.

The one place he had been previously convinced that he belonged.

On a sigh, he rose, pacing to the window that overlooked the road below, where the world was just beginning to come back to life after a night of world-weary slumber. Once, this view, this building—a commanding, palatial, expansive edifice holding court over Pall Mall—had been his greatest pride. And yet, he saw now with sudden, abject clarity the truth of it.

All the clout he had amassed, all the hard work he had poured into Bellingham and Co., achieving his loftiest dreams and settling comfortably atop a pedestal as the proprietor of the greatest shop London had yet known, was a futile victory. Because true happiness was not to be found in the fans and furs and pocket watches and fine fabrics and jewels lining his shop. It was not to be found in societal position, nor in banknotes and gold, and nor was it found in that elusive chimera of legitimacy he had been seeking. His father's approval, an earl's daughter as his wife, his debts forgiven, *none* of it mattered compared to the sheer miracle of Lily in his arms.

Leaving her this morning had felt wrong, as if he were abandoning the most important part of himself. One night was not sufficient. *Good God*, one *lifetime* would not begin to appease him. Tarquin rested his forehead against the cool pane of glass, staring unseeing at the street, the hackneys and curricles passing below.

His mind was settled, and quite firmly on the matter, too. He was not going to marry Lady Clementia. He simply could not bear it.

He intended to marry Lily Sutton.

All he needed to do was figure out how to extricate himself from his father's rule. Until he was truly free, he was going to have to keep his distance from Lily. He did not dare trust himself to be in her presence now that they had made love, for he would not be able to resist her. And Tarquin intended to do right by her.

Because damn it, the woman who had stolen his heart deserved that, and nothing less.

∽

LILY WAS weary to the bone. The sort of tired that bogged one down like leaden skirts. And yet, she made her way to Hart's sickroom anyway, knowing that Emma deserved a respite and needing to ascertain her brother's welfare herself.

She opened the door and found Emma keeping vigil at a restlessly sleeping Hart's side, bathing his brow with a damp cloth.

"You ought to get some rest," Lily told her softly, trying to keep her voice from cracking as she took in her brother's appearance.

He was pale and feverish, covered in sweat, thrashing in the bedclothes. He looked terrible.

Emma started, glancing toward Lily as if just discovering her presence. "I do not need rest," she replied firmly.

Thank heavens for Tarquin racing them through the night to bring Caro to Hart's side, Lily thought. If not for Caro's swift arrival, Hart would be in even worse condition, she had no doubt. Thanks to Tarquin, Caro had come with her healing herbs and ointments and tended to Hart by dawn. In the flurry of the moment, the fear holding them all in its thrall, Caro had not questioned Tarquin's presence. And Tarquin had left them at The Sinner's Palace door like the gentleman he was, telling them he would pray for Mr. Sutton's swift recovery.

Hardly the words or actions of a lover. Although Lily had spent the ride to Caro's home on Tarquin's lap, her sister had been seated between them for the return trip. It had been a grim reminder of how their lives would continue.

*Separately.*

Lily forced her mind away from thoughts of Tarquin—never far—and instead back to Hart and Emma. The poor dear was going to make herself sick if she did not get some sleep soon. She had been tending to Hart tirelessly for hours, holding his hand as they had forced laudanum down his throat. Whispering in his ear as Caro had lanced the wound, thoroughly cleansing it before applying some herbal remedies she had brought with her. Lily's instincts about Emma were not wrong. She was a good woman, and she was clearly in love with Hart.

And Lily understood, for the first time, what it was like to lose her heart. It was painful and terrifying and glorious, all at once.

Lily crossed to Emma's side at the bed, dropping into an

empty chair with far less grace than she had intended. "Of course you need rest, Emma."

Emma's eyes were pinned to Hart, as if she could not look away. "I'll not leave him, Lily."

"It is morning now and you have yet to sleep," Lily reminded her quietly, reaching for Emma's hand and taking it in a sisterly grasp.

Emma blinked blearily. "Morning?"

"Aye, morning. The sun has long since risen." Lily squeezed her hand, feeling a deep kinship between herself and Emma, for anyone who cared for her brother as plainly as Emma did was a friend of hers. "You must be exhausted, dear."

"Thank you for your concern," Emma said stubbornly. "I will sleep when he is improved."

*Improved.* Caro's dire warning and grim countenance before she had left returned to Lily, making her stomach knot. For there was every possibility Hart would not improve. That the infection would weaken him until he slipped away.

"Emma," she choked out, trying to explain and not knowing how.

When they had lost Logan, he had simply disappeared. They had not experienced the anguish of watching him suffer. Both situations were agonizing, in their own ways.

"Do not say it," Emma said, shaking her head.

"He may not improve," Lily forced herself to say softly. "It is a reality we must face. He's in a bad way, 'art is."

And there went her carefully polished speech. But it could hardly be helped. Lily had lost her heart to a man she could never have, and now she could lose another of her siblings as well.

"I am staying," Emma insisted sternly, though her voice broke with emotion. "I'll not leave until he wakes."

Someone she loved more with each passing day.

"I do believe I shall name you Sir Bellingham," she told the feline, stroking along his back, uncaring that her hand was becoming soiled.

She could not have the cat's namesake, but she had every intention of taking the newly christened Sir Bellingham into The Sinner's Palace, cleaning him, and keeping him safe. No more darting about in alleys, desperate for rats and mice, dodging wheels and angry tosspots. She would love them both, one from afar.

"I reckon hisnabs would like you as well," she told the cat, who was busy gobbling the meat and demanding more pets.

Tears stung her eyes, but Lily blinked them away, refusing to shed them or think of how very much she missed Tarquin. It was for the best that they remained apart, that he had not come to see her since the night he had taken her to fetch Caro. They had reached an agreement, after all. One night.

One glorious, life-altering, soul-changing night.

And a week later, Lily had much to be thankful for. Hart's fever had broken and he was steadily healing. He had also fallen in love with Emma and was courting her. While Lily could not help but be a bit envious of her brother for being able to marry the one he loved, she was no less happy for him. Exuberant for the both of them, for they deserved to wed and have a dozen adorable, bright-haired, hazel-eyed babes. Just because *she* was in misery, loving a man who would be marrying another, did not mean that she wished for everyone to dwell in the same despair.

But Hart's recovery wasn't the only piece of good news stirring the Sutton family. They had also discovered their lost brother Logan was not dead as they had all believed. Instead, he was alive, and working with a vicious money-lender right here in the East End. While he had claimed he wanted nothing to do with the family, there remained hope amongst them all that he could be brought back into their fold. That whatever had taken him from them would prove surmountable, and he would come home.

Yes indeed, the last week had proven a tumultuous one.

Biting her lip, she continued stroking Sir Bellingham's back as he finished his feast. Tarquin had not been without contact, although he had ceased to abruptly appear at The Sinner's Palace. She could not lie—each time she walked past the family parlor, she peered inside, hoping to find him within. And whenever Randall or any of the guards called her name, she hoped in vain it was to hear she had a caller who was tall, handsome, and icy-eyed.

But Tarquin did not call. He did, however, send her notes. Missives inquiring after Hart's health. And yet, after seeing him every day for so many days in a row, and after falling in love with him and having him in her bed, she could not deny that the correspondence paled in comparison.

The cat had finished his supper, and Lily was not taking any chances with this particular Bellingham. She scooped him neatly into her arms and carried him into The Sinner's Palace. He put up no fight, purring madly instead and jamming his head into the crook of her shoulder. The poor little lamb smelled terrible, but that could be settled soon enough.

"Miss Lily?"

Sir Bellingham began to shift in her arms, his concern clear as his claws sank into her shoulder. Lily clutched him to her tenderly, whispering hushed nonsense into his ear to let him know he was safe as she turned to see Randall stalking toward them, wearing what seemed to be his customary glower these days.

He was also bearing a missive. Lily's heart leapt at the familiar scrawl.

She held out her hand. "For me?"

"Aye." Randall's fingers tightened on the missive, and for a moment, she feared he would not relinquish it. But then he extended his arm, offering it to her. "It's just come."

Holding Sir Bellingham in one hand, she snatched the missive from Randall with the other. There was no time to read it now, and she had no wish to do so with an audience.

"I'll be needing a box for Sir Bellingham," she told Randall, tucking the missive into her pocket along with the pistol.

"Sir Ballocks-ham?" Randall repeated, frowning menacingly.

"My cat," she said, pinning him with a glare of her own. "You heard his name, Randall. 'Tis Sir Bellingham, not Sir Ballocks-ham. I'll need a box and some sand. He'll be staying in my attic rooms now. No more alley dwelling."

"Too soft, you are."

His muttered words reached her, making her shoulders stiffen, Sir Bellingham's claws digging deeper. "I am not soft."

"Easily fooled by an 'andsome dial plate and lordly airs," Randall said coolly. "Begging your pardon, Miss Lily, but Bellingham ain't going to marry you."

"Plummy," she snapped, ire coursing through her. "Because no one ever said I wanted to marry 'im, did they?"

Losing her polish again. Blast Randall for cutting to the heart of her fears. For taunting her with what she already knew and hated.

"The box for my cat," she added. "Tell one of the others to bring it to my room. Anyone but you."

"Miss Lily," Randall began, his tone pleading.

"Enough," she bit out, tears threatening her vision. "You've said enough."

Turning, she moved through the hall, still holding Sir

Bellingham in her arms. To her relief, he clung to her tenaciously, breaking skin and cutting through the layers of her undergarments and gown with his impressive claws, and yet not attempting to flee. Although the tears threatened to fall, she held them in check with valiant effort. Through the labyrinth of the private halls, up two sets of stairs, and finally, she and Sir Bellingham were alone in the quiet confines of her attic rooms.

She lowered the cat to the floor and made her way to the tinder box. The day was yet another gloomy one, and the light filtering in the eaves was insufficient for reading. Lighting a candle took far longer than she wished. But at last, she had flame. Sir Bellingham had disappeared beneath her bed, taking his unfortunate smell with him.

She unfolded the missive, reading.

*To the Queen of Thieves,*
*I have something that belongs to you. It will be awaiting you at Bellingham and Co.*
*Yours forever,*
*T.B.*

Hers forever.

*If only.*

Those words, his bold, dark scrawl, swam before her eyes. Because she was weeping. The tears she had been withholding had burst forth. He wanted to see her again. And how could she deny him? He was all she had thought about, all she had dreamt of, since they had said their farewells. Helping Emma tend to Hart had been a welcomed distraction; she had been caring for her brother and diverting her attention from all thoughts of Tarquin, too busy to wallow in despair over what she could never have.

But now, she had no such distraction. Hart was well. He

and Emma were in love. And Lily...well, she was existing. Carrying on with each day, waiting for the moment another note would arrive from Tarquin.

Until it had.

And now, Lily was going to call upon his shop.

## CHAPTER 12

"Lord Brownley has paid a call upon me."

The announcement from his father came as no surprise. If anything, Tarquin was startled that the call had been placed with such a lack of regard for immediacy. He had cried off on Lady Clementia some four days prior, after all. And now, at last, the Duke of Hampton had deigned to pay a visit to Tarquin's shop. Although this time, it was not to demand an expensive trifle for his conquest of the moment, as it had been the last.

Seated at the broad desk in his office, where he had been working through financial scenarios with quill and ink at hand, Tarquin regarded the man who had sired him with new eyes. He had spent the past few days testing theories. Poring over numbers and suppositions. And he had come to the conclusion that if his father chose to call in the entirety of his debts, Tarquin would have to leave Bellingham and Co. behind forever.

He was prepared to do it.

Life without Lily was not a life at all.

"Am I to presume the call was concerning Lady Clementia?" Tarquin asked calmly.

"You know it was," he hissed. Whilst he customarily liked to affect an air of imperturbability, the Duke of Hampton was seething. "How dare you defy me, after all I have done to help you, you insolent, ungrateful whelp?"

"You have helped me by loaning me funds to force me into obeying your will," he countered.

"And you were more than happy to accept those funds in return," the duke bit out.

He had been, it was true. Initially, Tarquin had not realized his father's aid came with a price. But when he had, it had been too late. Telling himself it was for the greater good to please his sire had been far easier before he had fallen in love with Lily.

"I find myself no longer happy to accept the conditions of the loan," he said, careful to keep his tone even, not allowing even a hint of anger.

"Who do you think you are?" the duke demanded, his voice trembling with fury.

"Someone who no longer wishes to be the puppet of the man who sired him," he answered coolly. "I never should have accepted your loan. It was wrong. Nor should I have agreed to court Lady Clementia when it was apparent to me that the two of us would not suit."

"She is the daughter of an earl," the duke growled. "You are nothing but a bastard. Taking her as your wife would have been a blessing to you. Yet instead, you defy me, scorn my wishes, humiliate Lady Clementia, and leave me to answer to her irate papa why you have cried off."

*You are nothing but a bastard.*

There it was, the truth. What a fool Tarquin had been for supposing he might forge a relationship with his father. For thinking the duke would ever see him as something more than an unwanted child born on the wrong side of the blanket. Those words should not have the ability to cut into his heart like a knife, and yet they did, even after all these years.

"I did not cry off," he corrected. "There was no betrothal between Lady Clementia and myself."

"There was an understanding," the duke raged, twin patches of red rising in his cheeks. "You have been courting her."

"I am in love with someone else," Tarquin said. "Marrying Lady Clementia has become insupportable to me. I will pay the debts I owe you as quickly as I'm able, but I'll not be marrying anyone other than the wife I have chosen for myself."

"Love?" The duke scoffed. "Love has no place in a marriage."

He did not doubt that love had not had a place in his father's marriage. Tarquin himself had never met the duchess, and from what he understood, Her Grace lived a separate life, leaving the duke free to pursue mistresses to his heart's content.

Tarquin held his father's irate stare, unwavering. "You are entitled to your opinion on the matter. However, my decision has been made."

The duke stormed to his feet, leaning heavily on his cane, and it did not miss Tarquin's observation that he was slower to rise than he had recently been. Tarquin rose as well. Age was taking its toll upon the Duke of Hampton. But then, so, perhaps, was bitterness. It was difficult to believe his father had ever truly been happy. Instead, he spent his days attempting to control everyone around him and bend them to his will.

That ended today for Tarquin.

"I am also entitled to require your repayment of the loan," the duke snapped. "I was willing to forgive it, as you know, in exchange to your marriage to Lady Clementia. No longer. I shall expect the funds within the week."

Tarquin had expected a swift retribution from the duke in return for defying his wishes. But one week to remunerate his father the substantial sum he yet owed would be impossible. He had hoped for more time.

Still, he would not allow his emotions to show. Instead, he kept his countenance carefully blank.

"Within the week," he agreed, though he knew that gathering such an amount in so short a time was an impossibility.

Now was not the time to allow his father to see any hint of weakness.

"If you do not present me with the funds by Monday next, Bellingham and Co. will be mine." The duke's lip curled. "You will regret betraying me for your own foolish whims, Mr. Bellingham. You could have had a lady wife and a debt forgiven."

"But I would not have had the woman I love," Tarquin said firmly.

The duke sneered. "You are a fool, Mr. Bellingham."

With that terse insult, the duke turned and thumped from the office.

∼

LILY WAS in the furs and fans department of Bellingham and Co., pretending to admire the selection of fans, when Tarquin came striding over the threshold. He was dressed, as always, to perfection, his cravat expertly knotted, his coat molding exquisitely to his broad shoulders. His dark hair was neatly combed, and he was stunningly handsome. His jaw was tensed, his well-formed lips thinned into a grim frown until he spied her, and his demeanor changed.

She knew the feeling, for when she saw him, it was as if she could breathe again.

He was before her in an instant, offering her a courtly bow.

"Miss Sutton."

She dipped into a curtsy, an answering flutter of awareness sparking to life within her. "Good day, Mr. Bellingham."

How odd it was to maintain propriety and address one another formally, as if they were strangers instead of lovers. She thought of his carefully worded note, of his mouth on sinful and forbidden parts of her body, of him atop her, inside her, and heat rose to her cheeks. She cast her glance over his shoulder as she attempted to compose herself, feeling giddy as a girl.

"You came," he said softly, taking care to keep his voice from traveling.

"Yes," she answered in kind, her gaze seeking his. "Your note…"

She faltered then, wondering if she had misinterpreted his missive.

"You are alone?" he asked, frowning.

Lily shook her head, for after the cutpurse incident, her brothers had decided to rein in her freedoms. Wolf had escorted her on this particular shopping expedition, and he was currently awaiting her in the carriage outside. "My brother Wolf accompanied me."

"Ah, and what an appropriate name for a brother of yours, my dear. He is in a different department, then?"

"In the carriage," she corrected. "Waiting for me to complete my shopping."

Tarquin raised a brow, his lips quirking. "Will he eat my liver if I speak with you for a few moments in private? I should point out that it is far past the customary hour for breaking one's fast, and based on our previous conversations,

I am given to understand breakfast is your brother's preferred meal for the consumption of livers."

She could not quell her laugh in sufficient time. It rang loudly, echoing off the shelves of expensive wares and drawing the attention of a few fellow customers. When she realized several pairs of curious eyes were upon her, she pressed a gloved hand over her lips.

"Forgive me," she murmured to Tarquin, knowing he would not wish to draw undue attention to them, and she had just unintentionally done the opposite.

To her shock, Tarquin merely smiled, and it was one of his rare, beautiful smiles, the kind that never failed to nestle its way into her heart. "You have a lovely laugh. I should like to hear it more."

Of course, that was an impossibility. They were not even meant to be seeing each other now. But Lily held her tongue, following Tarquin through his shop and to the paneled door where she knew his office resided. Taking advantage of the distraction of the ladies in that department, he opened the panel and Lily followed after him.

It was a risk, being alone in this fashion. Particularly for him. He was marrying another. Lily swallowed against a rush of misery at the reminder.

"How long do we have before your brother grows impatient enough to look for you?" Tarquin asked softly, leading her to his office.

"One quarter hour," she said, knowing Wolf too well. "He insisted upon accompanying me after..."

"I am glad for it," Tarquin said, closing his office door and turning toward her with a frown. "Someone needs to look after you."

For the first time in a week, they were alone. No one watching them. He was so handsome in that austere way of his. Her heart was pounding hard. Harder than it had on the last occasion he had brought her to his private office, when she'd been carrying a purloined fan within her stays.

"I look after myself well enough," she told him, feeling flustered by his nearness, the intensity of his stare, and the surge of emotions whirling through her.

"You could have been injured or worse that day," Tarquin said grimly, a muscle in his jaw tensing. "My God, when I think of it..."

She waved a dismissive hand, for her siblings had been fretting over her similarly, and she did not like the sudden lack of freedom that blasted incident with the cutpurse was causing her. "You sound like my brothers."

His mouth kicked up into a half smile. "My feelings for you are not brotherly in nature, my dear."

Awareness unfurled.

Their gazes held, and she saw reflected in his ice-blue eyes everything which had passed between them that glorious night one week ago in her attic rooms.

"And mine for you aren't sisterly either," she countered boldly, although she knew she had no right to entertain those feelings. To voice them. Their night of passion was over, and soon enough, he would marry another.

A full, sensual smile bloomed on his lips. "So I noted."

Her cheeks went hot. He was teasing her. The air between them was different. Changed. And yet, nothing had altered except the passage of time and the exchange of a handful of missives. He had his shop and the woman he would wed, and she had The Sinner's Palace and the girls at the foundling hospital.

"Why did you send me the last missive?" she blurted, not certain she could withstand any more of this new, charming Tarquin.

He was softer. More tender. The frigid businessman had

been replaced by an ardent lover. A man who seemed somehow younger. *Gentler.*

Dangerous to her ability to resist him.

"As I said in the note, I have something of yours." He swept past her, striding toward his desk.

With the added distance between them, she could breathe easier.

He pulled open a drawer and extracted a fan, before returning to her, the fan resting on his flat palm. "Go on, take it."

Hesitantly, she retrieved the fan. It was very fine, crafted of ivory. She owned no fans so dear.

"This is not mine," she told him, frowning down at it before chancing a glance back into his vibrant-blue eyes. "You must be mistaken."

Disappointment sliced through her. Perhaps she had read too much into his note, his demeanor. Had he truly sent her the missive merely to return a fan to her that was not hers?

"Open it," he urged her softly.

She slid the ivory blades apart gently, keenly aware of just how ornate the piece in her hand was. It was a brisé fan, she realized, its individual sticks pierced with a pattern that, fully spread, became apparent. Lady archers with their bows drawn bedecked the ivory, accompanied by intricate flowers and birds. The piece was beautiful, quite unlike any fan she had ever previously seen—or thieved—at Bellingham and Co.

"It is quite lovely," she said, lifting her gaze to meet his again. "But as I said, it's not mine."

"It is yours now. Lady archers for my lady Robin Hood. When it arrived, I knew of only one woman suited to own it."

A gift, she realized. Tarquin was giving her the fan. No one had ever given her something so elegant and intricate before, so obviously costly.

Her heart leapt at the gesture, even as she closed the fan and held it out to him. "I cannot accept it, I'm afraid."

Because looking at it would break her heart, and besides that, Lily Sutton would never grace a ballroom or anywhere suitable for such an elegant fan. And Tarquin ought to know better than anyone that such an extravagant gift for a woman he was neither betrothed nor married to was *outré*. He ought to save the fan for the woman he would wed.

"I want you to have it."

"Mr. Bellingham," she protested, attempting to cling to formality in the hopes it would be easier to resist him.

"I hope we are beyond formality, Lily," he said softly, the heat in his gaze forcing her to remember the intensity of the passion they had shared. "Do you not agree?"

"Tarquin," she tried, thrusting the fan toward him, poking him in the chest with it in her eagerness to be rid of the lovely piece. "I'll not be your mistress."

"I don't want you to be my mistress." His long fingers closed round hers, in a gentle grasp, staying her frantic attempts to make him accept the fan. "I want you to be my wife."

Lily blinked, certain she had misheard him. "Are you dicked in the nob?"

"Perhaps." He flashed her a self-deprecating grin. "But the sentiment remains the same."

"You can't marry me," she reminded him.

He was stroking her fingers gently over the closed fan, a caress that she felt to the soles of her feet. "I've told my father I won't be marrying the lady of his choosing. I've also informed the lady."

"But you…" Lily sputtered, struggling to make sense of his words. "What of the loan your father gave you? Will he not rescind it if you do not do his bidding?"

"Yes." Tarquin's countenance grew somber. "He has given me a week's time to gather the funds."

"Will you be able to gather them?" she asked, astounded at the magnitude of what he was revealing to her. "What happens if you do not?"

"I am not certain just yet." His thumb slid beneath the sleeves of her gown and pelisse, finding an especially tender place where she was certain her heart beat as fast as the wings of a bird. "I will do everything in my power to repay him, however I must. If I fail, I may lose Bellingham and Co."

"Oh, Tarquin." She shook her head, tears rushing to her eyes as the full ramifications of his decision hit her. "This shop is everything to you. You've worked so hard to make it yours. You cannot lose it."

"I thought the shop was everything to me, as you say," he said, his gaze holding hers, searing in its intensity. "But I realized I was wrong. Because *you* mean far more to me than this shop ever will. If I don't have you, I have nothing of meaning."

Her heart ached, bursting with love for him. He was willing to surrender everything to marry her. Lily's mind could not quite fathom it, but even as part of her rejoiced, another part of her knew she could not expect him to make such a drastic sacrifice.

"But I cannot ask you to give up everything for me," she denied. "I would never forgive myself."

And he would come to resent her, she feared.

"I have to do this, or *I* shall never forgive myself," he explained patiently. "I'll need some time to make certain I can provide you with the life you deserve, but I hope you will wait for me, and take this fan as a reminder of my devotion to you until I am able to make you my wife. Supposing that you will have me, that is."

It occurred to her then that it was possible his sense of

honor was prompting this sudden decision. Lily could not bear the notion of Tarquin giving up his shop and severing ties with his father because he felt obligated to do so.

She searched his implacable stare. "Is this because of what happened between us? I gave you myself because I wanted to, Tarquin. Because I care for you. Not because I expected you to marry me. I absolve you of your obligations to me. You need not feel as if you must wed me to make amends for doing the feather-bed jig."

She was being crude, it was true, but if that was what it required to remind him of who she was, and who he was, so be it.

"This is not about obligations," he said, frowning as he released her hand and took a step back. "I can understand why it may seem that way. But I assure you, I am a man of deliberate action. I would not undertake these measures without knowing they are necessary. I never wanted to marry Lady Clementia. Not before I met you, and most certainly not after. But it was you, Lily, who made me realize I had to take a stand against my father. All my life, I've wanted nothing more than his approval, his love. And all my life, I have been nothing more than a pawn to him. Useful when he required someone to do his bidding. Forgotten and scorned when I am not."

She understood the frustration and hurt in Tarquin's voice, for she had not had a loving relationship with her own father. He had been a cruel man, a tyrant and a tosspot, until he had died. She was forever grateful she had her siblings who loved her as much as she loved them. Yet, Tarquin was alone in life. No siblings. No mother.

Still, she had to be certain this was truly what he wanted.

"You have become a grand gentleman in your own right," she told him. "What would happen if you were to marry me, a Sutton born in the rookeries? A woman who doesn't always mimic the speech of her betters, who has never seen the inside of a drawing room?"

"I would be content," he said simply. "I would be your husband. And that, far more than any of this, is what I want. I have made my decision. Would you have me, Lily? Would you be my wife?"

She wanted to say *yes* with a desperation that seized her in its crushing grip. But he had made an important omission.

"Why?" she asked, even as everything within her urged her to accept, to throw herself into his arms and rejoice in the future she had believed beyond her reach mere moments ago.

But she was hesitant. She needed to be certain. She needed Tarquin to be certain, too.

"Do you not know?" His velvet baritone slid over her like a caress, his expression softening once again with infinite tenderness. "Can you not tell?"

She swallowed hard against a rush of welling emotion, shaking her head. "No. I'm afraid you'll need to say it."

He took the hand that was not clutching the fan and raised it to his lips for an ardent kiss. "I love you, Lily Sutton. I told myself I was angry with you for stealing from my shop, but in truth, all the bits and baubles were nothing compared to something else you stole. My heart. And I don't want it back. It's yours now. It's not nearly as pretty as the fan, but I hope you'll keep both."

*Oh.*

He loved her.

Tarquin *loved* her.

Lily's fingers tightened on his instinctively. "You can't love me."

It was a silly thing to say. Nonsensical. But she could scarcely believe this handsome, self-assured gentleman who had not long ago looked upon her with irate scorn in this very same office was now looking at her with such affection. That the beautiful words he had just spoken were true and from the heart. That he had not offered for her out of a sense of obligation, but because he wanted her to be his wife. Wanted it enough that he was willing to give up everything he had worked for just to make it so.

He smiled. "I assure you that I can and do love you. And I want nothing more than to make you my wife. I cannot promise you that we will be wealthy. But I do promise you that I will do everything in my power to make you happy."

What could she say then, to such a heartfelt revelation?

"Yes." So great was the tide of her feelings rising, rising, that all she could initially manage was one coherent word, throwing her arms around his neck.

He caught her in his embrace, lifting her so that her feet dangled above the floor, his exuberance nearly crushing as he spun her in a circle.

"Thank God," he breathed. "You had me worrying."

She pressed her cheek to his, thwarted slightly by the unwanted intrusion of her bonnet. "You have my heart as well. You made it yours, just as you made *me* yours. I love you, Tarquin Bellingham, and I'd be honored to be your wife."

Tarquin returned her to her feet, staring down at her, looking as if he could scarcely believe the words she had uttered. "You'll marry me?"

"If it's truly what you want, yes."

"It is all I want," he said urgently. "*You* are all I want, all I require. Now and forever. I'll need some time before we can wed. This business with my father must be settled, but as soon as we are able, I want to make you my wife. That is, if it is what you wish, too?"

Lily smiled back at him, blinking away tears of happiness

which had blurred her vision. "Of course I will be your wife. There is nothing I want more."

His mouth lowered then, his lips taking hers in a slow, lingering kiss. A kiss that robbed her breath and would have stolen her heart as well were it not already his. She clung to him, kissing him back, showing him with actions what she wanted to say with words but was too unpolished to say. She had never imagined he would be willing to give up his entire life for her. That he would take so bold and big a risk.

That he loved her.

But she was grateful, so very grateful, humbled by the enormity of it all. By him.

A sharp knock suddenly intruded on the moment. Someone was at his office door.

Tarquin's head lifted, his eyes stormy with desire.

"Who's there?" he called.

"It's Mr. Withers, sir," answered an unfamiliar male voice.

"Blast," Tarquin muttered softly. "I am sorry, love." Louder, he called, "Just a moment, Mr. Withers."

The interruption reminded Lily that Wolf was yet awaiting her in the carriage, likely to soon grow impatient and come looking for her, if indeed he had not already done so.

"I should return to my brother before he comes searching for me," she murmured.

Tarquin winced. "And finds his sister being thoroughly compromised by a blackguard shop owner. That shan't do, but I must speak with your brothers to ask for your hand."

Lily wondered how Jasper, Rafe, Hart, and Wolf would feel about her marrying Tarquin. They were protective of her, terribly so, and particularly since she was the youngest. Before he had disappeared so suddenly, Logan had been the same, hovering over her, watching her far more than the rest of her siblings. That had ended, of course, with his defection, and although he was alive, from what she understood, he was now a mere husk of himself, bitter and angry. Wanting nothing to do with the Suttons.

But she hoped her other brothers would see that Tarquin was a good and honorable man and that she loved him, and he loved her. No matter what happened with his shop, they could find happiness together. She had no doubt.

"I'll speak to them first," she offered. "To prepare them for the nature of your visit."

"And spare my liver." He smiled again. "I do suspect I'll be needing it for some time yet."

She chuckled, and then kissed him again, because she could not resist, happiness bubbling up inside her like she had never known. He held her to him, prolonging the moment until they were both breathless.

"Now then," he said in hushed tones. "I'll go out first. You follow discreetly after."

"Yes." She nodded her agreement, hating to leave him so soon and yet knowing she must if they were to go about this properly. She very much wanted the approval of her brothers. "When will I see you again?"

"Soon." He kissed her. "I'll send word."

He moved to go, and then strode back to her for one more frantic kiss. Her lips answered his with a similar urgency and fire. And then, too soon, he broke away and was gone.

## CHAPTER 13

The town house was unassuming enough. Grand, even. It hardly looked like the abode of a ruthless moneylender. But, after all the inquiries Tarquin had made, he had been assured he would find Archer Tierney within. And he was beginning to suspect Mr. Tierney was his only hope for saving Bellingham and Co.

Tarquin knocked.

A cold rain was falling, but it was the slow, thin sort of rain that was more mist than deluge. It gathered on the brim of his hat and dripped onto his nose as he waited.

No answer.

He knocked again, with greater determination this time.

The door swung open to reveal a scowling servant.

"Wot ye selling?" the man demanded.

Tarquin wondered if the fellow could tell he was a merchant by his attire—it was something he always did his utmost to hide. Instead, he wore the fine clothes of a gentleman, presenting an image of himself to those who frequented his establishment that made them believe he was truly gentry. But then, perhaps that was the manner in which the man always welcomed Mr. Tierney's callers. It was impossible to know.

He cleared his throat. "I would like an interview with Mr. Tierney. It is of grave import."

Tarquin extended his card, which the man rudely inspected before declaring. "Can't read. Ye could be the baker or a rum bubber for all I know."

"Tarquin Bellingham," he explained. "The proprietor of Bellingham and Co., a shop on Pall Mall."

The man's eyes narrowed. "So ye *are* selling something, then, ain't you?"

Tarquin wondered what manner of man Archer Tierney was, that he kept such an ill-mannered, foul-tempered servant.

"I am not selling anything," he explained patiently just the same. "I kindly request an interview with your master."

The man looked him up and down, sniffed, and then declared, "Ye'll wait 'ere."

With that pronouncement, he slammed the door closed, leaving Tarquin to stand in the rain and wait. After several minutes of enduring the damp, he was beginning to suspect he was being intentionally ignored when the door swung open, the servant gesturing for him to enter with another scowl.

"Mr. Tierney will see ye. Come along, then."

Tarquin followed the man through the entry, down a carpeted hall, to a closed door. The man rapped on it twice.

"Come," called a voice from within.

The butler opened the door, preceding Tarquin into the room. As he crossed the threshold, his gaze immediately lit upon Mr. Tierney. A tall, dark-haired, imposing man, he stood at his desk, a glowing cigar in his fingers.

"Thank you, Lucky," Tierney told the servant. "That will be all."

"And ye're certain?" the man asked, sounding dubious. "This one looks like a mace cove, 'e does."

Tierney cocked his head, his gaze settling on Tarquin in assessing fashion. "I'll be the judge of whether or not the good Mr. Bellingham is a swindler, Lucky. Carry on, now."

Grumbling something unintelligible, the servant took his leave.

Tierney took a contemplative puff of his cigar, exhaling a cloud of smoke. "I gather you have come to me for a reason, Mr. Bellingham?"

Tarquin told himself he could do this. That he must do this. He had exhausted every option for gathering funds. Outside of begging Lily's family for aid, which he would not do, there was no other choice for repaying the loan to his father in a week's time. Everyone he had consulted had pointed him in one discreet direction.

This man.

"I have," he said, removing his dripping hat, realizing that the foul-tempered servant had never offered to take it. "I have come to inquire concerning your moneylending services."

Moneylenders were vicious, and Tarquin knew it. All his life, he had managed to avoid the unscrupulous thieves. And yet, he had never had a greater need for funds than he did now. And it was his love for Lily, not his pride or even his common sense, guiding him.

"I regret to inform you I no longer offer such services," Tierney drawled.

*Damn it.* He had not been expecting such a response.

But he was not ready to accept defeat.

"Perhaps you are familiar with my business," he said instead. "Bellingham and Co. is one of London's finest shops. We are the largest of our kind, offering four departments. We sell everything from furs and fans, to every article of haberdashery imaginable, and jewels, clocks, perfumes, and fine furniture."

"I may have heard of it," Tierney said, his tone noncommittal. "What of it?"

"You may also know that it was formerly known as Mason, Whitley, Lodge and Co.," he continued. "I was able to buy out one of the partners several years ago. However, in order to grow the shop to the thriving business it has become, I needed to buy out the remainder of my partners. The value of the shop having increased thanks to my improvements, the remaining partners wished for an increased sum. One that was too vast for myself alone. I accepted a loan and bought their shares of the business, leaving me free to grow Bellingham and Co. as I wished."

"The history of your shop is bloody fascinating, Bellingham, but I don't see how it's of interest to me." Tierney took another puff of his cigar, his stare unrelenting, countenance harsh and hard.

"Because the loan I accepted is being rescinded without sufficient warning," he answered. "I have mere days left to gather the funds before I will be forced to sell my share of the shop and lose everything I have worked to build. While I have raised half the amount of the loan, I have exhausted my ability to pay for the remaining portion. That is why I have come to you."

"A shop containing ladies' fripperies? I cannot see how lucrative such a place would be." Tierney stalked across the chamber to where a fire burned in the grate. He tossed his cigar into the flames and then turned back to Tarquin. "Doesn't sound like a paying proposition, Mr. Bellingham."

"I am prepared to show you my ledgers," Tarquin said easily. "We are operating on a significant profit, which I have chosen to invest in the growing business rather than filling my own coffers. Much to my detriment, as it turned out, given the capriciousness of the man who holds my loan."

"Indeed." Tierney's eyes narrowed as he paced back toward Tarquin. "And therein lies a pertinent question, does it not? Why has he suddenly rescinded the loan?"

"Because I have refused to marry the woman of his choosing," he answered honestly.

"Ah. That would be an excellent reason." Tierney cocked his head. "And why have you refused? It seems that a wise man would simply take the woman to wife and save his shop."

"Perhaps," he allowed. "But I am in love with another, and I intend to marry her."

"Love is the reason you have refused to do as this man bids you?" Tierney sounded incredulous. "I regret to inform you, Mr. Bellingham, this ain't a good reason for me to lend you what I can only assume is a tidy fortune."

"If you have time, I would like for you to accompany me to my shop," he said. "I will show you the wares, the ledgers, answer any of your questions. You will see for yourself how exquisite the items we offer are and how well managed and profitable a business it is. All I require is more time to realize the full loan, but it will be repaid to you efficiently and quickly, at your terms."

Tierney considered him for what could have been a moment or could have been minutes, his gaze unwavering. Tarquin held his stare, unflinching and unblinking. Whatever the other man saw, it must have been persuasive enough.

For at last, he nodded. "Very well, Bellingham. Take me to this shop of yours. Mayhap I'll return to the business of moneylending, should it please me."

Relief washed over Tarquin. "Thank you, Mr. Tierney. I don't think you will be disappointed."

"See that I'm not, Bellingham," the other man quipped. "My time is a thing of great value."

∼

Lily cradled Sir Bellingham in her arms as the carriage swayed over the rutted road taking herself, the cat, and her brother Wolf to the foundling hospital. With Hart's wounding, Logan's stunning reappearance, and the work on the second Sutton gaming hell being well underway, Lily hadn't had an opportunity to visit with the girls since she and Emma had last called. She missed her darling, impish Marianne, and she also was seeking some distraction, it was true. A day had passed since Tarquin had proposed to her, and she could think of precious little else.

Part of her was overjoyed that he loved her and wanted to marry her.

The other part of her worried desperately over being the cause of him losing everything he had worked so hard to build. His little empire, Bellingham and Co. It was such a glorious shop, quite unlike any other, and now that she knew him—truly knew him—she could see all the ways he had influenced it. The elegant design within, the extensive offering of only the finest goods, the magnificence of it.

For him to lose it all…

Lily sighed, discontented despite everything.

And it appeared Wolf was in no better a mood than she, for he was muttering to himself.

"What are the bloody odds?" he grumbled.

She suspected she knew what he was talking about, even if it was clear the bulk of his conversation had been happening in his own head. Hart was not her only brother who had newly fallen in love. Wolf had recently been chasing after a lovely widowed countess, Lady Blakewell. Unfortunately for Wolf, it appeared that the widow was likely the unexpected half sister of Archer Tierney, an unscrupulous moneylender with whom their brother Logan had apparently become somehow involved.

"That you'd find yourself in love with Archer Tierney's sister?" she prodded Wolf, for although it was apparent that her brother had deep feelings for Lady Blakewell, he had yet to do anything about it.

Lily had never fancied herself a matchmaker, but there never seemed a better time to play the part. Wolf deserved happiness and love. If he required a nudge on the way to finding it, she could happily deliver it. Anything to distract herself from the turmoil within.

Her brother offered her his most intimidating glower. "Here now, Lil. No one said a damned thing about *love.*"

"You needn't say it explicitly," she told him, petting Sir Bellingham when he shifted as they bounced over a particularly pronounced rut. "You have spent the entirety of the drive fretting over your countess—"

"She ain't mine," Wolf interrupted her with a pointed glare.

His ire didn't bother or fool her. He was being defensive because she was right, and they both knew it. As a woman in love, she knew all the signs. *Oh, Tarquin*, she thought, her heart giving a pang. She hoped loving her would not cost him everything.

"Archer Tierney's sister, then," she allowed, attempting to keep her mind from heavier worries.

"Half sister," he corrected her with a harsh frown, "and we don't know if Archer Tierney and Avery Tierney are the same cove."

Wolf had learned that Lady Blakewell was seeking her lost half brother Avery Tierney, and the fact that the mysterious Archer Tierney had no past to speak of and such a similar name was telling to Lily. They were one and the same, she had no doubt.

"One syllable's difference," she pointed out, giving Sir Bellingham's head a scratch.

Now that he had been properly cleaned and was spending his days in her attic rooms—not to mention the occasional crafty escape to the kitchens, where Chef offered him scraps —Sir Bellingham's coat was shiny and fluffy and, best of all, no longer odiferous. He looked up at her now with his adoring green gaze.

"Where did you find that damned cat?" Wolf growled, his temperament not having improved in the slightest.

"Behind The Sinner's Palace," she answered calmly. "He was mewing quite loudly, but he was not readily seen. I searched for him everywhere, until I finally spied him hiding beneath a cart. The poor darling was terribly thin. I fed him some chicken and we have been friends ever since."

"Cats make me sneeze," her brother pronounced.

That was utter rot, and they both knew it.

The cat in question began to purr as she rubbed beneath his chin, scratching just where he liked. "Sir Bellingham shall take that into consideration. Won't you, my little darling lad?"

"Sir Bellingham?" Wolf's voice was sharp, drawing her gaze back to him as he adjusted his hat, his eyes narrowing on her. "Never say you named the cat after Bellingham and Co.?"

She should not have used the cat's name. Her brothers would learn of her romance with Tarquin soon enough when he approached them, but in truth, she was dreading the moment. Hoping their reactions would not be brotherly outrage. She hadn't garnered the courage to broach the matter herself just yet.

But there was no hope for it now, she had revealed too much.

The carriage traveled over another bump and Lily shifted Sir Bellingham in her lap. "And what if I did? I like to shop there, and its owner is a bit of a stray himself."

A stray she had found and loved, much like the cat in her lap.

Wolf continued scowling, giving the brim of his hat a flick. "The owner, you say? And how are you acquainted with the high and lofty Mr. Bellingham?"

*Oh dear.* It was not as if she could confess to her brother that she and Mr. Bellingham were as intimately acquainted as two people could be. Wolf's protective fury would be instant.

Heat crept up her cheeks and she looked away from Wolf. "We are not acquainted," she lied, for it was too soon. She had no notion of when Tarquin would settle his finances enough to ask for her hand, and she had no wish to influence Wolf unduly before then. "Not at all."

But Wolf knew her better than that.

"Do not lie to me, Lily Sutton," he told her sternly, tapping the toe of her shoe with his boot. "Why is it you insist on shopping at that silly bleeding place with all the nobs? All of them looking down their aristocratic noses at you."

Because of Tarquin. But no need to admit it.

"Do you mean the silly bleeding place where you pretended you were married to your countess and had poor Mr. Smythe bring you all the gloves and lace as if you intended to buy it all?" she countered archly, for he was no more innocent than she was.

Wolf scrubbed his jaw with a gloved hand. "And what do you care to tell me about all the fans and slippers and lace and hats you've been keeping in your attic room?"

Well, *rantum scantum*. How did he know about that?

"Wolf Sutton, have you intruded upon my private room?" she demanded.

"I was looking for you," he said gruffly. "You were missing, if you will recall."

"I was at the foundling hospital," she countered, hoping that was indeed where she had been whenever he had gone looking for her.

And thank the heavens above that he had not ventured to her room when Tarquin had been there! What a disaster that would have been.

"So you say," he allowed.

"Yes," Lily agreed cheerfully. "Just as *you* say you are not in love with your countess."

As the carriage rocked on, they quibbled some more. Finally, when their arguments circled them back to the matter of love, Wolf's stubborn pride appeared to be receding.

"How can you love someone you've only just met?" he asked quietly.

An excellent question. One she might have asked herself, not long ago.

"Your heart recognizes itself," she told him, thinking of Tarquin. From the moment their paths had crossed, there had been an undeniable spark between them, burning steadily into an uncontrollable fire. "Regardless of what your rational mind wants, sometimes."

His brows snapped together. "What do you know about hearts and love?"

Nothing at all, it would seem. Only that her heart was finally whole with Tarquin in it, and she could not countenance spending the rest of her life with anyone but him as her husband.

"Precious little," she said instead of making that grand revelation. "I do read books."

For a moment, she feared her brother would press her for more information, ask her further questions she had no wish to answer just yet. But then, he relented.

"You never did say why you're bringing the bloody cat to the foundling hospital," Wolf said, turning the conversation to a safer subject.

"The children need more happiness," she answered easily as she cradled Sir Bellingham to her bodice. "I tried to secure some toys for them, but I was unsuccessful."

And she very much doubted the odious Mrs. Frost would allow such frivolity.

"More happiness," he repeated. "Ain't that what we all need?"

It was indeed. Lily hoped to find it with Tarquin, but until everything was settled with his loan and he sought out her brothers, the future was tinged with uncertainty.

Still, she very much wanted all her beloved siblings to find their own contentedness, and none more so than Wolf.

"If your happiness is to be found with the Countess of Blakewell, then you ought to pursue it," she urged him. "Pursue it, and her."

Her brother cleared his throat, looking uncharacteristically flustered. "You'll be wanting to hold tight to the creature so it doesn't escape and get trampled beneath the wheels of a passing carriage."

Another clear attempt to steer the conversation away from himself. Lily supposed she would allow it, for she possessed secrets enough of her own at the moment.

She raised a brow as the carriage rolled to a halt. "And how do you suppose I have been caring for Sir Bellingham all this time without your intervention, brother?"

The carriage door opened, then.

Shaking his head, Wolf rose from his seat. "You've a sharp tongue, sister."

Lily descended from the carriage, holding Sir Bellingham tightly. For of course, she very much did not wish her beloved cat to escape. Keeping him safe was paramount. But as she moved along the pavements, a fine post-chaise emblazoned with a gilded *B* on its doors caught her attention and she stumbled to a stop. She recognized the conveyance from the night Tarquin had rushed her to Caro's home.

Wolf was there, catching her elbow, keeping her steady.

"Tarquin?" she asked aloud, wondering if it could possibly be him, and why he would be paying a call upon the foundling hospital.

"What is amiss, Lil?" her brother asked at her side.

Blinking, she shook herself and forced a smile to her lips. "Nothing, of course. Let us go and see to the children, shall we?"

"Aye, let's see to the children," he agreed, a slight hint of menace creeping into his voice. "And to this Tarquin, whomever the devil he may be."

Biting her lip, Lily accompanied her brother inside the foundling hospital. It would seem one of her brothers was about to meet with the man she loved, and sooner than she had anticipated.

∼

TARQUIN WAS TOURING the sparse quarters of the foundling hospital under the eye of its head matron, Mrs. Frost. This was his final call to be made before the last, most important one.

The call to The Sinner's Palace to meet with Lily's brothers and ask for her hand in marriage.

First, he had one more mission to complete.

"And this is where the girls do their sewing work," Mrs. Frost announced, gesturing to a room filled with uncomfortable-looking wooden benches.

He had some chairs which had arrived damaged in his warehouse. Those would do far better for the girls to sit upon, he thought, wondering what else he might donate that was no longer of use to his shop.

It had not taken Tarquin long to discover the head matron of the foundling hospital, Mrs. Frost, was a dreadful woman. His dislike for her had begun the moment he had been escorted into the entry hall and she had appeared before him. Her cunning gaze had swept over him, judging the cut of his coat, the price of his hat, the sheen of his boots. That, coupled with his calling card, had led her to deem him a gentleman worthy of her time.

"Mr. Bellingham of *the* Bellingham and Co.," she had said, her cap fluttering about her narrow face in her excitement as she dipped into a hasty curtsy, clutching his card as if it were fashioned of gold. "You honor us, sir, with your presence."

She was the sort of person to whom appearance, and the suggestion of wealth, was of far greater import than a man's character. And she most definitely was not alone. There were plenty more of her ilk. He recognized it well, for not long ago, he had been little better, striving toward being perceived as a member of the gentry. Concerning himself solely with the approval of his father, the increase of his own wealth and influence.

Until Lily Sutton—with the unintentional aid of one mischievous scamp—had changed him forever.

"I would be more than happy to provide some new seating for the room, Mrs. Frost," he said.

For his life had taken a new and glorious turn, and he wished very much to repay his good fortune however he might.

Archer Tierney had accepted his bargain. Bellingham and Co. had been saved. His own coffers would be brought perilously low in the process, but Tierney had surprised him by offering reasonable terms. He now had sufficient time to fund the loan using his shop's profit, and he would be able to take Lily as his wife with a clear conscience.

Doing business with a cutthroat like Tierney was not a perfect solution, but then, there was not a perfect solution to be found in such a circumstance. Tarquin was grateful for the chance to keep his doors open, to keep his shop growing, and to marry the woman he loved.

He had taken great pleasure in paying a call upon his incredulous father, who had been shocked to find Tarquin possessed the entirety of the loan, and well within the time he had specified. The duke had reluctantly accepted the banknote and told Tarquin he never wished to see him again, after the shame he had brought upon him by refusing to wed Lady Clementia. The feeling had been mutual.

"We would be pleased to accept your generosity, Mr. Bellingham," Mrs. Frost said.

"Your foundlings mend as part of the payment for their board and food, do they not?" he inquired, looking around the shabby interior, thinking it could benefit from a great deal more light. He could gladly donate some of the candles in his own home. He scarcely needed them all. "My shop will be taking in pieces for mending soon, and I would be pleased to send the garments here, paying more than what they presently earn per piece."

"Why, Mr. Bellingham, that would be most appreciated," Mrs. Frost said. "I cannot begin to express my gratitude."

"I am more than happy to help however I am able," he told the head matron, meaning those words. The foundling hospital and its girls meant a great deal to Lily, and as such, meant a great deal to Tarquin as well. One of the children perhaps more than the rest. "Consequently, I was wondering if you might inform me of the familiar process for taking in one of the orphans."

"Our oldest girls may be placed as maids," Mrs. Frost said. "They are all equally adept."

"I am not seeking a servant, Mrs. Frost, but am intending to give the child a home rather than a situation," he explained. "Her name is Marianne, I believe."

"That imp." Mrs. Frost frowned. "You'd not be wanting that wretched child."

He wondered what manner of trouble the girl could have caused at the foundling hospital to warrant such a reaction. If her pickpocketing and clever deceptions were any indication, a great deal. But Tarquin knew what it was like to be a child no one wanted or loved. To be alone in the world. And he knew that Lily cared for her, that no good would come of the child running wild in the foundling hospital on her own. She needed guidance. A loving home.

"Nonetheless, that is the child my betrothed has her heart set upon," he said, invoking Lily without using her name. "She was quite clear on it."

"You are going to wed, Mr. Bellingham?" the head matron asked.

"Soon," he hedged, "and when I am married, my wife and I would be honored to bring Marianne into our household."

Mrs. Frost led him to the main hall, where he was startled to find Lily herself, along with a tall, broad-chested man with eyes that matched hers. One of her infamous brothers, he reckoned. But Tarquin's gaze quickly flitted back to Lily, his heart thudding in his chest as he drank in the sight of her, belatedly taking note that in Lily's arms was a squirming orange cat, held tightly. What the devil was she doing with a feline?

"Mr. Bellingham," Mrs. Frost said with great enthusiasm

which distinctly fled her voice as she turned to Lily and her brother, "may I introduce you to Miss Sutton and her brother, Mr. Sutton? Miss Sutton often offers her time in assisting with the girls. This is Mr. Bellingham, of Bellingham and Co."

"Bellingham," Lily's brother greeted coolly, his eyes assessing as they flicked between Tarquin and Lily. "Mrs. Frost."

He wondered what the brother knew, if anything.

Just then, the cat hissed at Mrs. Frost.

"Oh dear," the head matron said, pressing a hand over her heart, her cap fluttering yet again. "What is wrong with that creature?"

Lily dipped into a curtsy which was quite fair, considering she was juggling the cat. "Mr. Bellingham, a pleasure to make your acquaintance. My companion is frightfully shy, Mrs. Frost. I brought him to take a visit with the girls, thinking they would enjoy a visit from him."

Mrs. Frost frowned. "Miss Sutton, I fear the girls are otherwise occupied at the moment. They haven't the time for a silly visit with a cat."

Undoubtedly because they needed to be put to work.

"Surely a small visit will not be remiss?" Tarquin suggested smoothly, his dislike for the forbidding head matron growing.

The head matron huffed a sigh of displeasure, but relented. "I suppose not, Mr. Bellingham. I shall assemble the girls in the sitting room. If you will excuse me for a moment?"

Mrs. Frost bustled away, leaving Tarquin, Lily, and her brother alone. Well, alone with the cat, who was watching Tarquin in a distrustful manner.

"And how do you know my sister, Mr. Bellingham?" Lily's brother asked, eyes narrowing.

*Blast.* Was their familiarity that apparent? Had he gazed at Lily too lovingly? Likely so. This was decidedly not the manner in which he had hoped to first make the acquaintance of one of her siblings.

"Wolf," Lily said softly. "Not now, if you please."

"She's named the cat after you," her brother pointed out, his voice hard. "Care to explain why?"

"Tarquin?" he asked, confused, for he had not known Lily had a cat.

Then, knowing Lily, the feline was likely a newfound friend. And how like her. She collected the lost. Marianne, himself, the orange cat in her arms.

"Lil, is there something you'd like to tell me?" her brother asked her.

This was not how he had envisioned approaching Lily's brothers, but he supposed it would have to do. He was not going to begin in lies. The truth was all he could give, and hope for the best.

"I want to marry your sister," he said baldly before Lily could offer a response of her own.

Wolf Sutton turned a ferocious frown upon him. "Marry my sister?"

"Yes," he said simply. "I meant to go about this in a far different fashion, but circumstances have brought us here together now, and I see no reason to deny my intentions."

"And Lil, you wish to marry this cove?" Wolf Sutton asked Lily, sounding shocked as he nodded in Tarquin's direction.

Lily held his gaze, smiling softly. Tenderly.

"Yes," she agreed. "I do want to marry him."

The cat hissed again, effectively shattering the moment.

Lily's brother chortled. "Seems like he ain't too fond of his namesake."

"I have only just made the little chap's acquaintance," he informed Sutton, as if it were every day that he frequented foundling hospitals and indirectly proposed marriage before angry orange felines who were named after him.

"I know that in no time, he shall love you as much as I do," Lily told him.

"Love?" Wolf snorted. "Is this what you were pattering on about in the carriage? I ought to have known. Makes everyone touched in the upperworks, it does. Here, now. This is what you've been doing when you disappeared, aye? Chasing after a cull?"

Lily flushed. "Of course not. If anything, Mr. Bellingham has been chasing me."

That was true, but Tarquin would have preferred if Lily hadn't admitted it aloud to a brother who looked as if he might dearly long to rip off Tarquin's left arm and beat him about the head with it.

Wolf Sutton started forward, his expression thunderous. "If you've compromised my sister—"

Lily jumped between them, keeping her brother from attacking, and Sir Bellingham leapt from her arms with an angry mewl. In the next moment, Mrs. Frost reappeared, a trail of girls following in her wake. The cat ran directly beneath the head matron's skirts. Mrs. Frost screeched.

And hell decidedly broke loose at the foundling hospital.

## CHAPTER 14

"You want to marry my sister."

Not for the first time, Tarquin found himself in the pleasant confines of The Sinner's Palace's private family parlor. But unlike previous instances when he had been ensconced within these four familiar walls, he was not alone with Lily. Rather, this time, they had an audience of her brothers.

It was the eldest brother, and the most dangerous looking of them all, Jasper Sutton, who had growled the pronouncement.

"Yes," he answered.

"Of course he does," Lily, seated at his side, said with an air of great frustration. "He has just said so, has he not?"

Fortunately, the miscreant Sir Bellingham was locked away in her attic room where he could not set the gaming hell on its ear. But Tarquin still felt rather as if he were facing a wall of enemy soldiers, about to do battle.

"What we're all wondering is how the two of you 'ad cause to meet," said another of her brothers, the one who sported a head of blond curls and resembled nothing so much as a pirate.

Tarquin considered the question, wondering how best to answer.

"I was filching from his shop," Lily answered for him, unabashedly. "Mr. Bellingham caught me with a fan stuffed down my...well, it was not as if he found it. Nothing as scandalous as that. He merely suspected..."

"Thieving?" roared another of her brothers. "Christ, Lil. What were you thinking?"

"Well, it's quite simple. I thought he was Marianne's heartless brother and that he'd left her to the foundling hospital. She was stealing fans and other small items and selling them when it was her turn to deliver the sewing, so I decided to help her."

"Who the devil is Marianne?" growled Jasper Sutton.

Tarquin cleared his throat. "She is one of the children at the foundling hospital. A charming imp. Not truly my sister, as it happens. She was bamboozling Miss Sutton. When we marry, your sister and I intend to bring the girl into our household so she can receive a proper education."

"And we also hope to aid the other girls as well," Lily added, sending Tarquin a secretive smile of approval. "We are going to help the girls learn to better themselves, rather than being forced into servitude when they're deemed too old for the hospital."

Somehow, in the melee which had followed Sir Bellingham's abrupt dash through the foundling hospital—which had ended when Marianne had finally caught the beast and calmed him—Tarquin and Lily had managed to have a moment to speak with each other. Lily had been pleased with his suggestion they bring Marianne to live with them, and also excited at the notion they might work together to help the rest of the foundlings.

It was the right thing to do. Tarquin knew how dark and dangerous the world could be for children forced to work for their suppers. He had no wish to see anyone preying upon the foundling hospital girls. Not as long as he could do his part, and with Lily at his side, he knew that together, they could. They were united. One in heart and mind, and he had never felt so strong, so joyous, as he did now.

Even facing all these furious, protective Sutton brothers as he begged for their sister's hand in marriage.

"Bleeding hell," swore the eldest Sutton, rubbing his jaw. "And after the thieving, what happened then? Don't think to lie, Bellingham. I know you've been sniffing about The Sinner's Palace, paying Lil calls. If you ruined 'er, I'll eat your liver for breakfast."

Well, then. It would seem Lily's threats concerning her brother's reactions were founded in more than a modicum of truth. Tarquin tamped down his guilt as he forced his countenance to remain blank.

*Do not think about that wondrous night in Lily's bed*, he warned himself. *Do not think of all those kisses, of lying naked and entwined together...*

"Jasper," Lily chided with a frown. "That ain't any way to speak to my future husband."

"He needs to know where things stand." Her brother shook his head, scowling. "Do you love him, Lil?"

"Aye," Lily said simply. "I do."

"And you," Sutton said, pinning Tarquin with a menacing glare. "Do you love her?"

"More than words can express," he said earnestly.

So much that he had done everything in his power to make it possible for them to marry, all but selling his soul to the devil. Selling his debt to a moneylender was scarcely any different. But every sacrifice was worth Lily as his wife, his love, his future.

"You'll make our sister the 'appiest bleeding woman in all London," one of the brothers warned, cracking his knuckles. "Or you'll answer to us."

"All I want is to make her happy and to spend the rest of my life with her, if she will have me." At the last, Tarquin turned back to Lily, who was gazing at him with so much unfettered love that he was at once humbled and astounded.

"Of course I will have you," Lily told him softly. "It would be my honor to be your wife."

How hollow his life had been without this vivacious force of a woman. She had stormed into his shop, intent upon championing an orphan, and had changed him forever instead. Because of Lily Sutton, Tarquin Bellingham was a better man.

Because of her, he understood that life was not about amassing wealth and influence. Not about pleasing the father who had never given a damn for him. Not about titles or waltzes at Rivendale's. His endless quest to grow Bellingham and Co., to show the Duke of Hampton how worthy he was, had ultimately proven meaningless. Because life was truly about loving others, purely and simply. It was about caring for an orphaned girl. About taking in a stray orange cat. Life was about finding happiness and holding it tightly, and Tarquin intended to do precisely that.

"I reckon," Jasper Sutton said suddenly, his voice sharp yet laden with a wealth of underlying emotion, "that if the two of you love each other, there's naught more to be said on the matter."

Lily beamed at Tarquin, and he knew there was likely a similar, ridiculously thrilled, thoroughly besotted smile on his own face. He didn't care. Lily Sutton was going to be his wife.

"Is that a tear I see in your eye, brother?" one of the brothers teased Jasper.

Tarquin was truly going to have to learn all their names, or face their wrath.

The eldest Sutton sniffed. "Of course not, you arsehole."

"Your cheek is wet," observed another impudently.

"Well, hell," Sutton grumbled. "It ain't every day that the last of our sisters announces she'll be caught in the parson's mousetrap."

"We have your blessing, then?" Tarquin pressed, for there was a difference between *nothing more to be said on the matter* and approval.

"Aye," Jasper Sutton relented, another wet track appearing on his other cheek. "You've our blessing."

Lily reached for Tarquin's hand, and he grasped it, their fingers tangling. He longed to haul her into his arms and kiss her breathless, but that would have to wait since they had an audience of fiercely protective brothers.

"When can we marry?" Lily asked him, her thoughts apparently not far from his.

"Not soon enough," he told her, bringing her hand to his lips for a chaste kiss, all he would allow himself.

"Might I have a moment with my betrothed?" Lily asked her brothers.

"Not on my bleeding watch," Jasper Sutton said darkly.

"Come now," said the brother with the blond curls. "They'll be married soon enough."

The eldest Sutton cursed beneath his breath, but finally relented with a sigh. "Ten minutes, and nothing untoward. I've a dagger with your name on it in my boot, Bellingham."

Tarquin had no doubt the man did have a dagger in his boot, and likely one with a sharp and unforgiving blade. "Nothing untoward," he agreed. "I would prefer to keep my liver intact."

"Now you're understanding the way of it," Jasper said,

nodding in approval as he rose, along with the other brothers. "I'll return in ten minutes."

With that final warning, the Suttons departed the parlor, leaving Tarquin blessedly alone with Lily. They had stood together in deference to her brothers, and the moment the door clicked closed, Lily threw herself at him. He caught her around the waist, holding her tightly, pressing his face into the sweetly scented crown of her hair.

"Do you truly wish to marry me?" she asked, tipping her head back to look up at him.

The blue-green-gray of her stare seared him to his soul.

"Need you ask?" He brushed a tendril of hair from her cheek. "I have never wanted anything more."

"What about your father?" She searched his gaze. "What of the loan you must repay? I did not want to ask you before the others."

"I have secured the funds to repay my father," he assured her. "I saw him today and delivered the banknote. I won't lose Bellingham and Co."

"Oh, thank heavens," she breathed, before frowning. "But how were you able to find the funds so quickly?"

"A moneylender," he explained, wishing he could offer her a different answer. "It is not an ideal bargain, but it was the only way to ensure I would not lose the shop."

"A moneylender." Her frown grew. "Who?"

"A gentleman by the name of Archer Tierney."

Lily gasped, her grasp on his shoulders tightening. "Archer Tierney? Oh, Tarquin. You mustn't accept any aid from that ruthless scoundrel."

He caressed her cheek, needing to touch her. "It is already done, my love. The terms are fair. I will see the new loan promptly repaid. You needn't worry."

Her lovely face was wreathed in concern. "But he is a dangerous man. My brother Logan disappeared over a year ago, and we believed him dead. Instead, all this time, he has been involved in something nefarious with Mr. Tierney."

Tarquin struggled to comprehend the full implications of the news she had just imparted. "You've another brother? How many Suttons are there?"

"Eight of us, in all," Lily answered. "But Tarquin, Tierney is a dangerous man. You mustn't involve yourself with him. Is there no other way to gather the funds you require? How much do you need? I have some funds of my own, set aside from The Sinner's Palace. My brothers could help, if you but asked."

"No." He shook his head, for on this, he was firm. "I will not enter a marriage owing you or your family. I must do this on my own, Lily. I dug myself this terrible hole by trusting my father, and I alone will get myself out of it."

"Do you not see?" She grasped his lapels, her frustration evident. "Involving yourself with Tierney will be a far deeper hole. My brother Logan has wished us all to the devil. He won't speak to any of us, and my other brothers fear what he has become embroiled in with Tierney."

"You need not fret." He cupped her face, holding her stare. "I promise you, Lily. I have no involvement with the man, aside from the repayment of the loan. The agreement is clear, for I've learned my lesson well. He cannot rescind the funds for any reason save my inability to pay him. And with Bellingham and Co. thriving, that shan't be a problem. Trust me, my love. I would never do anything to jeopardize our future, our happiness."

She bit her lower lip, still looking worried. "If only you would have spoken to me first. Why did you not seek me out? I could have warned you away from him."

"There was no other way," he told her softly. "I was running out of time."

"Tarquin." She blinked, tears glistening in her eyes.

The sight nearly unmanned him. He kissed her cheeks, her lashes, feeling the cool wetness of her teardrops on his lips.

"No, Lily. Trust me. Trust in me. All will be well." He took her mouth then, just a quick, chaste kiss of reassurance. "I love you."

"And I love you," she said, sadness tingeing her voice.

He hated the sound, despised being the source. But he had made the right decision. The *only* decision. In time, she would see.

A knock sounded on the door then, a harsh rap of knuckles on wood. "Ten minutes is over."

They jumped apart guiltily as the door swept open to reveal Jasper Sutton.

"I must go now," Tarquin told Lily gently. "But begin your preparations. The sooner we wed, the better."

"Yes," she agreed, still looking troubled. "The sooner, the better."

With a bow, he took his leave.

∼

LILY SAT in the low-lit confines of Tarquin's post-chaise. The hour was late. If her brothers discovered Sly Jack had driven her to Bellingham and Co. so that she could secret herself in Tarquin's waiting conveyance, they would not be pleased. Indeed, she had no doubt they would be furious over the gamble she had taken.

But it was worth it, because she needed to see Tarquin. The ten minutes Jasper had afforded them earlier was not nearly enough.

And afterward, she intended to take the biggest risk of all.

The door to the post-chaise opened, and the flickering

glow of the carriage lamps illuminated the planes and angles of Tarquin's handsome face. His eyes went wide.

"Lily? What are you doing here, love?"

"Waiting for you," she answered.

Fortunately, his coachman had remembered her and had been willing to allow her to remain in the post-chaise until Tarquin emerged from his shop. Sly Jack, ever loyal and protective, had waited until she was safely ensconced within before driving off.

Tarquin disappeared for a moment, giving orders to his coachman, before returning.

"But why?" He climbed inside, shutting the door, effectively enclosing them in privacy. "Is something amiss?"

"Nothing is amiss," she reassured him. "I merely wished to see you. Is that not reason enough?"

"For gadding about in the midst of the night alone?" He frowned, settling himself on the bench at her side and gathering her onto his lap, his arms banded tightly around her as if he feared she might disappear. "No, curse you. It is dangerous."

"I wasn't alone." She looped her arms around his neck and settled herself more comfortably, nuzzling his neck above his perfect cravat. "Sly Jack brought me here."

"Do your brothers know of this?"

She kissed his ear. "Of course not."

He growled low in his throat. "I'm going to have to marry you tomorrow just to keep you out of trouble."

Lily moved to his jaw, kissing along it as she inhaled deeply of his scent. "I missed you. Ten minutes alone was not sufficient."

"This was reckless, my love." His countenance was stern. "You shouldn't have slipped away alone. If something were to happen to you…"

"Nothing happened to me." She sent him a wicked smile. "Yet."

"Good God, what am I to do with you?" he asked, cupping her cheek with reverence.

"Kiss me first," she suggested. "Love me. Marry me."

"I'll do all of those things," he promised. "But we are not doing them in the proper order."

"Why should it matter which order we do them in? We are marrying anyway."

He grinned, and it was the carefree grin of the man she had come to love. "Indeed."

He kissed her then, his mouth angling over hers with almost bruising intensity. And she kissed him with equal fervor, thrilling to his touch. Their earlier, hasty joining of mouths had not been sufficient, and she reveled in the way he parted her lips with his, claiming and consuming.

The post-chaise lurched into motion. She didn't know where it was taking them, and nor did she care. After so much uncertainty, she was in his arms where she belonged. No frowning brothers to deny her what she wanted. No hovering head matron at the foundling hospital looking for a hint of scandal. It was only Lily and Tarquin as it had always been meant to be.

As they rocked together, feeding each other frantic kisses, an acute hunger blossomed to life between her thighs. She wanted him, and the rising ridge of his cock along her bottom suggested he wanted her every bit as much. His hands were moving, traveling over the layers of her pelisse and gown, finding her breasts and palming them.

All the pent-up desire which had been bedeviling her since he had made love to her rose to a fervent, furious pitch. She needed to be closer to him. Needed less fabric between them. Needed him inside her, quelling the ache.

She tore her mouth from his, her breath already ragged,

meeting his gaze in the dim glow of the carriage lamp. "I want you, Tarquin."

"Yes," he hissed, breathless as she was. "I have been thinking of nothing else all these days we've spent apart."

"Too many days," she said, shifting on his lap so that her knees were bent on either side of his thighs, and the place where she ached was almost perfectly aligned with his thick length.

He tugged at the ribbon keeping her bonnet in place, sending it to the floor. And then, his fingers were flying over the fastenings of her pelisse, pulling them open, working the garment down her arms until it pooled in a heap below. He cupped her nape, guiding her lips to his for another long, voracious kiss before his mouth traveled in a hot, delicious pattern over her jaw, down her throat. With his other hand, he plucked at the buttons of her gown until her bodice loosened.

"My God," he breathed against her skin. "You bring me to my knees."

"I like you there," she told him wickedly, thinking of how he had buried his face between her legs that night, remembering the agonizing pleasure of his tongue on her intimate flesh.

His head lifted, his blue stare stormier than a hurricane-tossed sea. "Now? Say the words, Lily, and I'll get down on my knees for you and lick you until you come."

She swallowed hard, his words sending a pulse to her core. "Yes."

His hand slid inside her bodice, gloved and warm, his fingers slipping within her stays and chemise to cup her breast, rolling her aching nipple between thumb and forefinger. "Tell me."

"I want you on your knees," she said. "I want you to pleasure me until I spend."

With another guttural sound of raw pleasure, he moved her, sliding her onto the seat before going to his knees before her. "As my queen wishes. But you must promise not to be too loud. We'll not want my coachman to overhear and know what we are about."

"That would be wicked," she agreed, the forbidden nature of their tryst heightening her need.

"Yes," he agreed. "Now take what you want, love. Show me your beautiful cunny."

Grasping handfuls of her skirts, she raised her petticoat, chemise, and gown, the fabric brushing past her ankles, along her calves, and then higher. To her knees. The slow, sensual graze of the fabric while Tarquin's hungry stare devoured her was enough to make her hands tremble. Watching her, he removed his hat, then slid a finger between his cravat and Adam's apple, loosening the knot. The sight of him on his knees in the carriage, ready to do her bidding, to pleasure her, was unbearably erotic. The carriage rocked over a bump in the road, and the sudden motion was a stimulation in itself, making her rock back and forth on the leather bench, seeking more friction.

Higher, she lifted her hems, the gentle swaying of the post-chaise and the confined space combining with her anticipation, making her almost dizzied with desire. Her skirts reached the tops of her thighs, and she paused, feeling momentarily shy. He had seen her before, of course, but this was all still new.

Tarquin tugged off his gloves, abandoning them to their other discarded garments. The night air was cool, but she felt nothing but heat as his bare hands coasted over her calves, up to her garters, toying with the ribbons which held her stockings in place.

"You're so lovely." He pressed a kiss to each knee as his

fingers moved higher, sweeping tentatively over her inner thighs.

She slid her legs open, giving them both what they wanted, and his mouth traveled greedily along the new flesh she had exposed. Lily could not withstand the urge to touch him any longer. Still holding her hems in place with one hand, she threaded her fingers through his hair with the other, drawing him nearer.

"Good girl," he praised.

And then, his head dipped. His tongue slid over her seam, hot and wet. Her fingers tightened on his hair, gripping, holding him in place. Gently, he licked, fast swipes up and down her sex, teasing her unmercifully as he avoided the place where she wanted him most. His tongue glanced lower, finding her entrance and swirling inside with shallow thrusts.

She moaned softly, her head falling back against the squabs, bottom sliding to the edge of the bench to grant him greater access, thighs widening, boots flat on the floor so she could arch into his beautiful face. The scent of her desire perfumed the air, and the lusty sound of his tongue traveling over her wetness rose above the din of travel.

"You taste so good," he murmured against her, kissing her mound. "Sweeter than any dessert."

She whimpered, nearly half mad with wanting him, the only response she could muster. Finally, he parted her folds, flicking his tongue over her aching pearl in steady lashes that took her swiftly to the edge. The flutter of his tongue, combined with the subtle abrasion of his teeth sent sparks of pure bliss up and down her spine. It was…oh heavens, she was going to…

Lily came apart, the pleasure almost too much for her to bear, her thighs clamping together as she rolled her hips to meet his mouth, pressing herself shamelessly against him. A ragged cry escaped her involuntarily, and she released her skirts to press a hand to her lips, muffling the sounds she could not seem to stop making.

Tarquin kissed her inner thigh and then moved, taking a seat beside her on the bench. His lips glistened with the evidence of her desire, his eyes dark with passion. Her heart was pounding, an inner warmth glowing deep inside her, like the sun. Her sex was pulsing from the aftereffects of the orgasm he had given her.

Still holding her gaze, he unbuttoned the fall of his trousers. His cock sprang up, demanding and ruddy, a bead of his mettle already leaking from the slit on the tip, glistening in the light. He gripped his shaft hard, stroking himself.

"I need to spend, love," he ground out, the tendons in his neck standing in relief from the strain.

"Just from…" She allowed her words to trail off, not certain how to phrase what had just happened between them politely.

"Licking your cunny," he gritted. "Yes."

The knowledge that she had such a tremendous effect on him filled her with warmth and pride. Followed closely by the need to give him pleasure as he had done for her.

"Let me," she said, reaching for his shaft, curling her fingers over his.

"I'll finish myself off. You needn't."

His voice was thick with desire.

Lily was already sliding to her knees, taking his place, pushing his thighs apart so she could insert herself between them. Holding his gaze, she said, "I want to, Tarquin."

He released his grip on his cock with a groan.

Her fingers replaced his on the base, and she mimicked his motions, moving up and down his shaft before bending her head to run her tongue along the underside of his cock, licking him as he had done to her. She had no notion of what he liked, what would feel as exquisitely pleasurable for him as what he had done to her. But she moved instinctively, tasting him, her tongue pressing to the head of his cock where the moisture seeped from him, tasting his mettle on her tongue. She laved him, glancing up to find his gaze hot and piercing upon her.

"Tell me what to do," she murmured. "How to please you."

He reached for her, running the backs of his fingers along her cheek in a tender caress. "Take me in your mouth and suck."

Holding him with one hand, she tentatively took him between her lips. The sensation of him in her mouth was at once foreign and desperately rousing. It stirred the ache between her legs back into a fever. She took him deeper, loving the rigid smoothness of his cock, the way he filled her mouth and there was still more of him.

He groaned again, his fingers sinking into her hair as his hips began to pump in shallow, measured thrusts.

"Yes," he murmured. "God, yes. Just like that, love. Take me as deep into your throat as you can."

She lowered her head, taking more of him into her mouth, until the tip reached the back of her throat and she gagged. Lily retreated, taking a breath, working the root of his shaft, hoping she had not insulted him with her instinctive reaction.

But Tarquin's countenance was slack with pleasure, and he appeared drunk on desire. No hint of hurt to be found.

"More please," he begged.

And that was all she needed to hear. Lily took him again, engulfing his thick, beautiful cock in her mouth and sucking hard. His hips jerked. Following the cues of his body, she moved up and down on his cock, mimicking the act of lovemaking with her mouth. Sucking, licking, taking him deep into her throat. He undulated against her, his movements less controlled, the hand in her hair tightening as he began to lose himself.

One more suck, and he stiffened beneath her, the hot spurt of his seed shooting down the back of her throat. She swallowed and fell back upon her knees, breathless from her exertions, drinking in the sight of him, legs splayed, head back against the squabs, his cock glistening from her mouth. She had done that, she thought, pleased with herself. She had brought him to the peak of pleasure.

"Lily," he said, reaching into his coat and extracting a handkerchief, handing it to her. "I didn't intend to do that. Forgive me."

She accepted the linen square, using it to dab at her mouth. "I loved it. And I love you."

He tucked himself discreetly away and then reached for her. "Come here, darling."

She crawled into his lap, settling there, wrapping her arms around him and listening to the steady, reassuring thump of his heart.

"How long do we have until your brothers notice you are gone?" he asked softly.

She smiled, for she did not want the night to end just yet either. "A few hours."

He kissed her crown. "Good. I'm going to take you home with me, and then I'll see you back to The Sinner's Palace before dawn."

That sounded perfect to Lily. She held him tight as his post-chaise continued lumbering on.

## CHAPTER 15

Because she didn't wish to incur her brother's wrath or cause any trouble for Sly Jack, Lily decided to hire a hack to take her to Logan's lodgings. The hour was desperately early, and she'd had scarcely any sleep, having spent most of the night in Tarquin's bed, but she had ventured out anyway, knowing she needed to leave under cover of darkness. If any of the guards or Jasper, Rafe, Hart, or Wolf learned where she intended to go and why, she knew they would stop her.

Their lost brother was not the same man they had known, they had already warned her. He was a cold, distant stranger who wanted nothing to do with their family, and he had made that more than apparent.

But Lily was worried about Tarquin's loan from Archer Tierney. The notion of him or his shop becoming entangled in whatever nefarious dealings the man was involved in made her sick with worry. And she had been close to her brother once. She refused to believe that he would be entirely unmoved or unwilling to help her.

He was still her brother, whether he liked it or not.

As the hackney came to a halt, she thanked the driver and paid him his fare. She leapt down without fanfare, her reticule, pistol within, firmly at her side. One never knew what manner of trouble awaited, and it was always best to be armed and prepared. She was a Sutton, after all.

She approached the front door, hastening up the pavements. It was dreadfully dreary at this early morning hour, the air damp with mists, a thick, pervasive fog having settled in overnight. She could scarcely see the buildings before her, and uneasiness rolled down her spine, settling in her gut.

Perhaps she should have waited until later in the day, when the fog and mists had dispersed. When there were more people about. But there was no help for it now. It was far too late to change her mind. The hack had already rattled off into the fog, leaving her stranded.

Nothing to do save stride forward. She reached the door not a moment too soon, seizing the brass knocker and delivering a sound rap.

She heard rustling within, and then the door opened to reveal the tall, shadowy figure of a man.

A man who was not Logan. She would recognize her brother even in the dark.

"No molls wanted here," the man told her. "You've come to the wrong door, madam."

He assumed she was a doxy.

"I'm not a moll, sir," she said hastily. "I've come to speak with Mr. Martin."

That was the name Logan had adopted, choosing to eschew the name Sutton, and it was the one she hoped would prove she knew her brother well enough to find her way to him.

"Martin ain't here," the man said. "You'll have to return later."

He began to close the door, but Lily reached out with a

splayed hand, stopping him from snapping it shut. "Please, sir. May I wait for him, if he is not within? My hackney has already gone, and the air is cool."

To say nothing of the dangers that could be lurking in the shadows.

"And who are you?" the man demanded coldly.

"His sister," she said, for that was the truth.

"Sister. He hasn't a sister I've ever heard of."

"Nonetheless, I am," she insisted. "Now, I shall wait for Mr. Martin, if you please."

The man finally relented, taking a step in retreat and opening the door. "Come inside then, if you must."

Lily stepped over the threshold, relief washing over her that died abruptly. A sudden flurry of movement happened behind the man, and he was roughly seized, an arm around his throat, the barrel of another man's gun pressed to his temple.

She gasped in shock, backing away, into the night, knowing she had to escape.

When she felt the undeniable end of a pistol prodding her in the back and a hand seized her upper arm in a punishing grip, she froze.

"You'll be coming with me," said an unfamiliar voice that was harsh and hard.

Emotionless.

Lily felt as if all the air had been sucked from her lungs. Her mouth went dry.

"No," she managed to say, turning to see into the mists behind her. "Please, sir, release me. This is a mistake."

"Oh, it ain't a mistake," the man said, cruelly digging the gun deeper into her back. "If you scream, I'll kill you. Understand?"

"Yes," she managed to whisper, still clinging to her reticule, thinking of her own pistol within. If she could only reach it. Her fingers crept nearer.

But her captor sensed the movement and ripped the reticule from her, tossing it to the pavements.

"No more moving," he warned. "That's your last chance, Mrs. Martin."

Mrs. Martin? Did Logan have a wife? Who did this man think she was, and why was he taking her?

"I'm not Mrs. Martin," she tried to argue. "My name is Lily. You've mistaken me for another."

"Shut up," the man growled. "I'll not believe a word of your lies. Come with me, now."

He shoved her, and Lily nearly lost her balance, pitching headlong to the pavements. At the last moment, she righted herself, eyes darting around into the shadows, hoping to find a means of escape. Or someone passing. Anyone who could help her. But the street was barren as far as she could tell, the fog so thick she could scarcely see past her hand.

"Please," she tried again. "I'm not who you think I am."

He struck her in the temple, and pain blazed through her, sharp and hot.

"No more talking," he bit out. "You'll be coming with me, and you'll be holding your tongue, or I'll cut it out myself."

Fear sank through her, heavy as a stone.

Knowing it could be her last chance at escape, Lily screamed.

Something hard and sharp came down on the back of her head, and then all she knew was darkness.

∽

LOGAN RAPPED on the door of The Sinner's Palace and waited.

Bloody odd, the feeling of returning to a place that had

once been his home as a stranger. He wasn't certain of the welcome he would receive. He was weary, covered in the blood of his aid, Chapman, and he hadn't slept all night. He was also desperate.

So desperate that he was here, in a place he had vowed never again to frequent after he had taken the oath of allegiance. Acknowledging his family only put them at risk and undermined the cause. He had no choice but to shun them. To disappear. For their own sakes more than his.

But he should have known that remaining in London, where he needed to be for his missions, would have made him vulnerable to discovery. Should have known that his determined siblings would have never surrendered to defeat. And he damned well should have predicted they would find him.

Which they had done.

And when they had, the danger had come.

A small door within the larger portal slid open to reveal a pair of eyes. "Hell's bleeding closed today."

The door snapped shut.

Logan rapped again, with greater insistence. "I'm not here to gamble. I need to speak with Jasper."

The door slid halfway open. "Tradesmen round the back, but he ain't seeing tradesmen today. Come again tomorrow."

"Damn you, I'm not a tradesman," Logan snarled, losing his patience. "I'm his goddamned brother. He'll want to see me."

"All the brothers are within," said the voice of the guard.

Logan was tall, and it wasn't difficult to peer into the viewing slot. "Randall, is that you?" He tore off the hat that had been shielding his face. "It's me, Logan."

The large door swung open with a creak.

"You're bloody," the guard observed, lip curled. "You been hushing culls?"

Not a warm welcome from one of the family's most trusted men, then. Fair enough. He deserved no less, especially for the peril he had brought to Lily.

"Not today," he told Randall honestly. "Where are my brothers? I need to see them. It's concerning Lily."

"Miss Lily?" Randall's eyes narrowed. "No one's been able to find 'er all morning. Missing, she is. What do you know of where she's gone?"

Far more than he should. Of all the nights Lily had sought him out, it had to have been the same night he had been sent on a mission to die. Betrayed by his own men. If she had come to him any other night, she would have been safe.

If anything happened to her, he would never forgive himself. The fault would be his, and his alone.

"I don't answer to you," Logan reminded the guard sharply, for he did not know who he could trust after last night. But he did believe he could trust his brother. "Take me to Jasper, or I'll find him myself."

He moved to skirt the stubborn guard, knowing that every moment wasted was another that could be his sister's last. Because of him. Because of the risks he had taken. The promises he had made and broken.

"Aye." Randall nodded, his tone steeped in reluctance. "Follow me, then."

The guard led him down the familiar hall to what had been the family parlor when last he had been within these walls. Randall paused to knock, and Logan recognized Jasper's voice.

"Come," he barked, sounding tense.

Logan pushed past the guard, throwing open the door to the room, stopping on the threshold. Within, his brothers had gathered. Jasper, Rafe, Hart, and Wolf. And another man, one he realized belatedly was the cove who had come to Tierney for funds. Logan had been concealed in the office, hiding behind a panel in the wall, when Tarquin Bellingham had arrived. He wondered for a fleeting moment what Bellingham was doing within, what his connection was to the Suttons.

"Loge?" Jasper asked, frowning. "What the devil are you doing 'ere?"

"And why are you soaked in blood?" Rafe asked grimly.

"One of my men was killed this morning," Logan explained, his voice rough with emotion he could not quite conceal—grief for Chapman, fear for Lily, so many regrets. "He was stabbed in the guts. I found him as he lay dying, and he told me they'd taken a woman who said she was my sister. He heard her tell them her name was Lily."

Logan had known, then and there, as Chapman breathed his last, that it had been his sister Lily who had been taken in the hopes of luring him out. Mace would stop at nothing to destroy him, and he would not stop at harming a woman. Especially not if he believed she was Logan's wife.

"Lily." Bellingham went pale, looking as if he'd been stabbed himself. "Who has taken her?"

"An enemy of mine," Logan explained grimly. "One who wants me dead."

"Why would she 'ave been taken?" Jasper asked, urgency creeping into his voice as it lashed out like a whip.

"Because they mistook her for my wife," he answered.

But he would not think of Arianna now. She was safe. And Lily was not. His sister was innocent. She did not deserve to die.

"Wife?" Hart repeated. "You've wed?"

"I'll not speak of it," Logan said curtly. "It ain't important. What matters is finding Lily before it's too late."

"Why should we trust you?" Wolf demanded, speaking for the first time since Logan had entered the room.

Logan deserved his brother's scorn, his mistrust. Once, he and Wolf had been inseparable.

"Because you want our sister to live," Logan said, holding his gaze. "Time ain't on our side. If we want to find Lily before it's too late, you're all going to have to trust me."

"He's right," Jasper said grimly. "We've gathered to form a plan, to find Lily. And no matter what the arsehole says, Logan's got Sutton blood running through those veins."

The acknowledgment sent an odd rush of relief through Logan. He hadn't considered himself anything other than a member of the Guild for so long now. It felt good to be a Sutton, if only for this moment.

It felt *right*.

Logan nodded to his oldest brother. "We'll need all the men we can get. And we'll need to act fast."

"Where is he?" her captor roared, spittle raining from his lips and splattering on her face with the force of his words.

Lily braced herself for another blow. Her hands were tied behind her back. The last two had sent her to her knees, but she had withstood them. Her cheek was bruised, her lip split, her entire head aching. But she would not relent.

"I've told you," she managed past her painful, swollen lip. "I don't know."

"Lying whore." The man slapped her again, more viciously this time.

White stars speckled her vision, pain making her cry out even as she tried to remain strong, to show him that she would not bend, would not break.

"You know where your husband is," the man said. "I'll have it from you if I have to kill you. Do you understand me?"

Lily blinked, refusing to allow the tears that had blurred her vision to fall. After she had been taken from Logan's lodging that morning, she had come to with her wrists and ankles tied, on the floor of a conveyance that took her to an unremarkable building. Her captors had carried her inside and proceeded to take turns inside this dank room with her, demanding information she did not possess.

It was painfully clear that they were looking for Logan, that they believed she was Logan's wife, and that they would not stop until her brother was dead. Even if it meant killing Lily, too.

"I'm not married," she managed to say, although part of her knew it would be easier to stop fighting.

To tell them what they wanted to hear so they would stop beating her.

The other part of her feared that if she lied, they would simply kill her immediately rather than torturing her slowly to death.

"You're lying." He struck her again with the back of his hand. "What do you think to accomplish? You're only making me angry."

"I'm telling you the truth," she said, her ear ringing with the force of the blow.

His nostrils flared. He was a tall man, with a hawkish nose and blond hair and massive, cruel hands. "Do you know what I ought to do? I ought to stick my cock down your throat and see if that brings out the truth."

Bile rose in her throat.

"No," she begged. "Please."

He grasped her hair and yanked. "Then tell me where your bloody husband is, or I will."

Tears stung her eyes at the pain, the roots of her hair feeling as if they were on fire. She was utterly defenseless, at this man's mercy. She had to escape. If she did not, she would die here. At last, he released her hair.

"Have you nothing to say?" he demanded.

She thought of Tarquin then. Of the life they were meant to have together. Of the future awaiting them, of the love they shared. She could not surrender to this vile man so easily. She had to fight.

Summoning all the remaining strength she possessed, she lowered her head, willing him to come nearer to her so she could strike. She remained silent and still, watching from beneath the fringe of hair that had come free of her chignon. Waiting for his booted feet to move nearer.

"Well?" he demanded. "Speak, or I'll fill that pretty mouth of yours with something more useful than your tongue."

Another step closer.

Lily lunged forward, using the top of her head to strike him between the legs with as much might as she could muster. Her blow sent him staggering backward, hunched over, the breath knocked out of him.

Taking advantage of his surprise, she struggled to scramble to her feet, knowing it was now or never. But her bound wrists and ankles made the struggle nigh impossible. Fear raced up her spine as she attempted to rise. She was running out of time. At any moment, he would come for her.

Suddenly, the door to the room burst open. And there, on the threshold, as if her frantic hopes had conjured him, was Logan. He was covered in blood, and he looked as fierce and frightening as she had ever seen him. He was holding a pistol, its barrel trained on her captor, his stare unwavering.

"Stay where you are," Logan warned sharply, speaking to the man, who was still doubled over, breathing heavily from the damage she had inflicted.

Without warning, her captor lunged, growling.

The sharp report of the pistol firing echoed through the

room. The bullet found its mark. The man fell forward, slumping to the floor, struggling for breath.

"You... bastard," the man gasped out, blood trickling from his lips. "I should've...killed you...when I had...the chance."

Logan stalked forward like a beast of prey. "But you didn't, did you?" He stopped before the man, shooting his pistol again.

And the man went silent and still.

Violent, uncontrollable trembling overtook her as shock, pain, and terror intertwined. Her mouth was dry, her tongue incapable of finding words. Her body seemed unable to move. Arms came around her, hauling her up, and she instinctively fought, fearing the man was not dead. That he was coming to hurt her again.

"Hush," Logan said soothingly. "It's me, Lil. You're safe now."

And then her brother cut her bonds and lifted her into his arms as if she were a child.

∼

Tarquin held Lily tightly in his arms as his post-chaise rocked over the rutted road leading out of the seedy den where she had been taken by her captors. When she had emerged, safe but bruised and bloodied in her brother Logan's arms, he had never been more relieved in his life. Nor more furious. He had stormed forward, along with her other brothers, a collective wall of protective rage, determined to tear her assailant limb from limb for daring to lay a hand upon her.

But Logan had stayed them all with a raised hand. "The bastard's already dead."

More relief had surged, along with the satisfaction of knowing the man who had taken her would never again cause her harm or pain. When they had arrived at the dilapidated home where she was being held—a location discovered by none other than Archer Tierney, who was far more than a mere moneylender—it had taken every bit of control Tarquin possessed to allow Logan Sutton, Tierney, and their men to sweep inside first. Their warning of danger had been sufficient to persuade Tarquin and Lily's other brothers to stand guard outside.

But doing so—entrusting her welfare, her *life*, to others—had been nigh impossible.

Hating the pain she must have endured, Tarquin had taken her from her brother, gathering her in his own arms, before carrying her directly to his carriage. Her brothers had offered feeble protestations. He and Lily were not yet married, after all. But Tarquin had refused to bend. He had almost lost the woman he loved today, and he was not going to allow her out of his sight.

To the devil with the scandal it would cause for a gentleman shop owner to bring his betrothed into his own home by the light of day. Tarquin did not care who saw them. Did not even care if every customer he had refused to return to his shop on account of his complete and utter disregard for what was proper. Last night, he had slipped Lily inside his home under the cloak of darkness, attempting to at least keep tongues from wagging.

Today, he felt like a soldier who had just been to battle. And he did not care about anyone or anything but the beloved woman in his arms. He was going to carry her into his town house in full sight of anyone who dared to look. Because she was here, thank God. She was *alive*.

"Are you in very much pain, darling?" he asked now, gently smoothing a stray strand of hair from her battered cheek with the greatest of care.

She attempted to smile, but winced at what must have been the pain in her swollen, bleeding lip. "Some."

"I'll send for your sister Caro to attend you," he said. "If I thought you would trust anyone else, I would gladly call for a physician."

"Caro will do," she said stoically.

"I hate what that bastard did to you," he said, unable to keep the viciousness from his voice as he thought again of her nameless, faceless captors. The evidence of the pain he had inflicted upon Lily was written in mottled bruises and blood. "If your brother had not killed him first, I would have gladly done so. My God, when I think of what might have happened had Logan not come to The Sinner's Palace..."

"He came to the hell?" she asked, sounding surprised.

"Logan is the reason we found you," Tarquin explained gently. "And he is the one who saved you, along with Archer Tierney and some others."

"Archer Tierney?" Confusion laced her voice. "Why? How? He is the reason I sought out Logan. I was worried about your involvement with him, that he would put your shop at risk."

"I had wondered why you had gone to see your brother." Tarquin placed the tenderest of kisses on the top of her head, where there were no visible injuries. "I feared it was because of me. If anything had happened to you, I never would have forgiven myself..."

His voice broke on the last, for he could not contemplate the full ramifications of his own words. If Lily had been killed, it would have been his fault. She never would have gone to her brother Logan if Tarquin had not taken a loan from Archer Tierney. He could never have known what Tierney and Logan Sutton were truly a part of when he had gone to the moneylender. He could scarcely believe the truth of it now. But none of that mattered when faced with the terrible thought of losing Lily forever. If this bold, pure-hearted woman who championed orphans and cats and broken men like himself had been extinguished like a candle's flame, his own life would have been over, too.

"Nothing that happened to me was your fault, Tarquin," Lily told him, caressing his cheek with a dirty, bloodied hand. "I'm still here. I'll heal."

"Thank God," he said. "You are so damned brave, my love. Brave and kind and good."

She made a soft sound in her throat. "Not always. Sometimes I'm terrified and quite wicked. I knocked that bastard in the tallywags."

Lily was trying to make him laugh. *By God*, she had just been through hell, and it was she who was trying to reassure him. That was his Lily.

"Good," he said, his tone vehement. "You should have bloody well chopped them off and fed them to him."

"You cursed," she observed, resting her head against his shoulder with a small sigh.

"So I did. Almost losing the woman I love turns me into a beast."

"You didn't lose me," she reminded him. "I'm yours."

*His.*

"I love you so much," he told her, voice raw. "When your brother Jasper came to me this morning looking for you, I was sick with worry. I knew you'd not simply disappear."

"I should not have gone," she admitted weakly. "I was only trying to help. I should have listened to my brothers when they said Logan was involved in something dangerous."

Dangerous was one word for it. There were others, but Tarquin had no wish to trouble Lily with the truth when she was injured and weak.

"Promise me you'll never do something so reckless again," he said sternly. "I cannot lose you, Lily. I need you."

"I promise." She tilted her head back, that mysterious gaze that always held him in its thrall meeting his. "What is Logan caught up in? And Archer Tierney? The men who took me thought I was Logan's wife. They were trying to hurt him."

"That's a tale only your brother can tell," he said grimly. "The danger to you is gone. The bastards who took you are both dead, killed by Logan and his men."

And the rest would have to wait for another day. For now, all that mattered was that Lily was safe, in his arms where she belonged, and no one was ever going to hurt her again.

Lily nodded, tears glistening in her eyes. "I'm glad for that. Thank you for coming to find me. For loving me."

Careful to avoid the bruising on her cheek, he brushed his fingers over her skin, catching a teardrop as it fell. "Lily Sutton, I will forever come to find you wherever you go, no matter how far. And I will always, always love you."

"Oh, Tarquin," she said softly. "I will always love you, too."

He kissed her brow. "Rest now, Queen of Thieves. I'm taking you home."

# EPILOGUE

"Marianne," Lily called, walking into the drawing room with as much haste as her ungainly body would allow. Movement was rather difficult these days, as she neared her confinement. Her back ached, and her feet were nearly too swollen for her slippers. "Have you seen Sir Bellingham? I cannot seem to find him…" Lily halted at the sight of the dark-haired child curled up in a chair by the window, the orange cat nestled in her lap. "Anywhere," she finished.

"Here he is," Marianne said, grinning. "He scratched at the door after I returned from my lessons, and I let him in."

Although Sir Bellingham had been making the town house his home instead of The Sinner's Palace for over a year now, he still tended to wander and become lost. Once, he had been hiding in the attic for two days before he had been found. As a result, Lily preferred to keep watch over him. Much as she kept watch over Marianne, who had truly blossomed after coming to live with Lily and Tarquin when they had wed.

"I should have known I would find him with you," Lily

said with a smile, stopping at the chair and giving Marianne's thin little shoulder a loving pat. "You spoil him so."

Marianne had a tendency to hide scraps from her meal, tucked away in a napkin and taken to her room. It was an old habit from her days at the foundling hospital, when she had been forced to ration her food and had often gone hungry. Every time she saw the girl discreetly hiding bits of food in a handkerchief, Lily was newly pleased that she and Tarquin had been able to make certain the foundling hospital was supplied with sufficient food for all the girls within. They had enacted many improvements thus far, including the replacement of Mrs. Frost, with more to come.

"He loves chicken," Marianne said, giving Sir Bellingham a scratch between the ears. "Fish, too. He is always hungry. I suspect he's part cow."

Lily chuckled, petting Sir Bellingham too. "Whatever you do, don't let him hear you say that. You'll hurt his pride."

Marianne covered Sir Bellingham's ears. "There. Now he shan't know."

Sir Bellingham looked quite cross, but he held still, Marianne's small fingers cupped over him.

"Ah, but what if he has already heard?" Lily asked with mock concern, playing along.

Marianne huffed an exaggerated sigh and removed her hands. "Perhaps he has. I reckon if he wants his chicken, he'll forgive me."

"I reckon he will." Lily shared a smile with Marianne. "And how were your lessons today?"

Marianne had begun taking lessons with Jasper's twin daughters, Elizabeth and Anne. Since the three of them were close in age, they adored spending time together. And all three of them were natural-born imps.

"Quite boring until the toad."

"Toad?" Lily asked, wondering what manner of mischief the girls had been making now.

The poor governess had the patience of a saint.

"Yes, Anne said Elizabeth released it, and Elizabeth said Anne was the one who did it," Marianne explained. "It went hopping about and scared Miss Smithers, who screamed and tripped over her hems and fell on her arse."

Lily bit her lip to keep from laughing, as much at the poor governess's plight as at Marianne's curse. The girl's language had grown steadily more ladylike, as had her elocution. But occasionally, some of her old life spilled through.

"Marianne," she chided.

"I know, it ain't nice to laugh at Miss Smithers falling on her arse," Marianne said with a sigh.

"It also is not done for a lady to say *arse*," Lily explained patiently.

"Why should a lady not say arse?"

Tarquin's familiar, deep voice had Lily turning to find him crossing the threshold of the drawing room.

Lily pinned a mock frown to her lips. "Mr. Bellingham, you ought to be ashamed of yourself for uttering such a vulgar word."

He grinned, reaching her and dropping a kiss on her cheek. "But you have just done so, Mrs. Bellingham. Has she not, Marianne?"

"She has indeed," Marianne agreed sagely.

"Then I suppose I should be ashamed as well," Lily said, shaking her head as she looked from Tarquin to Marianne.

The girl had blossomed, and the three of them, along with Sir Bellingham, had forged a wonderful family. A family that was about to grow larger in size by one. Lily rested her hand on her immense belly, happiness bubbling up within her.

"You should," Tarquin and Marianne told her in unison, their voices teasing and light.

Lily was pleased with how well the girl and her husband had bonded. They had all come a long way together from deceptions and misunderstandings and filched fans. Bellingham and Co. was thriving more than ever, so much so that Tarquin had been able to repay the loan. And Lily, Tarquin, and Marianne were thriving, too.

Sir Bellingham mewled loudly, not to be forgotten.

"I've brought a gift for both of my ladies from the shop," Tarquin said then, reaching into his coat and extracting a pair of matching fans and offering one to Marianne, then another to Lily. "I saw them when they arrived and knew they had to be yours."

Lily opened the fan, which was another delicate brisé fashioned of ivory sticks. A beautiful painted scene revealed itself of a mother and daughter tending to a garden surrounded by flowers. Her heart gave a pang, for the mother and daughter even resembled herself and Marianne; the girl had dark curls and the mother possessed hair of blonde.

"It's beautiful," she told Tarquin, so moved by the depiction of mother and daughter on the fan and his gift that she was near tears.

She was ever in a weepy state these days. Lily blinked furiously to clear the sheen from her eyes.

"Oh, look at mine!" Marianne exclaimed excitedly, holding her fan out for Lily to examine.

The scene painted on hers was that of two sisters tending a garden together as a mother and father watched on.

A fresh wave of tears stung Lily's eyes.

"They reminded me of our family," Tarquin said softly. "And knowing how much my ladies adore fans, I couldn't bear to offer them for sale."

*Our family.* Two sweeter words Lily had never heard uttered.

"But this picture has two children in it," Marianne said, her enthusiasm waning as she pointed to the two girls on her fan.

"Indeed," Tarquin told the girl solemnly. "The painting is not perfectly representative. It is missing a fat, spoiled cat. Perhaps you might add one yourself, hmm? You have become quite skilled with your watercolors recently."

Marianne had. The child had a talent for everything she tried, which was really quite remarkable. Lily was inordinately proud of her.

"Perhaps I could," Marianne allowed hesitantly. "But the two children…"

"Represent *our* two children," Lily told her, heart full. "You and whomever shall be here with us soon."

"But I'm not your daughter," Marianne said. "Not truly."

"Yes, imp," Tarquin told her fondly. "You are. If you wish to be, that is."

Marianne's eyes went wide. "Do you mean I might call you Papa?"

"It would be my honor," Tarquin replied, his voice thick with emotion Lily recognized all too well.

*Love.*

"And mine too," Lily added, "to be your mama."

"I would like that." Marianne gently lifted Sir Bellingham —who protested with a low mewl of disapproval at being dislodged from his present situation—off her lap. "Very much so."

Then, she sprang to her feet and caught Tarquin and Lily both in an enthusiastic embrace. Lily slid one arm about her husband and the other around their daughter, the movement only slightly made awkward by the intrusion of her large belly. Tarquin's arms wrapped around them both, and they stood together, in a circle of love, Sir Bellingham satisfying himself by weaving his way through their ankles.

~

Lily was seated comfortably on an overstuffed chair by the fire in her chamber, book in hand, when the door opened and Tarquin entered. Although *The Silent Duke* by F. Kirkwood was a thrilling adventure, its allure could not compare to that of her husband. She placed it on a table at her side and rose to her feet, not without some additional effort thanks to her belly. She was rounder than an apple.

"Remain as you are," Tarquin urged as he hastened across the room. "You needn't rise on my account, love."

But Lily had already hefted herself from the chair. "It does me some good to move about. I've been planted in that chair for the better part of an hour. Besides, I can't embrace you if you're towering over me."

"You could embrace me with your mouth," he teased with a wicked grin.

Lily laughed at his unexpected humor and looped her arms around his neck as he pulled her close. "I fear I have corrupted you beyond redemption. Where has the frigid, cold-as-ice Mr. Bellingham gone?"

"Melted by his beloved wife's fire," he said easily, gazing down at her with such tenderness and love that it made her breath catch. "Forever a better man because of her."

She smiled up at him. "And your wife is a better woman because of you."

They had grown together in love and happiness. She never could have known, the fateful day when she had slid the last pilfered fan into her bodice, the turn her life would take. That she would end up here, in her husband's arms, loved and more contented than she had imagined possible.

She rose on her toes to press her mouth to his. With a low rumble of need, his lips brushed over hers, slowly at first, and then with greater insistence. Her condition had rendered her overly sensitive everywhere, and all it required was the touch of his tongue to hers for the flames of passion within to ignite. She sucked on his tongue, tasting the sweetness of the wine he had consumed with dinner, and moaned.

Her nipples were hard and aching, her heavy breasts straining against her loosely flowing dressing gown. Beneath it, she was nude, the encumbrance of a night rail one less burden she could not bear; her body was ungainly enough, in her estimation. The smooth fabric of her robe abraded her tender nipples as she moved, seeking to deepen their hungry kiss.

Tarquin's palm pressed the small of her back, bringing her more snugly against him, the protrusion of her round belly keeping their bodies from coming together as she wished. The thick prod of his cock, jutting from beneath his green silk banyan, told her he wanted her every bit as much as she wanted him and sent an ache of longing between her thighs where she was already wet and ready. Her fingers sank into his soft, dark hair, loving the crisp sensation, the warmth emanating from him. Their tongues played together, hot and wet, the kiss turning distinctly carnal.

She was glad her hair was unbound, her nightly preparations already performed, scarcely anything keeping her naked body from his. He nibbled on her lower lip, tugging, the action sending a fresh rush of desire streaking through her. She moaned, head tilting back, and Tarquin took it as an invitation, his hot lips coasting down her throat to deliver a path of open-mouthed kisses to her skin.

"I want you inside me," she told him, the desire throbbing between her legs almost unbearable, needing to be assuaged.

If he did not touch her there soon, she was sure she would die.

"Patience, darling." He kissed to her ear, tonguing the dip

behind it as he caught a handful of her bottom and gently squeezed. "God, I love your sweet curves."

In Lily's delicate condition, her body had changed as much as the rest of her had. But whilst she felt ungainly and large, Tarquin reveled in her larger breasts and rump and thighs. He never failed to make her feel beautiful, worshiped, and loved.

"Mmm," she purred, hooking her leg around his hip, seeking to align her aching cunny to his cock. "More, please."

Her belly intruded, however, keeping her from the prize she sought.

Tarquin chuckled at her shameless eagerness, dragging his teeth along the sensitive cord of her throat as his fingers finally sought the buttons on her dressing gown. "I'm afraid I'll have to remove this if I'm to fuck you properly."

Her proper husband scarcely ever cursed. But when he did, and particularly when he said that thoroughly sinful word, it made her mad with desire.

"Let me help," she said, reaching for the dressing gown and grasping two handfuls.

Without ceremony, she yanked, sending buttons raining to the carpets.

"I'm afraid we shall have to buy you another of these, Mrs. Bellingham," he drawled, his warm hands caressing her shoulders as he pushed the tattered garment to the floor. "Or perhaps not. I must admit, I prefer you naked."

He caressed her breasts, his fingers finding her hard nipples and tugging until her knees went weak.

"I prefer you naked too," she told him breathlessly, working at the belt of his banyan next.

His clever hands coaxed a response as they traveled over her, sweeping down her sides, over her belly, to her hips. When his fingers dipped into her sex, unerringly finding her swollen pearl, she cried out, bucking into his touch, seeking more as she frantically worked to remove his robe.

His head dipped, and he took one of her nipples into the wet, velvet heat of his mouth, sucking hard as he continued to work her slippery, aching flesh below. As he drew on her breast, a crescendo rose within her, impossible to ignore. Lily had not intended to find her climax so quickly, but her body had a will of its own. She came hard, the force of her pleasure making her shoulders curve inward, her body stiffening as the wild beauty of her orgasm rocked through her.

"There's my queen," he said, his voice low with erotic approval. "So wet and hot. Your cunny is dripping, my love."

Ah, not more filthy words. How could she withstand the agony? She loved her icy, proper Tarquin to turn into a decadent sinner. Just for her.

Lily whimpered, clutching him for purchase as her knees threatened to give way and more licks of pleasure swirled through her.

"All for you," she told him, feeling bold and wicked, too. "You should get on your knees for me. Taste it."

He growled and withdrew his fingers, dropping to the carpets before her. "Take your pleasure from me. Tell me what you want."

Gripping the back of the chair for purchase, Lily raised her foot to the seat she had vacated, opening herself to him. "I want your tongue on me. Make me spend."

And then, she reached for his head, gently guiding him to where she wanted him.

"Yes," he praised, and then his tongue was on her, lashing her pearl with fast, wet strokes.

She gave herself over to the pleasure. The new shape of her body meant that she was denied the sight of his dark head buried between her legs, but there was an eroticism to not being able to see what he was doing, to only feeling. And *dear heavens*, the sensations. His tongue worked over her frantically, then licked down her seam to her entrance, lapping there before dipping inside.

She clutched the chair tighter, struggling to keep upright. It was too good, too glorious. He latched on to her pearl and suckled her, groaning as if he could not get enough, his enthusiasm heightening her own desire. When he nibbled on her clitoris, she almost came out of her skin. But Tarquin did not allow her a moment of respite, for in the next breath, he had plunged two fingers inside her, thrusting in and out as he sucked and bit her pearl until she came apart with a strangled cry, nearly falling into the chair as the shudders of ecstasy wracked through her body.

She had scarcely recovered when he rose to his feet and clasped her hand in his, wordlessly guiding her to the looking glass perched atop a low chest of drawers. He settled her before it, positioned facing her reflection, hands splayed atop the polished wood. He took his place behind her, his face starkly handsome over her shoulder, his lips dark and glistening with her dew.

The size of her growing belly necessitated some creative positions for coupling, but this was new. They had never made love standing up before. She could not lie, the sight of them together, her breasts full and heavy, her nipples pink and hard, and Tarquin so beautiful, his dark hair tousled, his proud jaw taut as he struggled to rein in his own need, was deliciously sinful.

"Look at how beautiful you are," he told her, cupping her breasts, toying with her nipples until she made a desperate sound of need.

"Inside me," she managed to tell him. "Please."

He nudged her legs into a wider stance, and then he pressed himself against her fully, his cock nudging her opening from behind. "You are even wetter now, my love."

He slicked his cock head up and down her folds, until she was whimpering and thrusting herself shamelessly into him as she sought more. Just when she thought she would perish from need, he guided himself to her entrance. With one tip of his hips, he slid deep inside her cunny, gliding easily through her wetness. The angle was exquisite.

"Oh," was all she managed to say, half moan, half plea.

Holding her hips in a tender grasp, he began moving, anchoring himself against her as he thrust in and out of her welcoming body.

"Watch us," he said breathlessly as he canted his hips, sinking deep. "Watch me taking you."

And she did. Watched as he lowered his head, kissing a path of fire from her shoulder to the base of her throat. Watched as he nipped and licked and sucked. As her breasts bounced. Watched her hard nipples and parted lips, her hair a wild, gold curtain around her face. Felt him filling her, taking her, claiming her.

One of his hands slid from her hip to her sex, parting her folds, finding her throbbing pearl. She slumped forward against the sturdy piece of furniture, crying out as wave after wave of pleasure buffeted her. Tarquin thrust faster, harder as she clenched around him, and then with a cry, he spilled inside her, the hot rush of his seed sending her spiraling over the edge, helpless as she spent yet again.

They remained as they were, bodies pressed together, breathless and flushed with pleasure, watching each other in the looking glass as the furiousness of their releases ebbed and gentled. And then Tarquin nuzzled her throat, pressed a kiss to her cheek.

"God, I love you," he murmured.

She smiled, rubbing her cheek against his. "And I love you too, my darling."

Their bodies were still joined, and she did not think she

ever wanted to move again. He was her husband, her lover, her friend.

Her *everything*.

Lily Bellingham was one happy woman indeed.

~

Dear Reader,
Thank you for reading Lily and Tarquin's happily ever after! I hope you loved them (and Marianne and Sir Bellingham!) as much as I did as I wrote their book. Please read on for an excerpt from Logan's long-awaited story, *Sutton's Secrets*!

~

*Sutton's Secrets*
*The Sinful Suttons Book 7*

LOGAN SUTTON LIVES in the shadowy underworld of London, rooting out evil before it can strike. He's a nameless enigma prowling the streets to keep the innocent safe. His next mission? Seducing a beauty with ties to the villains he's out to destroy. It ought to be simple. Learn her secrets and then never see her again. And yet, there's something about the midnight-haired temptress that won't allow him to walk away.

Lady Arianna Stewart is living a lie. Forced to do her father's bidding to give her sister a chance at a future, she has no choice but to sell the secrets of dangerous men. She never imagined she'd fall for a charming mercenary along the way, but one wicked kiss from Logan is all it takes.

Thrown together by deceptions and peril, the spy from the wrong end of London and the lady who can never be his fall head over heels into an impassioned affair. But as carefully guarded secrets unravel and deadly enemies hunt them both, they must fight to keep a love that's worth sacrificing everything.

## **Chapter One**

Logan took a puff of his cheroot, watching everyone, trusting no one. Smoke hung in the air, a silver shroud providing him with a momentary screen as he surveyed the chamber. The Onyx Club was a stunningly plummy establishment. A place where sinners congregated to partake in any vice they chose, assured of their privacy.

The walls were hung with scarlet damask, offset by elaborate French curtains draped over the windows to create an illusion of seclusion from the outside world. Even the chairs, Grecian affairs fashioned of mahogany with inlaid ebony and red Morocco leather, were a marvel. The matching card tables were carved mahogany, enhanced by scrollwork and gilt.

One had to only step one foot inside to know it was for the well-equipped. Only culls flush with coin would be able to afford the games being played within this lair. And aye, by comparison, it made his own family's gaming hell, The Sinner's Palace, look like a tumble-down, second-rate den for vagabonds and filching coves.

But it had been some time since he'd last been within those once-familiar walls, and he wasn't here to fret over the competition. Nor to gamble or sample the fine swill or attract the even finer quim.

Rather, he was here on deadly important business, awaiting the arrival of a man known only as *the major*. The exchange—information about the next secret meeting amongst the remaining members of the London Reform

Society in return for two hundred pounds—had been arranged by Logan's superior at the Guild, Archer Tierney.

The group of revolutionaries behind the Reform Society were as depraved as they were brazen. They were willing to commit any crime, regardless of the victims, in the name of their proposed revolution. Attacks on the Tower of London, murdering prominent members of the government. And that was just the start. All of which necessitated a great deal of care in the negotiations which would ensue this evening.

Nothing had been left to chance.

The major was to meet Logan here, sit at the table, and tell him that he heard the port at the Onyx Club was particularly fine. The major had been previously informed concerning the details of Logan's appearance; the color of his hair, the coat and cravat he would be wearing, the table at which he would be seated.

Logan and the major would share a glass of port. At some point during the course of their interview, a missive would be passed to Logan from the major. Logan would pay the man the agreed-upon sum. He was then to linger at the Onyx Club, to avoid drawing undue attention to himself and his mission, lose a game of *vingt-et-un*, and subsequently depart. He would then take the communication immediately to Archer.

But the appointed hour for the major's arrival had already come and gone. The fellow had either been waylaid or had experienced a change of heart. It wouldn't be the first time an informant failed to appear since Logan had begun his covert work for the Guild. And he knew it wouldn't be the last.

Feigning *ennui*, he extracted his pocket watch and consulted the time.

The major was one quarter hour late. Logan reached for his port, taking another slow, small sip.

And that was when he saw her.

She was not the only woman in the club's main room. Nor was she the only beauty. There were petticoats aplenty to distract, for the Onyx Club was a place where men and women mingled freely.

But this woman was different from all the rest in a way that was indefinably alluring. It was a delicious combination, he thought, of the way she carried herself and the way she dressed. She simmered with intelligence and boldness, and a glance at the other coves proved he was not the only one captivated by her.

But inevitably, his gaze returned to her. She moved through the throng of gents with grace and poise. She wore a gown of vibrant, red velvet that showed her figure to perfection, her pale breasts on display above a bodice bedecked with silver rosettes. Her shoulders were bare, her arms concealed in white lace sleeves that hugged her wrists, and a necklace of triple pearls with gold ornamented her throat. Rubies glimmered from her ears, her hair a profusion of glossy jet curls framing her face and caught at her crown to trail in further ringlets down her nape.

From across the chamber, her gold-brown gaze collided with his.

Logan felt the intensity of that stare, that marrow-deep connection, to his soul. It was as if he were looking at the other half of himself, someone who was meant for him. The acknowledgment was tacit, but he swore she felt it too, simmering between them, as tangible as a touch.

But as longing arose, he suppressed it with force. He was not here at the Onyx Club tonight to be distracted by a woman, regardless of how enticing she was. He was here to meet with the major. To gain information that could ultimately prove priceless.

It was imperative that he remain clear-headed and calm.

He could not afford for lust to addle his wits. When he had first joined the Guild, a clandestine group of mercenaries who reported directly to Whitehall, he had never imagined how deep London's secrets ran. Nor how entrenched in them he would become...

Want more? Get *Sutton's Secrets* here!

# DON'T MISS SCARLETT'S OTHER ROMANCES!

Complete Book List
**HISTORICAL ROMANCE**

Heart's Temptation
A Mad Passion (Book One)
Rebel Love (Book Two)
Reckless Need (Book Three)
Sweet Scandal (Book Four)
Restless Rake (Book Five)
Darling Duke (Book Six)
The Night Before Scandal (Book Seven)

Wicked Husbands
Her Errant Earl (Book One)
Her Lovestruck Lord (Book Two)
Her Reformed Rake (Book Three)
Her Deceptive Duke (Book Four)
Her Missing Marquess (Book Five)
Her Virtuous Viscount (Book Six)

DON'T MISS SCARLETT'S OTHER ROMANCES!

League of Dukes
Nobody's Duke (Book One)
Heartless Duke (Book Two)
Dangerous Duke (Book Three)
Shameless Duke (Book Four)
Scandalous Duke (Book Five)
Fearless Duke (Book Six)

Notorious Ladies of London
Lady Ruthless (Book One)
Lady Wallflower (Book Two)
Lady Reckless (Book Three)
Lady Wicked (Book Four)
Lady Lawless (Book Five)
Lady Brazen (Book 6)

Unexpected Lords
The Detective Duke (Book One)
The Playboy Peer (Book Two)
The Millionaire Marquess (Book Three)
The Goodbye Governess (Book Four)

The Wicked Winters
Wicked in Winter (Book One)
Wedded in Winter (Book Two)
Wanton in Winter (Book Three)
Wishes in Winter (Book 3.5)
Willful in Winter (Book Four)
Wagered in Winter (Book Five)
Wild in Winter (Book Six)
Wooed in Winter (Book Seven)
Winter's Wallflower (Book Eight)
Winter's Woman (Book Nine)
Winter's Whispers (Book Ten)

DON'T MISS SCARLETT'S OTHER ROMANCES!

Winter's Waltz (Book Eleven)
Winter's Widow (Book Twelve)
Winter's Warrior (Book Thirteen)
A Merry Wicked Winter (Book Fourteen)

The Sinful Suttons
Sutton's Spinster (Book One)
Sutton's Sins (Book Two)
Sutton's Surrender (Book Three)
Sutton's Seduction (Book Four)
Sutton's Scoundrel (Book Five)
Sutton's Scandal (Book Six)
Sutton's Secrets (Book Seven)

Sins and Scoundrels
Duke of Depravity
Prince of Persuasion
Marquess of Mayhem
Sarah
Earl of Every Sin
Duke of Debauchery
Viscount of Villainy

The Wicked Winters Box Set Collections
Collection 1
Collection 2
Collection 3
Collection 4

Stand-alone Novella
Lord of Pirates

**CONTEMPORARY ROMANCE**
Love's Second Chance

DON'T MISS SCARLETT'S OTHER ROMANCES!

Reprieve (Book One)
Perfect Persuasion (Book Two)
Win My Love (Book Three)

Coastal Heat
Loved Up (Book One)

## ABOUT THE AUTHOR

*USA Today* and Amazon bestselling author Scarlett Scott writes steamy Victorian and Regency romance with strong, intelligent heroines and sexy alpha heroes. She lives in Pennsylvania and Maryland with her Canadian husband, adorable identical twins, and two dogs.

A self-professed literary junkie and nerd, she loves reading anything, but especially romance novels, poetry, and Middle English verse. Catch up with her on her website https://scarlettscottauthor.com. Hearing from readers never fails to make her day.

Scarlett's complete book list and information about upcoming releases can be found at https://scarlettscottauthor.com.

Connect with Scarlett! You can find her here:
    Join Scarlett Scott's reader group on Facebook for early excerpts, giveaways, and a whole lot of fun!
    Sign up for her newsletter here
    https://www.tiktok.com/@authorscarlettscott

- facebook.com/AuthorScarlettScott
- twitter.com/scarscoromance
- instagram.com/scarlettscottauthor
- bookbub.com/authors/scarlett-scott
- amazon.com/Scarlett-Scott/e/B004NW8N2I
- pinterest.com/scarlettscott

Printed in Dunstable, United Kingdom